To

Mother —

A Happy Easter

1964 —

Evelyn & Bill

The Hack

By the same author:

A MIDDLE CLASS EDUCATION

The Hack

BY WILFRID SHEED

The Macmillan Company, New York

The Macmillan Company, New York
Collier-Macmillan Canada Ltd., Toronto, Ontario

Library of Congress catalog card number: 63-16129

Printed in the United States of America

To Missie

Part One

"Where pagans go wrong is that . . ."

FLAX. *Thoughts.*

1

He crawled into the car, took off his gloves and gave the ignition a resigned twitch. The radio, still half-alive from the night before, resumed its mumble of vague, weekend music. He slid around the corner and turned off the motor; popped, flipped, aimed a cigarette at his mouth; rolled the window down; wrapped the tails of his overcoat round his knees; yawned.

The Texaco station to the right was spanking bright and empty. It said, "Get your antifreeze." Beyond that, rows of trees, some bare, some golden, on what principle he didn't know. Beyond that the library. Beyond that the school. Beyond that the church. Everything quiet, of course. Sunday was death rehearsal in Bloodbury.

Bert Flax paid no attention to the crisp blue air which maundered gently between his hat and his dark red muffler. It wouldn't keep away the boredom for long. He was already ten minutes late by the town clock. Of course, he could just sit here for the rest of the hour and drive home again. But he knew from experience that he would feel terrible all week if he did that. Besides, it could get pretty dull in the car, too.

So he started the Studebaker up again and idled along to the church. It was always dark in the vestibule. He could just stand back there and peep at the notices, the condemned films, the outings. And he could beat the rush of chic, tranquil people on the way out. Overcoats coming at you from every direction, a plague of fur.

Father Terwilliger was reading the notices when he looked in . . . "The Holy Name will . . . the Children of Mary have just . . . all the men of the parish . . . Communion in a body." Oh, great. It was no use pretending it was just the notices, though. The boredom had started there, but fanned out in all directions, an obscene plant. He couldn't even pretend it was just the suburbs, although the suburbs had plenty to do with it too. The suburbs and the jokes about the suburbs. "The mortgage on the new buildings," said Father Terwilliger: a special collection, dingy little envelopes. Three new films on the condemned list. The annual dance for all the men of the parish—that was more like it. Brigitte Bardot, indeed! when the men could be right here, having a good dance. The C.Y.O. The women of the parish. Decent literature. The girls of the parish.

It had nothing to do with the girls of the parish. A surprising lot of coughing was going on this week. Sixteen. Seventeen. And a sneeze. Whoops. Winter. The sermon on purgatory for All Souls' Day. Terwilliger would get it all wrong, because he got everything all wrong. "Imagine the worst pain in the world, my dear brethren"—the numbers game again—"and double it" right double it, "and multiply it by a thousand" . . . OK, now take away the number you first—"And it would be less than the least" . . . yes, yes. Go to it, Father. Give them purgatory. "But God in his infinite mercy . . . and compassion . . . and—" ouch! hiss and sizzle went the souls in purgatory. Father Terwilliger was a museum piece—there couldn't be many left by now. But maybe Bert Flax was a museum piece too. The sermon lasted twenty-three minutes.

It wasn't exactly Father Terwilliger that was bothering him. You could always explain Terwilliger in terms of recent immigration or something.

He took his Missal out of his overcoat pocket. It was the part now that counted. The words. He braced himself without hope. Boredom during the notices, swelling into irreverence during the sermon, but still the words had held up. For two, three years he had clung to this consolation. "Wash my hands among the innocent . . . to us also, sinners" and then sometime during the past summer, with all the fans going, the strain of depending on just the words had proved too much, and they had gone sour on him too. He looked, sightless, at the Missal.

From the vestibule, he could watch them coming back from Communion. Their faces vacant, foolish by design. They might be knocking themselves out to look exalted, but most of them just weren't the type. He ought to know: he had played the same game himself, once upon a time. It was his old friend Dave Gilhouley who put him on to how funny he looked. Pious, gloomy—"where does it hurt, Bert?" He always felt funny about looking pious after that, and never knew when he was doing it right.

In a different kind of church, big, old, city church, he remembered how Dave Gilhouley scuffled the hours away. It was a bad sign, remembering him. A terrible restless fellow, Gilhouley, used to smuggle in books inside his Missal, although he never read books anywhere else, and pinched people till he was past the age for it. He thought about Dave for a while: his oafish irreverence used to offer a grotesque contrast to the piety Bert felt in his own heart, and give it value. (When he got bored, he could always disapprove of Dave for a while.) And he thought about the black, crumbling church where Dave performed. A far cry from Terwilliger's antiseptic comfort station. A *real* church, boy.

The congregation settled itself by inches for the last part of the Mass. He found himself looking at a woman's legs. That was what was known as "small" behavior and it brought on suddenly the cold, gray emptiness of another spoiled Mass. The playground outside was cold and gray and empty, too, and he thought about that for the last few minutes. A small boy solemnly dribbling a basketball, shooting, and wheeling his bicycle away into the autumn dusk. He stopped looking at the woman. She wasn't much anyway, although that isn't the point, is it, Bertram?

The first drippings were beginning to come loose down the aisle. Mothers who had to get back to their children, and mothers who had to get their children out of there; in a moment, the rout would be on. He whispered a frantic piece of prayer, "Sorry to mess it up again," and slid out ahead of them. Another Sunday shot to hell.

(If only he could stabilize the boredom, but it grew wantonly, insanely; every week, it flung another wet arm around him.)

He picked up the paper and drove it home. Waffles awaited him, and curling coffee steam, and pulpy forgetfulness in the Sunday papers.

And above all, a wife who took a morbid interest in his churchgoing; who didn't go herself, but who would be obscurely dismayed if he gave it up—a wife (and this was really crazy) he would give what was left of his soul to convert.

Betty Flax was waiting at the door, brushing away children: Bertram, Jr., age six, Betty, Jr., Rosemary, Patricia and Kevin. That's how it was at Bert's house. He strode at them over the frosty grass.

She made a clearing for him in the dining-room and brought him his standard stuff. Steam and smell. And questions.

"How was the sermon, darling?"

"Terwilliger riding roughshod again."

Betty laughed, "At least your people believe in something, enough to ride roughshod."

"Yes, I suppose so."

Terwilliger, for instance, believed in witches at this time of year. His boss, Monsignor Flanagan, believed in the Sugar Plum Fairy. It might be better than nothing. But did it really justify riding roughshod?

"I just couldn't take our people seriously," said Betty. "That's why I left. Or rather, never really went. Or rather . . ."

"Yes, I know."

"Of course, you don't take Father Terwilliger seriously, either. But that doesn't seem to matter so much."

"No. It doesn't seem to."

Betty pushing hair out of her eyes; Betty more girlish than ever in her moribund dressing gown. He wanted it to be right for her, whatever it was for him.

"Father Terwilliger isn't the point," he said slowly. "A thousand Father Terwilligers wouldn't make one point."

"I know that's what you believe," said Betty, so pretty when she was trying to be irreligious and full of doubts. "Oh, if only I could believe in something."

"It isn't so difficult. Pray for faith." The words tasted like ashes. Betty could believe in anything she wanted to, of course; her world was a great feast of possible beliefs. He hung on to what he could, fingers on a wet rock.

"Tell me about purgatory," she asked.

"Some other time." He smiled thinly. A man should be willing to tell his wife about purgatory. It was the least he could do.

She took out his plate, and Sunday afternoon set in right away. Gray wastes of paper piled their way across the study floor; a whine of children, unreflectingly discontented, came from downstairs; and there on every side stood the rows of Sunday books, books that had lost their punch one by one: the latest spirituality, the earliest spirituality, all bent and broken straws. (Who was he fooling with the books? They had never helped much.) Brown leather smells like a priest's sitting room. He had to get out of this stinking room.

Bertram Flax was out in the hall again before he even knew why. He thought he could hear Betty's mother downstairs which settled it. He could still make it down the back stairs. Betty would explain. As he tiptoed down on woolen socks, he could hear "the voice" through the back wall, like wood breaking. Betty's mother was one subject he had spoken his mind about. (Humorously, of course—always humorously.)

Oh God, yes, humor. It was just, he supposed, another sign of the staleness life had temporarily taken on in this his thirty-third year, that his high point of candor was a mother-in-law joke.

2

*Bert Flax inserted his Studebaker among the un-*congealed lumps of traffic on Route 46. He didn't know where he was going. In his line of work the Christmas jitters came early and he often worked them off in the car. Industrial blight embowered him, billboards covered in soot, rows of underprivileged gas stations—the whole damn country was spilling over with gas. New Jersey was a parody of the total situation. He turned on the radio. The Giants' game would be on in a minute or two. It was no use getting mad at New Jersey.

Betty's mother would just be hitting her stride behind him, making the doors and windows rattle and the china bounce. She came over on Sundays, straight from Service, to do battle, so he supposed, for Betty's soul, with a voice like a trench mortar. (Humor kept you sane, the jokes about Mrs. Forsythe were a form of therapy—nothing personal.) At times, Bert had half a mind to let her win; but Mrs. Forsythe would not, he sensed, make a graceful winner. Putting aside the merits of the Catholic Faith, life would be impossible if Mrs. Forsythe won. . . .

Back to that, then, the merits of the Catholic Faith. The merits of the, so to speak, Catholic Faith. He was so tired of all that, didn't want to argue. If you could just give it up for a year, you might get excited again. But you weren't allowed to give it up for so much as a week. It got in your teeth and hair. And meanwhile, the whole thing was getting to be more and more like New Jersey.

Then, on the other hand, if you didn't think about the Church, you had the Giants' game, and turn right for Hackensack, and a word from our sponsor, and haven't you heard of signals?—it wasn't just religion that had gone flat, anyway. It had all gone flat at the same time. Fellow in the next car strung, strang, to hell with it, out his grievance over Bert's driving to an unreasonable length. "You want to get us all killed or something?" Bert hoisted the window and silenced the snivels.

Things looked better from the George Washington Bridge. The graceful sweep of the Hudson and all that. There was oafish industry still visible on the New Jersey side, but what did you expect? Jersey had to make a living, just like everybody else. The New Jersey whine.

Down there, beyond the Riverside Church, lurked his old friends, Dave Gilhouley and Matty Flynn. He hadn't seen them in years, but the Bishop Mahoney alumni magazine said they were still hanging around—how about let's go see them, then?

One good thing about Dave and Matty: they probably didn't know who he was. He could be himself with them (in his quote official capacity, he had to tread so carefully, even with his own wife). He could see incognito how Dave and Matty were holding up under the glorious gift of the Faith, to hell with carrying this thing around by himself. He headed down the drive.

Actually, Gilhouley might be quite a help. Dave used to strengthen one's faith wonderfully, just by ridiculing it. (Pious people often had the opposite effect, didn't they?) But seriously, you needed an enemy, you needed persecution. Religion was dying of politeness, *watch* out, you bastard, Sunday drivers were a reaction to church.

Gilhouley lived in the same ratty apartment as always. It reminded Bert of a Chinese laundry because there were always piles of clothes on everything, dirty shirts ready to go, fresh pajamas that had just arrived and hadn't been sorted. He had never bothered to work out why Gilhouley had this problem.

Dave was slumped in front of the television, where Bert had left him years before, watching the Giants' game. He was a fleshy, smiling man with high shoulders.

"What are you doing in pajamas, you lazy bastard?" asked Bert. "Didn't you go to church?"

" 'Fraid not," said Dave. "Not today. Party last night, and *you* know."

"When are you going to grow up, Gilhouley?"

"Not for a long, long time."

In no time fellows began to drift in, in pairs, and asked what the score was. Everyone brought a quart of beer—it was like a badge—drank up, and said, "See you, Dave." Gilhouley asked them if they were going to be at the fraternity dance, the engineers' dance, or whatever was right, and they said they were, or hoped to be, if sexual commitments permitted. Bert was reminded of the Holy Name spaghetti dinner next Thursday night. He should be able to make that all right.

"How often do you skip Mass, Dave?" he asked during a lull.

"Pretty often."

"OK. How often do you catch Mass?"

"Pretty seldom. All right, maybe once, twice a year with my mother." Gilhouley smiled. "You still with it, Bert?"

"Uh, yes, sort of."

"You still believe that stuff?"

"Sort of. Some of it, I guess. It doesn't always seem too important." He realized that he wanted to draw Dave out, get him to say something sacrilegious. Then they could fight, and Bert would feel like a Catholic again.

"That's what I feel. It isn't too important," echoed Dave.

"You bear down for a while, and then you give up. Is that what you find?"

"Yeah, well I never bore down all that hard."

Gilhouley went out to the kitchen, before they could settle an agenda even, to make his breakfast. A fried egg and some canned peaches. "Don't tell Matty I don't go to church," he said. "It would most likely kill him." Gilhouley was more delicate than he used to be. "If someone believes, that's fine. I won't say a word," said the new, gallant Gilhouley, from somewhere in the kitchen.

In the old days at Bishop Mahoney High, Dave had pursued different methods. It was his stated purpose to drive Matty Flynn out of his mind. "You don't believe that bread and wine bit, do you? Oh come now, Flynn. Let's not be adolescent." Matty was transparently shocked and thrilled. Gilhouley always made his criticisms sound blasphemous because just the words got Matty all excited. "For christsake, Flynn, you don't buy that crap about indulgences?" "Think you're being so smart," Flynn was all atremble, "think God is shocked by a pipsqueak like you." Maybe not God, but Flynn, definitely.

"Yes, I remember that," said Gilhouley, coming out of the kitchen with his defaced plate in his hand. "The difference is, I guess I must have believed some of it myself in those days. Or at least, I didn't not believe. I just liked to put a little fun in Flynn's life."

They kept rolling in, in raincoats and leather jackets. Dave certainly kept in touch. It wasn't as exciting as Bert remembered it though. It was more like an old men's club. In the old days, Bert used to turn up himself at Gilhouley's, with his quart of beer, and watch them making obscene gestures at the commercials and frigging around. Now it was all talk. They were thumbing through exactly the same girls—Barbara who put out, Ruth who might put out—as if it still mattered, who put out; Gilhouley had the shades down as usual, and there was something subterranean about hearing these girls' names, among Gilhouley's dirty clothes.

But they talked so slowly and respectfully, as if putting out was an aptitude like playing the piano. As if Sin had been repealed. Bert was getting terribly restless. "You seen Flynn lately?" he asked at the next intermission.

"Yeah, I see him around. He lives over on 95th. Still rattling his beads. Four kids—none of dat filt'y birt' control for Flynn," he said in housekeeper-Irish.

"I've got five, myself."

"So? Well," Gilhouley scratched himself politely, "all right, I guess, if you're built that way."

It was beginning to look as if Matty Flynn might be closer to what he wanted this afternoon than fun-loving Gilhouley. "You're an irresponsible crud," he said, and Dave laughed. "You live a tirrible empty life, Gilhouley. Nothing but pleasure." He punched Dave's arm wistfully.

They could hear a rustle of paper shopping bag in the hall, and the sound of a key probing against the door.

"That'll be Jane," said Gilhouley, and so it was. A buxom girl in jeans, sneakering in under a load of groceries. What kind of people bought groceries on a Sunday?

"I'd like you to meet Jane," said Dave. Jane smiled and ducked into the kitchen and told him he shouldn't eat canned peaches all the time. It was bad nutrition, she said. Even childless voluptuaries had to have balanced diets. They owed it to themselves.

Bert got up to go, by way of the bathroom. It was hot and cramped in there, smelling of several different kinds of soap. The bath mat was wet and there were old clothes on the laundry box. Bert's eyes looked bad in the mirror. He pushed glumly at his thin brown hair.

On the way out, he noticed a box of feminine napkins on top of the medicine cabinet. Just like that. Gilhouley had come a long way from smuggling books into church. It had something to do with the rhythm of life, he supposed.

Right now, it reminded him of New Jersey and Route 46. The box was covered in soot, another victim of industrial blight. Things weren't so much better across the river, not so much better outside the church. The whole country was suffering from creeping New Jersey, that was what it was, and he managed a smile on that to see himself out.

3

He said, "See you, Dave," and made off over the tiled floor.

He would have to tackle Gilhouley again and find out if that was all there was to it. But, he thought, five children never left a bathroom looking worse than that. To live for pleasure and wind up with a soggy bath mat, oh my.

His walk took him past the Columbia buildings, which had their own kind of Sunday. Professors' wives, interfaith groups, good taste; mild, high-domed parsons drafting thoughtful sermons and mimeographing them in their rimless spectacles. It was an import-export thing. Bavarian theologians threshed out the latest subtleties, came grunting with them out of the Black Forest—they were behind the whole thing, kept it going. Then the parsons distilled it and wrapped it in cellophane and the professors' wives took it home and gave it to the cat. Protestants were our brothers now, but you couldn't help laughing.

He liked the air around Columbia. His skin would have recognized it blindfold: brisk, light air, carrying anecdotes about Nicholas Murray Butler to all corners of the world; twenty vapid, barmy years he had spent in this neighborhood, over on Amsterdam Avenue, and he would feel superficially grateful for the rest of his life. For a few minutes, as he walked along Broadway, things seemed to make a little sense. His tongue cooled and slowed. Ha, ha, trick.

Matty Flynn's place was five floors up in a dark building off Broadway. It used to be his mother's place, then his mother's and his, and finally, with the arrival of his fourth child, his mother had moved downstairs.

The self-service elevator refused to leave the basement for several minutes, and after it did, it died peacefully on the third floor and Bert had to take the last bit on foot.

Matty had never been a gregarious man, but he greeted his old friend with a startled kind of enthusiasm, swarming around him and taking his hat. "You old son-of-a-gun," he said. "Good to see you, man."

Bert kicked past the toys that pointed to the living room. The Giants' game was flickering to a close at last. A sallow boy sat in front of it, adrift in his pajamas. "Jimmy has a cold," said Matt, "Mary took the other kids over to her mother's." He paused. "So. Some game, huh?"

Bert nodded.

Matt sat on the couch and said, "So."

He was thin, dark, somehow folded wrong, as if he had been forced to sit in an unnatural position all his life. But he had a kind of wizened charm, which had made him a lot of unlikely friends in the old days.

"I've just been to Gilhouley's."

"So?"

"Still the old Gilhouley."

"Yeah, I guess so."

"That's some—" Bert looked at Jimmy, whose back was safely turned, and made two distended curves in the air.

"Yeah," said Matt, "Gilhouley hasn't changed." There was sadness in his voice, but whether over Gilhouley's lost soul, or over the toys in the hall, or what, was hard to tell. Matty seemed very tired.

"I half envy a guy like Gilhouley," said Bert.

That would have aroused Matt once upon a time; he would have whinnied, "Envy a guy like that? He only *thinks* he's enjoying himself." Now he just shrugged and said, "Yeah, well I don't know about that."

Bert got the antic notion that it might be a good idea to have a look at Matt's bathroom and see how *he* was doing. Instead he said, "So, I hear you got four kids."

"That's right. Four." He took his wallet out of his back pocket, thumbed through the pictures and, when Bert didn't ask to see them, put them away again and the wallet back.

"Geez, did you see that?" snuffled Jimmy.

"No, what happened?"

"Pat Sumerall just booted a field goal, from his own forty-seven."

"That's great, Jimmy. Now you better get back into bed before your mother gets here."

"A fifty-three-yard boot."

"Yes that's very good."

Jimmy went off and the two men were left alone. Matt said, "So," and didn't look embarrassed at having said it for, what, the fourth, fifth time?

"This is a nice, big apartment," Bert told him.

"Yeah. It belongs to my mother."

Bert nodded. That seemed conclusive. Mrs. Flynn was

actually an old sofa in real life. He was sitting on her right this minute.

"What are you doing now, Matty?"

"Uh? Selling insurance, I guess. I'm on the road a lot. Upper New York State, Rome, Syracuse, all around there."

"Well, for goodness' sake," said Bert. "Anyways, I guess Dave is the one who really has it made. That's some dame he's shacking up with."

"Is that so?" said Matt politely. "I've never seen her."

Small behavior again, still trying to get a rise out of old Matty. But he really needed to this time. He went on, "Sometimes I wonder whether you and I aren't wasting our time, being good guys, being good husbands and all that crap."

Matty smiled thinly, didn't say anything.

"Look at us, will you? Skinny, bags under the eyes, look at this hairline, boy. That's worry, that is. And for what?"

Matty shook his head. "That's a good question, all right."

"And meanwhile just take a look at that clown Gilhouley. He never looked better. Good tan, nice little pot."

"He's certainly in great shape," said Matt vaguely.

"Shape? I'll say he is. And screwing every good-looking babe he can get his hands on. For christsake, Matt, what are we *doing* with our lives?"

"Excuse me," there was a pained flurry of trouser legs, "I think I hear my wife." Matt was pale, worried, elaborately polite as he stood up. He walked out gently, as if the floor hurt.

The deflation came quickly. Bert hadn't meant to talk like that to Matty. That wasn't the way he talked to anybody. Not since Bishop Mahoney burned down. And Flynn so goddamn dignified about it. Not judging, just leaving the room when it got to be too much for him.

It wasn't Mrs. Flynn after all but her sister Kate. Fat, full of talk, by the look of her. Stepping into his mess. "Oh, I didn't mean to interrupt anything," she said.

"You weren't interrupting anything. Kate, I'd like you to meet Bert Flax."

Oh, wonder of wonders, for christsake. "Not *the* Bert Flax?"

"*The* Bert Flax?"

"The one who writes all those wonderful stories in the *Tiny Messenger* and the *Catholic Woman,* and I don't know where else."

Matty looked doubtful. "I don't think Bert would do that." Not after the way Bert had been talking.

"Well, it's such an unusual name, isn't it? Bertram Flax. And those beautiful poems about Our Lady and the Sacred Heart."

The best thing was to wrap your scarf around your face and pretend you had mumps. Failing that, Bert said, "Yes, that's me. I do a few things like that, from time to time."

"Oh, isn't he something?" said Kate. Funny how the men never read anything in these homes. It was the women who smoked him out. "Bertram Flax is only one of our leading Catholic writers, that's all."

"I never knew that," said Matt.

"His things are absolutely inspiring, just beautiful. I've read every word you've written, Mr. Flax."

"Thank you very much."

"I suppose you'll be doing your Christmas poem next. He does wonderful Christmas poems, Matt. The one last year was all about the innocent babe, you know, so small and yet, well, you know. . . ."

It was like having a tray of ice emptied into your socks. The coldness came up from there, then the desolation and finally the slow melting squish. Matt said, "Well I never knew that." "The little babe," crooned his sister-in-law, "the innocent babe." Well there were innocent babes and there were other kinds of babes. He had best go before he broke Kate's big, marshmallow heart.

"Good-bye, you old son-of-a-gun," said Matt at the door.

"I must read some of your stuff. I mean, it sounds great."

"It isn't all that great. You know me, Matt. It's just a knack."

Matt wasn't looking at him, but he wasn't looking at anything else either. It was a face Bert had seen once or twice in convent parlors. When the going got rough.

"Well, I think that's great, Bert. I'm glad you're doing so well." Matt was so charitable by now that he didn't know his old friends. No one could reach him.

The door shut. Bert imagined they would start saying the rosary right away. Or collecting stamps for the missions. Or subscribing to worthwhile magazines.

He might as well be getting back to New Jersey. His mother-in-law would have left by now and the children would be almost in bed. His pilgrimage to where it all started hadn't been a howling success. Time to take the old prig home then.

4

"They want you to give a talk in Paramus. The women's auxiliary, that is."

"I have nothing to say to the women of Paramus."

"They want you to talk about vibrant living. That isn't one of your subjects is it?"

"I don't see how it could be. Look, Betty, please not Paramus." Not industrial blight women, not Paramus women, not in his condition.

"They'll come and pick you up."

A horrible thought in itself. He shut his eyes. The children were beginning to file in to breakfast. Whey-faced, stringy hair, whining about its being Monday and all that.

And then, there was the pile of half-witted mail in front of his wife. You could tell it was half-witted by the way they put on the stamps. All in all, plenty to close his eyes about.

"*The Companions of St. Agatha* wants an article on sanctity in everyday living. Their policy does not, alas, permit payment. . . ."

"I always like the 'alas.' "

"And they realize that you have many commitments. . . ."

"Pass the sugar, Bertram. I can't see it."

"You've got your eyes shut, Daddy."

"Don't giggle." Bert Flax enjoying a repartee with his enormous family. They would be gone eventually. Time was on his side. Some of them went to school, others just disappeared. Bert knew better than to ask about it.

"This looks like a check. From the *Passenger*."

"Dirty money."

"Oh, Bert."

Four dollars for a book review. Four dollars for saying that Sister Somebody wrote beautifully.

The children were wiped away, and he faced his own morning. It was the season to rub his hands and be genial for the *Passenger;* moisten his eyeballs and be tender for the *Catholic Woman;* roll up his trousers and be childish for the *Tiny Messenger*. Must keep his roles straight.

"Betty," he called out a few minutes later from his study, "I want to try a different line of work."

She couldn't hear from where she was. But anyway, she would have known he was joking.

"Mr. Flax, you do so much good," he told himself in falsetto. Even when you don't feel inspired yourself, you manage to be a source of inspiration in others. Bushwa! Paramus, New Jersey! He was just too far in by now. He couldn't get out if he wanted to.

It had started way back in high school (poets mature

early) when religiosity came as easily as breathing. They told you to think of Our Lady whenever you had an impure thought, and this led him into some rather tense poetry. Sister Melody, the visiting Laureate from Iowa, got excited and said that he had a genuine lyric gift: on her recommendation, he submitted a fistful of his stuff to the *Passenger*, and Father Chubb confirmed all that Sister had said; adding in his gruff way that Bert had a voice of rarest purity. And Father Chubb was supposed to know about those things. All that remained to be done was to conceal this sudden glory from Dave Gilhouley. He changed his pen name temporarily to Winslow, and became two people for the first time.

Vance Winslow, boy-poet. He had struck just the right note for the magazines when he was sixteen, and the magazines were not about to change as he got older. When he was asked to do reviews, he glued himself together again and reconverted to Bert Flax. Nobody seemed to notice. Gilhouley was deep in *Playboy* by then and not to be disturbed. In due time came the stories, and the religious television scripts (if you were a writer you could presumably write anything), and finally, with time pressing, the "thoughts," which Father Chubb eked out with dots and stuffed into the interstices of his magazine. He was just getting out of college by then, with a lot of very vague plans, none of which included the role of spiritual hack. Little did he know.

He began sending some of his best things to secular magazines and the better Catholic ones, which meant mostly padding down the draughty stairs on frosty mornings to haul the manuscripts out of the mailbox and pat them back into shape. It also meant decomposed shirts and desiccated underwear and shredding pajamas on Horatio Street. Father Gonfallin of the *Tiny Messenger* called him a natural writer, though, so he kept at it for four, five years. A woman's fashion magazine said that he had an unpretentious charm; *Sport for Men* said he showed promise. He gobbled at the crumbs and kept running.

And meanwhile, Father Chubb was taking all he could do and panting gruffly for more. With enough dots, Bert could turn his "thoughts" into whole columns—all right with Chubb, anything to fill the magazine. The rate of pay was such that, so long as he didn't flag, he could never quite go under. Then, quick, quick, plan to get married, get married (fine Catholic man) one baby, two babies (way to go, big Bert) faster and faster, Father Chubb always just behind him with the day's needs; and Sister Melody, with her gentle encouragement; and Father Gonfallin with the towels. Gad, what a farce. And here one was, thirty-two and doing a Christmas story (like an adult lisping) out of tired, empty bowels, hoping that jovial Uncle Chubb would fill the stockings once again.

"It was snowing cruelly and the little girl had nowhere to go." Pissing down as usual—words were a dangerous medium. You had to shake them loose to get them to come at all, and then look what happened. "A kind stranger came up and said. . . ." Flax, for godsake cut that out. It isn't funny. I know, I just can't help it. Try to help it. Father, I had a thought.

Five children. . . . Now what was the point of that? Look it up in the files—you're not going to get anything done this morning. Away we go: "I was an eleventh child," story by Bert Flax. "And my mother used to say it was like having eleven guardian angels in the house, thirteen counting Daddy and me, and isn't it wonderful to have that many angels. . . ." Well, if you think of things like that, what's wrong with writing them down? It was just like being a lawyer or something. It helped some people.

He put the story back in the files, among the bales of desecrated paper. Every thin folder in there contained some attitude or homily that he had to live up to. He was being buried alive under thickening layers of hypocritical crud. He jerked the window up with a sudden violent spasm, to let the clean air blow on his fetid files.

"Brrr, it's cold in here," said Betty coming in with the coffee. "Writing going badly?"

"Mum. I can't seem to get the Christmas spirit as early as I used to."

"You poor dear. I think you're heroic."

She came over and put her arm round his waist. It flooded him with the only kind of warmth that still worked. He sat her on his knee and said, "I get tired," and she said, "Of course you do, dear. I think it's heroic."

"Don't keep saying that," he said sharply. "It annoys me."

"All right," she gave a startled jump on his knee, "call it something else. But, be honest, nobody can feel inspired all the time. Not even Billy Graham. You have to work at it."

"Never mind about that," he said, plucking her close. He seemed to be doing more and more things in spasms: talking, opening windows, loving his wife.

"You haven't had a rest in such a long time," she whispered. "Even inspiration becomes a grind."

"God, does it ever?"

"But the wonderful thing is . . . nobody sees it in your work. They still find it . . . as fresh, and moving. . . ." Of course she must know that it wasn't real writing. Just fresh and moving. He had seen through his own stuff years ago; it annoyed him that she hadn't yet: he felt it was a little dishonest of her.

"Never mind about that, either."

"Look at that wonderful letter you got from the woman with rheumatism."

"I don't want to hear about it."

"Bert, you're awful."

Now came the funny part. Betty pretended that she didn't mind having children. That was the ultimate boffo. She had trouble with them: they seemed to tear at her, wither at her from inside, like deathwatch beetles. And after they were born, they made her nervous in geometric progression. They kept at one so. But she had them for his sake. She knew how much it meant to him. She had read about it in the *Catholic Woman.*

And so, in the course of time, another lank-haired, listless grumbler would arrive, shabbier than the others, greeting each day with a whine. Toothless to begin with, then spotty and withdrawn, and all the time making the writing go faster and faster. And another guardian angel in the house. Cheers for that anyway.

It was sweet poison in his mouth. The only thing that did him any good any more was Betty. She could stop the endless, stinking flow of words for a few minutes anyway. Ah well.

"I'm sorry, Betty. I guess I don't feel like it today. Just tired."

"Poor dear," she said but with a certain coolness. "Poor, tired dear."

And that brought on the worst spasm of all.

5

It began to snow the next day, which figured. There was a brutal chill in the air, and he caught a cold right away, and handed it down to his heir Bertram, Jr., who would see to its further distribution. This was the kind of petty harassment that made Bert feel like a professional; if things got much worse, he could start turning out the Christmas cheer in earnest.

On Wednesday he gave a talk in Nutley. A woman dressed in lace curtains said, "I don't know how you think of those things," and her mother said, "Bless you, Mr. Flax." On Friday he spoke to a men's group in East Orange on the

Communist menace. He felt a bit sheepish about that one, especially when the chairman called him a fearless fighter against Communism—he could hardly call himself that; and it probably wasn't exactly true that the Communists hated his insides, or that he was No. 1 on their "must-get" list. But standing up there with his nose stuffed and his eyes streaming, he felt a little less outrageous than usual.

He had resisted the talks as long as possible. But with the arrival of number four, the extra fifty or a hundred dollars became irresistible. He and Betty made out a list of topics he felt competent to talk about—the Catholic literary revival, the Catholic intellectual revival, Catholics and TV, Catholics and decent literature, Catholics and better communications; he hadn't meant to talk about Communism at all, because he didn't know much about it. But men's groups in East Orange wanted to hear about Communism, so Communism it was.

"I don't say that the communications media are Communist-dominated and Communist-orientated. But I do say this . . ." his own grievances were ugly wounds showing through his dinner jacket ". . . it is sometimes difficult for a good Catholic to get started in these fields. I'm not condemning anyone, mind you, just asking questions."

His discontent was saluted by widely assorted faces around the room. Insubstantial men who wondered why things had gone so badly for them, fat men who felt chronically uncomfortable at the edges, the Monsignor to his right who was sick and tired of men's groups, and was bracing himself desperately for the nightly burst of *bonhomie*. Bert felt brotherhood with all of them: he addressed their nameless dissatisfaction, from his own.

"A young Catholic may find his chosen field closed to him. He may be obliged to settle for the second-best . . . waste of national resources . . . don't know who is to blame." It was a wild one tonight. But the faces continued to encourage him giving off an unreal glitter . . . and pretty soon he was hinting even more darkly ("Not unreasonable . . . to suggest . . . plot"). Oh what the hell, it was doing them all good, getting it out of their systems. And nobody really got hurt. "I'm sure you all know what I'm talking about. It wouldn't be charitable to mention names." Charitable or possible.

The chairman felt called upon to say just a little bit more. "Mr. Flax is a fine American. Coming all the way over here with a cold." The house rose. Except for the Monsignor who had fallen asleep, or was playing possum.

The next day Bert felt awful. He had taken another step down the primrose path, tried a new vice on his piano; and all at the expense of those pleasant, vacuous men in East Orange. Getting them all worked up like that. Tummies heaving with passion, little black ties askew.

"How was it last night?" asked Betty.

"It was awful. A complete fraud."

"I suppose it must feel like that sometimes."

"But so often?"

"It's always worse at this time of year."

True enough. Christmas cost more money every year, which meant that on top of the poems and stories, he had to take the stump more often too. Presents for the children, presents for the in-laws, food for millions, all had to be paid for out of trumped-up emotion and devalued language. This year was a bad one—toys were more expensive than ever, and the juicy women's clubs had left him for dead. And meanwhile, the Christ child came nearer.

Saturday. The week had a sting in its tail at this time of year. On Christmas Eve, Betty always wanted to go with him to Midnight Mass (like Dave Gilhouley's mother), which meant that pretty soon he would have to go to confession again. To round out the beauty of the ceremony, he was expected to go up to Communion and come back looking peaceful. And that meant once more into the little black box.

The funny part (all things considered) was that it did still mean that.

He went to St. Jude's at four that Saturday to look at the pamphlets. Possibly his momentum would carry him the the rest of the way. He pulled out the magazines and grimaced at Flax's material, which seemed to pervade them like fluff.

Serene fellow, Flax. A bit on the round, sleek side. Possibly a woman. Keeps hamsters and little bluebirds of some kind. A cheerful Christian ("Christianity does not call for long faces") but not too cheerful, of course ("We must watch out for our old friend Pollyanna"). Arrested development perhaps. Got stuck somewhere. Still, things being as they are, he or she serves a purpose.

A long line was shimmying toward Father Terwilliger's box—those must be the souls who liked to be scourged and pommeled for their sins. The comfort seekers waited patiently for Monsignor Flanagan. Granted that it didn't make any real difference, Bert opted for the Monsignor, and plunked himself down behind a covey of placid old women. You had to like old women, they took it all so seriously.

He put his hand over his mouth to stop the silent rush of words. Just to be still, and then slowly to work things out. Make useful notes.

It's been, what, six months? When was Easter anyway?

Useful notes. Winter afternoon in church. Prematurely dark. Steam heat. People subdued, creeping into the box one by one. Abasing themselves. Creeping home again drenched in humble gratitude.

He got up and walked out, just like that. Not today.

6

And so, back to Sunday again. Once a month, Betty took the kids over to her mother's place, as a kind of public service, and he stayed late in bed and did his damnedest to miss Mass. Just once. Prove he could. (What good did it do anyway, making wisecracks in the vestibule?) He shut his eyes hard against the morning light, but they kept flying open and by ten o'clock he was ready to hoist the white flag.

He got up peevishly and put on his brown tweed suit (for country living, three eternal years ago, when that bit still seemed worth doing). He watched Sunday morning television until he could stand no more. It seemed the point of the religious revival was to weave the dullness and flatness of church into the whole texture of life; bring the nervous cough into your own home. He ate breakfast so slowly it got cold and then crept, Betty having taken the car, like a snail unwillingly to church.

He missed the notices altogether. Monsignor Flanagan was giving a gentle sermon about Our Lady according to his wont. Bert backed and filled in the vestibule. He wasn't going to think blasphemy about the Virgin, or spill silly words about her.

He wasn't successful right away. He heard Flanagan say, "And her pain was ten thousand times greater than any pain experienced by you or I." He must have got that one from Terwilliger, right down to the "I." Look boys, one hundredth of that kind of pain would drive a human being out of his skull. Any human being, Ah forget it. "But her happiness was a billion, a trillion times greater." This must be the feast of the Meaningless Exaggeration. Not to mention the Unwarranted Assumption. Take it from a pro, he thought.

He got the audio off at last and watched Flanagan under glass. No wonder Catholics were so stupid, turning off their brains like this every week. No, Catholics weren't so stupid. They were recent immigrants, that was all. And there wasn't a population problem. There was lots of good seaweed to eat. And talking of that, the distribution of smut had grown immensely in the last few years, hadn't it? Communists bringing it in? He turned away from the diocesan papers which had caught his eye for a moment, and back to Flanagan.

The Monsignor was a good man. He had a good face. He loved his parishioners, even when he didn't know what they were all about, and he put up with Father Terwilliger. He had white hair. He had soft hands. He had a sorrowful voice, cracked for good in some forgotten confessional. Monsignor Flanagan was all right.

But Bert could only watch him through glass, because the

Monsignor lived in a music box or something. He was a little toy Monsignor, who scampered around on a groove and when you shook the box it snowed. Bert wished he could get in with the Monsignor and circle with him. The point was, Flanagan was a good man, but he didn't really exist.

Mr. O'Malley who took the seat money had been glaring at him balefully for some time, and Bert was afraid he was going to come over and say something. They used to be acquaintances and he was always afraid that O'Malley would want to start it up again. They faced each other every week like this, but today Bert was certain he was going to come over and say, "Hello there, Mr. Flax. My wife is still a great admirer of yours." After that, he would look pretty silly, not paying his seat money.

It occupied his attention for a while. O'Malley had his own construction company; he didn't know that Bert simply couldn't afford giving money to fly-by-night organizations. Then the bell rang, and the seat-money man struck his chest briskly, without taking his eyes off Bert. Sort of unnerving. "He thinks I'm going to break past him and vanish up the aisle." Bert opened his Missal and held it up between himself and the snoopy seat-money man. The worst thing about these childish diversions was that they only added to the ache of boredom. The service seemed even longer, as he played peekaboo with the moneychanger.

Monsignor Flanagan said Mass slowly anyway. His fingers shook, rattling the book, introducing a note of dramatic tension to everything he did. One could just picture his fingers groping for the host; the back was bent down over it, irrecoverably; old man's words were said, and then the arms came up triumphantly with the consecrated bread. The fingers trembled for joy. Bert pressed his nose to the invisible glass. How was it possible to feel so cold?

Monsignor Flanagan's arms slumped down and the sacrifice went on. Bert had long ago exhausted all his improving thoughts, all his burst of inspiration, to see him through the tapering-off part. He started to leave, then thought of the money man, reached over and dropped a dollar on his table. The man smiled seraphically, a good winner. Bert backed out of the church.

Father Terwilliger was waiting on the steps to intercept early departures.

"Good morning, Mr. Flax," he said in an icy little voice. Terwilliger too was excluded from Flanagan's feast, but didn't mind a bit.

"Morning, Father. Betty and the children. . . ."

"I was just reading your latest in last month's *Passenger*. A beautiful thing." He held Bert's sleeve with cold, chalky fingers. "Beautiful."

"Thank you very much."

"You have a great talent, Mr. Flax."

"Thank you, Father—I really must run."

"You must give a talk to our men. . . ."

Bert was off and running. What Terwilliger meant was, what are you doing out of church so soon, if you're so hot? Leading Catholic writer, eh? Then show us your medals. He was on to Terwilliger's tricks. Terwilliger had never read the *Passenger* in his life; why, come to think of it, Bert hadn't even *had* an article in last month's *Passenger*. It was the old school thing all over again. "A boy with your gifts, Bertram. . . . God has been good to you, Bertram. . . ." Keep in line, you snotty little boy, was what they meant.

And still meant. By God, he wasn't going to take much more of this. His Missal fell out of his pocket from running. He looked back and there was Terwilliger staring. Bert pocketed the Missal and walked slowly round the corner. He supposed he had pretended to be in a hurry for fear Terwilliger would remove all the magazines from the church rack as a punishment. It was a professional habit, keeping up appearances, but silly for a grown man and he wasn't going to do any more of it. "Wonder how many people keep up appearances for Terwilliger, keep it a good, live parish for Terwilliger?"

The house was exceptionally empty, which wasn't as much fun as it used to be. Betty kept the downstairs part as clean as a cemetery plot on Sundays. Upstairs, all was the usual dismal confusion. Vestiges of children: toys and clothes and water on the floor, pretty much like Gilhouley's place, in a roundabout sort of way.

As soon as you got out in the suburbs, Gilhouley's life began to look pretty good again. Not the Sunday sprawl in front of the televison set, and certainly not the quart of beer—that was like going back to your playpen for the afternoon; and not the pockmarked lads of the village who talked about making out, and who regarded their sex lives as some kind of sacred trust. Thank God it was not still part of his worries to envy that.

No, it was something he hardly dared say to himself, something to do after Mass on Sunday, something that went on in the cellar. It was like putting on woman's clothes and scratching blood from your arm . . . God, no, that was just the words again. He didn't mean anything like that.

All he really wanted to do was get away from Terwilliger for a while (do them both good), cuss a little—cuss, that was good; a little manly cussing among the boys—drink a little, talk the never-never language of making out and putting out, and in a word, clear his system for the Christmas poem. That's how it used to be at Bishop Mahoney's, obscenity over at Gilhouley's and the fruity voice of atonement afterward. Man had to relax sometimes.

He trotted through the empty house scooping at cigarettes and a bottle of rye, laying his Missal by the bed, jotting a note for Betty, checking the buses. He should have done this years and years ago. Instead of chewing his big, rubber problem, get to Gilhouley's, man, and spew it out.

And then what? Start again?

7

The bus ride to town on Sundays was an enriching experience. Bert was raised on the fetid, convulsive buses of Manhattan, and he could never get over this big, streamlined thing, exquisitely modulated to temperature and only about three other passengers to enjoy it. Chunks of Sunday newspapers had been stuffed into the crannies of the seats, so you could sit next to the section of your choice, and still be five rows away from the next man and his bleating urge to talk.

Good old bus line. It swept you away from the rising executives in their sandstone houses and the tweedy pediatricians and the pink-fisted dentists, with their teeth in everyone's neck. . . . While you were paying fleabite bills and raising automatic children and writing adolescent slop for Father Chubb, you got this silly feeling of being trapped. But on the nice airy bus, the barbed wire around your ears lifted slightly. Bert stretched his thin legs into the aisle and lit a cigarette, although the sign said not to. Bloodbury was unchristian, unnatural, but no need to get excited; the bus cost a dollar each way, but what the hell, Father Chubb would provide.

Gilhouley turned out to be much as before, changeless as a stone satyr. He hadn't put on his pajamas so carefully this time. His hair needed combing and sorting.

"Oh, hello, Bert old boy. Back so soon?"

"What's with the 'old boy'?"

"I thought we might have shocked you last week with our unconventional *ménage*."

"*Ménage*, old boy? What's gotten into you, Gilhouley?"

"Just a figure of speech. It means, never mind what it means."

"Why should I be shocked? By your . . . what you just said." Bishop Mahoney jokes. When Gilhouley was tired he talked about, oh, tonsorial parlors and intestinal fortitude, and Bert pretended not to understand.

"I thought you might be exacerbated, is all I meant to impute. Old boy."

"You know me, Dave. I don't mind about *ménages* and stuff like that. Within reason."

Gilhouley eyed him with mild curiosity. "I don't know. Aren't you the guy who writes all that religious stuff in the magazines, Bert? Jane remembered your name from her convent and dug up a batch of it."

"What do you mean, religious stuff?" The panic squirted down his arms and exploded in the back of his hands. He had never lost his fear of Gilhouley finding out.

"Yeah, sure, my mother sends me all those magazines.

Bertram Flax. We found it right away: that's you, isn't it?" He was very polite about it.

"Nah. That's my crazy uncle. You didn't really think it was me, did you?"

"I don't know. The guy writes a bit like you used to in school. You sure it isn't you?"

Bert laughed shakily. He wanted to find a way out of denying it three times. Just a superstition.

"Look, Gilhouley, I'm your old friend. Bert Flax. Remember?" Gilhouley nodded mechanically. "Would I lie to you, Dave?" Gilhouley nodded mechanically and said, "I don't know why you're so worked up over it. It's pretty good, some of it."

"Boy, they teach you tolerance in this goddamn place, don't they? I think it's cheap, hypocritical crap, myself. A disgrace to religion."

"Well, he's *your* uncle."

"That's what you like about him, isn't it? He's the kind of guy kills religion by inches, by pouring low-grade fertilizer on it." It suddenly seemed worthwhile to get Dave to blaspheme again. Then religion would be exciting again, and he could do the poem.

"No, I really go for his stuff. Hey, what you got in the bag, fella? You got something for ol' Dave?"

Bert unwrapped the rye and Dave gurgled with delight. "Hey, good stuff, good stuff." He scampered out and came back with the plastic cups. "Before the gang gets here. We'll have a wee nip, just the two of us." He pushed some shirts off the sofa. "Boy, for an inspirational-type writer, you got a very broad mind, Flax old boy."

"Cut that out, Gilhouley. I said it was my uncle."

"OK, OK, Uncle," he tiptoed round happily dropping ice in the tooth mugs. "For you, it's uncle. Ooh man." There was something a bit forced about that.

Bert perversely wanted to watch the Giants' game again, but they were playing at home this week, and New York was blacked out. So they turned on an old movie instead. "Boy, that Linda Darnell used to be something," said Bert. "Really something." Dave nodded. It sounded artificial and Bert didn't pursue it. Linda Darnell had been something, possibly still was. It was like pretending to be interested in electric trains.

"You ever marry Joan Furfy, Bert?"

"No. She married an architect."

"Too bad. She was pretty nice."

"I married a girl called Betty Forsythe."

"Oh. Did I know her?"

"I don't think so. She was after your time."

They drank fast. Bert felt the same rising excitement without substance, without content, that he felt last week. For some reason, Gilhouley seemed to be treating him like a priest or something. In fifty years or so, Gilhouley might want to make his peace with the Church, and then he would be able to say, "I was always reverent with the clergy, Father." Crap, no. Old Dave wasn't like that. It was just the old Columbia tolerance. If he had been a cannibal, Dave would have been reverent about that too. They'd really smoothed off old Dave.

"You know, if I'd left the Church like you have, I'd really hate it?"

"You would?" asked Dave courteously.

"I certainly would. I'd hate the guts out of it. Where are your friends?"

"I guess maybe they're not coming. No game."

"Oh. Yeah, well that's how I'd feel."

"I never felt about it that strongly. What's to hate?"

"What they do to you. The way they trap you."

"You mean all the rules? Is that what you mean?" Gilhouley got up and began to play with the channels. "Everybody has rules, don't they? It's not just the Church."

"You should have been a Jesuit, Gilhouley. You got more sense than imagination."

"I wouldn't mind being a Jesuit," said Dave, yawning. "They gave us a good education, boy. And it's not like being a Catholic, or anything." Dave found a movie about the *Wehrmacht* and went back to his chair. He used to be fatter than this, thought Bert, and more conspicuously sadistic. They had scaled him down in every way, at Tolerance U.

"Easy for you to talk, Fatso. You're out of it. You're out of the trap."

"What do you keep talking about, trap? You want a divorce or something?"

"No. Nothing like that."

"Rhythm giving you the jumps?"

"I don't know. We haven't tried it."

"So, stop giving me trap. How's your glass?" He took it. "You ought to read some of your uncle's stuff. He'd make you realize how lucky you are. With God's glorious gift of faith. No kidding, Bert. I sometimes wish I had it myself when I read your uncle."

"The hell you do. Frugaling your life away with every dame you can get." It was an acid fantasy. He didn't really care about the girls. It was just the only way he knew of getting at Gilhouley.

"Hey, if that's what's eating you, Bert—believe me, it isn't all that good."

"Yeah, sure."

"And it isn't that easy. *Heil Hitler!*" he jumped to attention and barked some German at the screen. He clicked his naked heels. "What was I saying?"

"You said you were fed up with girls and were going into a monastery."

"Oh yeah, that," Gilhouley grinned. "Well, not right now. I'm a sinful man, Bertram. You have to understand that."

Old friendship could be a drag. You had to talk the same old way, pretending to the same old lusts and amusements.

If you admitted that anything important had changed, pop went the friendship. You were just a stranger after that, making unreasonable claims.

"Where's Jane?" he asked idly.

"Over at her mother's. Spending the weekend."

"I didn't think girls like that had mothers."

"You bet they do. Goddamn useless mothers. Suspicious, lousy mothers. They're always just about to guess what their darling daughters are up to. I told you, Bert, frigging around isn't all a bed of roses." Yes, yes, he could almost sight his old friend surging up through flaccid layers of understanding, taking sides once more. . . . "But I guess you can't blame them. Somebody has to watch out for sods like me. Someday you'll be doing it yourself." Dave subsided, blub, blub.

"I guess so."

"Let's face it, Flax. It's a *bourgeois* world."

"I'll drink to that," said Bert, and emptied his tooth mug for the second time.

It looked as if his uncle had the right angle on all this. Pity, in a way, that he had no uncle.

8

A tropical beach with cardboard palm trees. Bert's dream of felicity was always the same. After making love, after working, he got out the beach and lay down on the synthetic sand. Not a very wide range of images for a creative writer but it brought extraordinary satisfaction. Silence and death, charming. Must have got the idea from an old calendar: there were no beaches like that around New York. For a moment, it was sort of duplicated on the screen. Water lapping, Tondelaya—I bring you filter tips. Well, anyway. Gilhouley's big thumb swept it away.

Gilhouley kept the windows closed, so the smoke from the cigarettes kept clouding up inside like incense. Sabbath observance. Gilhouley pouring the sacramental rye. Blasphemy was the occupational risk of the word business, you just changed the subject. Crank, crank. Gilhouley was to blame anyway, in a way.

"Why don't you grow up, Gilhouley?" Bert asked again suddenly, angrily. If he could denounce Dave coherently, it would clarify his own position.

Dave shrugged. "What's in it for me, if I grow up?"

"You could be out walking with the kids in the park right now. You could be at a meeting or something. Goddamn it, Gilhouley, I despise the life you lead."

"I guess it is pretty useless."

Bert grunted. You had to keep it a joke, or put away your knife. What was to get so angry about anyway? Well, the abstract painting over the television bugged him, for one thing. He focused on that.

"What's a lace-curtain Irishman like you doing with an abortion like that?"

"Wirra, wirra."

"You're not only useless, David Gilhouley, you're pretentious. I can never forgive that."

"That's it, that's what makes it so pathetic." Dave was fumbling with the channels again.

"You're a disaster, Gilhouley." Bert squinted at his friend, who was hiding somewhere behind a tight, patient smile. Gilhouley was bringing his tolerance to bear on the private life. Better change old Flax's channel while we're about it. On to a Sunday program.

"Ever see José Miranda any more?" he asked.

"No. What's he doing?"

"Priest."

"Huh."

"You could tell. Sanctimonious little creep."

Gilhouley didn't answer, damn it. Bert knew he agreed, but was squirming away from even the hint of a religious topic the way they always did. Lace-curtain reverence and

Columbia liberalism combined to produce this soft, sleek effect. Like Matty Flynn, Dave had the convent-parlor tactfulness. You couldn't talk to anybody any more, for tactfulness. If you could just talk, you might find out where you stood—strengthen your faith or give it up.

"Look, Gilhouley, just tell me one thing. Why *did* you leave the Church."

Dave looked embarrassed and ducked his head. "I guess it just didn't add up. I still have a lot of respect. . . ."

"Shit, Gilhouley, I don't want to hear any more about you and your lousy respect. Please." Gilhouley didn't answer. "You leave the damn Church and set yourself up like King Farouk, and you have the the stinking nerve to talk about respect. . . ."

The thin, tight smile again. Tight as a drum. Be nice to lance it and watch it burst, let some of the pus out. Bert held his temples. "I'm sorry, Dave. I don't know why I'm going after you like this. Must be something making me nervous."

"You seem to be loaded for bear this afternoon, old boy."

"The trouble with you is you're too damn good-natured. You invite unreasonable attacks."

"The fighting blood of the Gilhouleys," and so forth. It just got boring again after that. How did you get *into* people these days? Dave kept on glancing at the TV program guide and finding more movies to watch; Bert drank his rye and made tired fun of the commercials.

In itself a form of rerun. Gilhouley used to be a master of this art. Jumping up and down, making faces at Betty Furness, twisting her words with fiendish dexterity. Bert tried to remember some of his antics, but they were all gone, along with the smuggled beer, the autographed baseball on the mantelpiece, the picture of—who was it? Paulette Goddard, no doubt.

Little Gilhouley had been Mr. Worldly-wise-man in their

class at Bishop Mahoney. He was the one who brought in the jokes proper to each year. He was the one with the "party record" which he played upstairs on a muffled phonograph. Mrs. Gilhouley was a good woman, but so vague that she would dust off David's girlie magazines and put them back neatly without suspecting a thing.

This gave Gilhouley the edge he needed, and his room became a sort of clubhouse where pubescence could proceed undisturbed. Gilhouley had a brother in the navy who kept them abreast of biological developments. Dave read portions of his letters aloud every week to his friends. Matty Flynn sat there under protest, shaking his head and taking it all in. Matty was a treat.

Then to top it off, David's mother bought him a television set for his room and it arrived just in time, because his brother had left the navy and gone into dry cleaning. Nothing much to report on there. (Dry, dull brother, it turned out on meeting him.) But David came into his own as master of TV revels. What were some of the things he said? Bert groped back and memory retreated an inch farther. He could just see David crouched like a monkey in front of the set, chattering soundlessly.

It probably hadn't been as funny as all that. Dave himself didn't seem to think so. He sat back now, listening to Bert's retreaded jests, smiling on and off—for all the world as if he were the one who had grown up and Bert was the one who hadn't. Wonder what, if anything, amused him now.

"Remember," said Bert, "the way Matty used to look when you heckled Bishop Sheen?"

"Yeah." Dave made a perfunctory sound of amusement, a damp "huh" sound.

"He had a real hacking laugh, like it was killing him inside. And his eyes looked insane."

"That's right." Dave shook his head, as if remembering,

and shook out another sort of chuckle. No, he didn't think heckling Bishop Sheen was funny. What *did* he do for laughs these days?

"Almost empty," said Dave at last holding up the bottle soberly. "A sad moment."

Bert could think of only once when a bottle of booze had accomplished less. That was the time they hid gin in the cloakroom during the senior prom and drank it neat and got sick one by one from jogging up and down on the dance floor. No point in reminding Dave of that. He wouldn't think it was funny.

"I'm afraid I haven't got anything else to drink," said Gilhouley.

"You never did have anything," said Bert—and then, quickly, feeling a tactful smile coming on his host. "Never mind about that. You're a good fellow, Gilhouley, always very generous with your time."

Dave gave a small bow. He suddenly looked as if he was going to say, "I have a lot of work to do for tomorrow. I have a test," or something. Flax would have to go home alone, shivering and a bit flustered, minus a bottle of his entertaining-whiskey. His cold was gurgling back into place, as the rye cooled off.

"Let's go over to Matty's place," he said.

"*Matty's?*" said Dave.

"Yeah, over to Matty's. He may give us something to drink."

"I doubt it."

"Yes, well he might. Anyway it'll be good to get together again."

Gilhouley didn't appear to think so, which was interesting. Faced with his old target, he might forget some of this chintzy poise he'd picked up and let fly with some of the old Gilhouleyisms. Just one or two would clear the air wonderfully.

"Look, Bert—"

"I know, you got an important test tomorrow. Let's go see Matty."

"I should be doing some work."

"You got your midterm, semifinal preliminaries, I know, I know. Let's go see Matty."

The big man looked politely puzzled. Bert realized that he was tugging gently at Dave's pajama sleeve.

"All right, Bert. Take it easy. We'll go see Matty."

"I was only joking. We don't have to see Matty."

"No, we'll go see him. It'll be good to see Matty again."

He went to the bedroom to find some clothes. Bert watched him through the open door, moving slowly, rather solemnly around the room, picking up socks and weighing them carefully, as if it mattered about socks. Bert must have got hold of the wrong Gilhouley in the phone book, and the fellow he had found didn't know how to break it to him.

Or else the booze had stiffened Dave up unobtrusively.

Or else, and this was perhaps likely, he had been annoyed beyond endurance by those headlong sorties of Bert's. Ex-Catholics had little soft places, under the arms, between the toes. You never knew when you were going to land on one. Dave was being dignified to hide the discomfort.

Maybe over at Matty's. . . . He smiled to himself. That was what he wanted most of all for Christmas. A scene. One genuine, human cry of rage and pain. From somebody, anybody. Bert Flax would do in a pinch. Then he could go back happily to his world of chocolate icing and blueberry muffins and write his Christmas poem.

9

They took the subway down, and again the elevator didn't work when they got there. A platinum woman came down the stairs with her dog and looked in the mailbox, although it was Sunday. She held the dog up and it looked in the box too. Otherwise, Flynn's building slumbered in its own steam.

Matty greeted them with one of his surprising bursts of effusion—"Dave, you old son-of-a-gun, how are you?" and thump, thump on the biceps—which seemed to amuse Gilhouley slightly.

"My wife—" said Matty.

"Is visiting her mother, I know," said Bert.

"That's right," said Matty meekly, as if he had shot his bolt already. Gilhouley stood quietly in the doorway fingering his hat. It was up to Bert to get the meeting under way.

"You got any booze, Matty?" he asked jovially. Just like the old days, huh Matty? huh Dave?

"I guess we've got a little beer."

"Is that all?"

"I'll see what we've got." He slippered over to a big brown cupboard and took out his key-ring diffidently; looked at the keys one by one, chose a small one and plunged it in. There was one bottle inside. Matty had to read the label to see what it was.

"Look Matty, we don't want to drink your last bottle," said Dave.

"That's all right," said Matty. "I didn't know we had it."

"Yeah, but look Matty . . . what do you say, Bert? Matty's last bottle."

Bert chewed his lip, and it made him thirsty. The only thing was, you had to show *some* reluctance. "Yeah, Matty. Are you quite sure you don't mind?"

He saw, incredibly, Matty pushing the bottle back a few inches. He thought he saw it. "All right, then, if you don't mind," he stepped up heartily. "No use letting it sit there."

"I'll get some ice," said Matty.

Gilhouley sat on the sofa, his overcoat bunching up around him. He picked up a magazine off the coffee table, thumbed at it, put it back. It looked as if it might have some Flax in it. A boy in a torn dressing-gown peeped in and aimed his gun at Bert.

"Hey, you the kid who gave me this cold?"

"Bang you're dead," said the boy.

Just like Matty's boy, to say something bright like that. Bert played dead for a minute all the same because it seemed like a good idea, and didn't open his eyes again until he heard the nervous tinkle of ice overhead.

The boy went out again hitching up his pants through his dressing-gown.

"Nice boy," said Gilhouley. "Who does he look like?"

"We haven't decided."

Oh for godsake.

"He's got his mother's eyes."

And his father's backside, said Bert to himself. "Look, doesn't anybody want to talk about old times or something?"

"What have you been doing with yourself, Dave?" asked Matty.

"I'm still going to school."

"Uh-huh." Matty nodded thoughtfully.

"I get out in June. Then I have to start looking for work." Dave was thoughtful too.

"Too bad," said Matty.

"Yes, well. I like to eat," said Dave.

Oh, go on. You like to eat? You're teasing, aren't you? thought Bert.

This was where it all started, with these two. They were archetypes—Gilhouley the baddy, Flynn the goody. If they had a fight, Flax could join in on Flynn's side and stick a flaming sword in Gilhouley's rump . . . but they didn't seem to be archetypes any more, just nobodys. They wouldn't re-create the past if you paid them.

"How about you Matty?" said Dave, for instance.

"I sell. Upstate, Syracuse, all around there," said, for godsake, Matty.

"Like it?" Dave riposted. Over to Matty.

"It's all right, I guess. It pays for the groceries."

The whole thing was some enormous joke. People didn't talk like this when he wasn't around. They had some lookout man who said, here comes old Flax, we'll talk about paying for the groceries. We'll talk about selling, you know, upstate, all around there.

"Gilhouley left the Church," he said. It was meant to sound like the crack of a whip.

"Is that so?" said Matty conversationally.

"I wouldn't put it quite like that," said Dave.

"Oh, come *on.* For Christ's sweet sake, Gilhouley—you've left the Church and you know it."

They just stared at him. Whether you believed or didn't believe, it wasn't right to talk like this. Matty and Dave obviously agreed on that.

"Look Matty—that stuff is important to you, isn't it? Why don't you argue with him about it?"

Matty mumbled. "Arguing never solved anything."

"Right. It's example that counts, isn't it? I mean, like living in a crumby building and raising a lot of condemned kids—that kind of thing has a very profound influence. Boy, they say—hey, I don't mean you, Matty." Never, *never* make cracks about people's neighborhoods. Rules three, four and five for growing up in New York. "That was just a random example."

He suddenly realized that they weren't going to answer, whatever he said. It was all part of the arrangement. If old Flax tries to change the subject, from groceries and how've you been keeping, just don't answer him, that's all. Head him off somehow, get him back into line.

"You guys used to fight about religion. What happened?"

No answer.

"Gilhouley used to say that religion was for old ladies. Flynn used to say that Gilhouley was just trying to sound tough."

They smiled politely at the hilarious reminiscence.

"Why, you guys fought, really fought about it. One time. On the basketball court."

"Remember that, Matty?" asked Dave.

"Yeah, I guess so."

Bishop Mahoney had just lost a heartbreaker that particular afternoon, and for some reason this led to religious rancor. Matty was the team manager and paced the sidelines in a mighty overcoat. Gilhouley was tall for his age and second-string guard. A five-minute man, when Bishop Mahoney was riding high. Bert was a hard-hitting reporter.

They blew it in overtime because Gilhouley, who had come in when his overstudy fouled out, hacked a Mother-of-Sorrows man under the basket. Bony, anxious boys lined the keyhole for a moment. The Mother-of-Sorrows man bent his knees solemnly and flipped in the two points: 53–52.

Flax was some distance away and could only just make out what happened next. Gilhouley's hair was greasy and writhing with sweat; Flynn had on his little manager's hat. The fluorescent light made them both look green and half crazy. Gilhouley's lips moved, Flynn took off his glasses and made a woolly rush in his big overcoat. Gilhouley got all tangled up in Flynn's scarf. A lot of people didn't even know anything had happened.

Bert intercepted Flynn on his way out. He was still trembling and heaving with indignation. It seemed that Gilhouley had refused to say the team prayers at half-time. "You know, the Hail Mary and all. He wouldn't say them. I told him that's why we lost." Gilhouley had apparently not been as urbane as usual about it. He hadn't expected to get in the game anyway and had reasoned that refusing to pray would arouse his teammates to savage accomplishments; instead it had set the stage for his own catastrophe. So he called Flynn a superstitious——(Matty wouldn't say what the——stood for) and they scuffled and were easily parted, neither being notably warlike. End of anecdote.

"I remember," said Matty, "I guess."

"Crazy kids," said Gilhouley. "I can't remember what we were fighting about, though. It was something about a game, wasn't it?"

That does it! Bert poured himself another shivering slug and stalked toward the television set. They must be watching him like a madman by now; really scared he would say something and bring on the discomfort. Two old ladies simpering at each other and hoping for the best. I'll show them, by God. It was important then, it's important now.

He wheeled and took his last stand in front of the set. They could just see the screen between his legs, if they wanted to. "Matty, Dave, I want to have this thing out right now," he said firmly. "Right out. Once and for all."

"What thing, old boy?"

"This whole goddamn thing." He almost sobbed with vexation. "You know what I mean."

They looked at each other curiously. They shouldn't be doing that. They were enemies. He was going to choose up sides in a minute. Meanwhile, stop that.

"Look," he said, "you're my oldest friends, right? All right if I talk for a while? *Stop* looking at each other and answer me."

Matty nodded. "Go ahead and talk, Bert. We're listening."

"All right, then. I'm going to talk." He glared at them, warmed up his mouth and said, "Right now."

A clock started ticking for the first time. He could hear a cat that hadn't been there before, and smell flowers too, crazy flowers. A woman sent a shout into the courtyard and it caromed around like a bedspring.

Now what the hell was it he wanted to say?

10

Big Kate Dooley came in while he was talking and tiptoed around in a kind of ecstasy. Bert Flax had come back. Jubilation. She didn't hear what he was saying right away, just watched the pale ascetic face working, the thin pale lips: he might dispense joy to others, but for himself there was pain. That was what was so wonderful.

"It's a cruel joke," explained Bert, "they keep you a child until it's too late. That's what Dave should be saying. Look at Matty here, half a man, look at me, half of Matty. And Dave has a case, all right. These things are important."

Look at how he held them transfixed, thought Big Kate. The big sly man still in his overcoat, apparently too moved to take it off; Matty's face frozen in fascination. Kate hunched herself up to keep from making a sound and interrupting the train of thought. She was watching the others to make sure that Bert was going down well, getting his message across. (It must be a good message.)

"Why don't you just get out, if you feel like that?" asked Dave.

"It gets in your bones, that's why. You can't just get out, Gilhouley. Anyway, I'm not presenting *my* case, I'm presenting *your* case. If you had the guts. . . ."

Dave shrugged. He obviously wasn't fooled by that—he knew whose case it was. Matty was keeping prudent counsel. Sometimes quite good Catholics liked to sound off about the difficulties of the faith. Bert was obviously one of those. It didn't mean anything.

"They've got these rules against becoming a man, you see? You mustn't develop independent judgment, because that's pride. You mustn't be honest, because that doesn't square with the old *prudentia*. And you mustn't have any kind of experience, because experience is an occasion of sin. This is what Dave would say, and it isn't so easy to shrug it off. . . ."

What the hell was Kate Dooley looking so smug about? Bert had just noticed his swollen admirer simpering in the doorway. If there was one thing he hated it was fat demure women.

And Matty seemed to be working into a pious trance, too. "Isn't that right, Matty?" he shouted for attention. "Don't they shut you up in a little black box?"

"It sometimes seems like that," Matty conceded cautiously.

By now Kate was really trying to concentrate. But the face was so ugly-beautiful—there was a kind of torment in it, well, it was almost saintly—and the voice had a high, singing quality you could listen to without respect to the meaning. "Look at what the sermons do to you," said Bert. "They soften your damn brain. Take Kate Dooley over there. She can't *hear*. She can't *think*. She's all *soft*." Kate smiled at him uncertainly, at the face and the singing voice.

"But Matty here, that's the real tragedy. For years we watched this boy trying to grow up. Didn't we, Dave? And he couldn't get out of the cage, could he, Dave? He couldn't say an honest word, or feel an honest feeling."

Gilhouley looked over at Matty, who was scratching himself apologetically, acknowledging his faults. "And now he's so crippled with lousy humility that he can't just stand up and punch me—or you—in the jaw, like a man."

Flax weaved a couple of steps toward Flynn, then changed his plans and wheeled savagely on Gilhouley. "And you're no better, Gilhouley. Let's hear from Flynn for a moment. Why can't you be an honest-to-God atheist, Gilhouley? Flynn might be saying; only Flynn is a hundred percent noncontroversial. Let me tell you something, Miss Dooley, something about this big phony. He spent four whole years making fun of religion. Any doubts I have now, any trouble in church—there's the boy to thank for it. But now it seems, Gilhouley hasn't the grace, or the guts—*or* the guts—to follow through on it. Isn't that right, Matty? Isn't that right, Dave?"

"That's right," said Gilhouley tightly.

"He agrees with me, of course. God, how I despise a man who does that!"

"You'd better take it easy, Bert. You don't look too good." Matty reached out a tentative hand and watched it being swept aside. In a swirl of overcoat. Bert was back at the television, away from Flynn's suffocating gentleness. "Won't anybody fight about this? Won't somebody, for godsake, argue?"

It was hard to tell at what point Kate Dooley began to surface and see what was actually happening. Bert knew who *she* was, now. She was the big fat girl you had to take to the dance (mother's idea), for an evening's embarrassment. Naturally you ignored her at first and she sat stoically by herself; then you had two dances and made jokes that went over her head; and finally, on the way home, she said something that made you realize that she had known what you were doing all along. He bowed at Kate in anticipation —she was getting that look of squinty recognition they had on the way home. "You want to argue with me, Kate?" he asked almost gently. In a way, she was his responsibility; his flabby writing had helped to form her.

"You don't look very well, Mr. Flax," she said. "You've been working too hard."

They were coming at him from every side, fatherly, motherly, all great humanists, regardless of race, creed or color. He backed against the set, and it wobbled on spindly legs. "Get away."

For ten minutes or more they kept coming, in jerky waves, as if they needed repairing. Instead of giving him the contest he wanted, they had agreed to kill him with kindness. He clawed at them, but they came no closer and he couldn't quite reach them. From a safe distance they went on talking about him as if he wasn't there. "Bert was always a terrible drinker. Remember at the senior prom?" So now they remembered. He bet they remembered all along. "Poor Mr. Flax. He works so hard, you know." Gilhouley's face and voice were swimming in different directions; not so Kate Dooley's. Kate was merging, synthesizing, floating a merger; being more motherly than the Pope, all set to snuff him out like a cushion descending on a candle. "Poor Mr. Flax," a few inches away. "He writes those beautiful things. Yet he seems to be so troubled." "He does write them, doesn't he?" said Dave, from out in the hall it sounded like. "I was sure he wrote those things." Interesting eurhythmics. One two three kick, one two three kick. Bert Flax sank to the floor in his overcoat.

They tried to pick him up, but he pushed them away and sat there very dignified and knowing. A strand of thin brown hair had fallen across his forehead.

"Have you read his things?" whispered Kate. "They're lovely, aren't they?"

"Yes, he's a very fine writer," said Dave.

"Listen, all of you." Bert had to shout to make any sound at all. "I am not Bert Flax, I am not Bert Flax, I am not Bert Flax, I am not Bert Flax. . . ." How many times did that make it? Thing was, if they knew who he was, he couldn't speak his mind any more. Mustn't give scandal to the little ones.

"Of course you're not," said Diplomat Dave.

Bert tackled him round the knees for saying that and decided to go to sleep.

It was grim, even for a hospital. A colored man was cleaning his feet with a mop—pretty uncalled for at this time of the morning. He lifted his feet distastefully, and the mop shot under them and away. The amplifier was listing obscure complaints, "Nutley, Bloomfield, the Oranges . . ." a whiskery outpatient began to cry when he heard that "Verona, Pompton Lakes, Millbrook." An impossible sequence! Someone was doing if for a joke.

The bus terminal was a bit of New Jersey, one of the worst bits. The lights were so harsh. The people were so wretched. He wished he could cry too, but that was out of the question—since nothing had really happened. He put his head in his hands and stared at the tile floor for a while and said, "God help me," in an experimental sort of voice. But that was the worst of his case, the one that had all the doctors baffled.

In spite of all that excitement he had whipped up, and in spite of feeling so awful now, he still couldn't say "God help me" with a straight face. OK about the "help," of course, but he had used the word "God" a bit too often, and it was as hollow as a shriek in a fun-house, or a gong hit by a funny Chinaman.

He really must do something about that. Before Christmas at the latest.

Part Two

"A good Christian family is the highest repository of natural joy . . ."

FLAX. *Thoughts.*

1

Bert slept late on Monday morning, leaving Betty to galvanize the family. Bertram, Jr., went to school, Betty, Jr., went to kindergarten, the rest sat around and sniffled, while the family cold was passed sloppily among them. Betty wiped noses patiently and mapped out the day on her small blackboard. Food and medicine in reckless quantities, a trip to the doctor's, pretty much like a Monday.

She bundled them into red, green and blue snowsuits because, colds or not, they had to be hoisted out of Bert's way so he could do the Christmas poem. She stuffed them hacking, dripping and squealing into the Studebaker and made merrily off for the Safeway, leaving Bert to it: leaving him groaning in bed over his rhyming dictionary.

Betty had been brought up in Bloodbury and knew just about everybody. Women in red woolen hats waved from their stationwagons; and they had children pressed against the windows in the back, who had to be waved at too. And Canon Flood of the Anglican Church was out for his constitutional, and he wanted a wave. And so on.

She rather liked all this. Her own house seemed a bit dry and friendless toward this time of year. Bert had a lot of work to do, and he always got the same haunted (or was it deserted?) look. Once or twice before every Christmas he managed to get drunk, and then lay wheezing beside her, a strange, ugly man, smelling in the dark. He didn't seem to know her or want her. He just lay in a bundle looking, as far as she could tell, angry.

Bloodbury was the cure for all that. It was a shiny little town, with Tudor shop fronts and spiffy window displays; it had one genial policeman on every corner, and bargain shoppes run by punchy old ladies; it cooperated with the National Organization for Decent Literature—and how it cooperated!

She liked to drag her children in a chain past the bright windows: Christmas decorations, colored lights, quality furniture, everything polished and simplified, as it was in the *Saturday Evening Post* covers. She could join Bert in making jokes about this, but when he left her at Christmastime, it was a comfort to nose around and sop up the artificiality. Her religion against his.

Let's face it, he left her at Christmastime because of *that*. She had swung the car round by St. Jude's, and there was Father Terwilliger standing on the steps, blowing on his hands and taking in the scene. Bert left her for the principal feasts because she wasn't a Catholic. Once a year he came to his senses and got drunk with disgust. Her mother had prognosticated something of the sort.

"Good morning, Mrs. Flax," said Father Terwilliger. "It's very cold."

You could always park in front of St. Jude's. She hauled out the children, and found Father Terwilliger, blowing smoke. "It's got very cold."

Priests sort of frightened her. Mrs. Forsythe had told her years before that they were the enemy, and they certainly looked as if they might be. Terwilliger was particularly ominous. He kept standing around trying to look shy, when all the time he was laying frightful plans. Bluebeard. "Your husband seemed very tired yesterday," he said.

"He works very hard at this time of year," she answered tartly.

"Oh, yes, he's doing a great work, Mrs. Flax. A very great work. You must be Rosemary."

Rosemary took a step backward and fell on top of Kevin who was only just learning to walk. Father Terwilliger reached out his hand forlornly as the children fell away from him. "I mustn't keep you," he said. He looked sincerely uncomfortable and turned to go back into his church.

She peeped past him. It looked dark except for a finger of radiance at the end, a gaudy cross section of altar. It wasn't Father Terwilliger's fault that he was so sinister. It was this chamber of horrors where he spent his days. The waxworks dressed in satin, the red lamp that never went out, the confessionals that must be full of dead whispers. Terwilliger looked like a tiny curator slippering up the aisle of a mausoleum.

The problem was not so much believing (the world was going to have a farfetched explanation anyway) but believing that this was *good*.

"Are we going in, Mommy?" said Betty, Jr., who was already getting a bit sanctimonious it seemed to Betty, Sr. "Are we going to pray to God?" Kevin had fallen down again and his gloves had come off in the snow, so it seemed the only thing to do. They trooped in awkwardly, past the indecent movies and the war against smut (Betty smiled) and knelt, sat and sprawled in the back row.

Bert claimed to find St. Jude's very suburban, which always surprised her. What kind of churches must he be used to? It was all so dark and queer to a free-thinking Anglican. Terwilliger might suddenly pop out of one of the boxes; the tabernacle would fly open; the waxworks would start laughing—she looked as solemn as she could, and counted to thirty.

"Rosemary's pinching me. Kevin's gone to sleep," Betty, Jr., reported smugly.

"All right, children, let's go," said Betty.

She burst into the daylight, or so it seemed after that dark compression. The cold air broke against her cheeks. This, the outdoors, her mother had long ago told her, was where the real religion went on. The old lady was wrong, as usual. Outdoors was precisely where the religion did *not* go on—that was the charm of it, that was why you gulped it like water. The real religion went on in St. Jude's—dark, sinister, creepy-crawly religion. They took people like Bert and chanted and whispered over them, and said, "That will be ten dollars, please." She could tell from looking at Bert after he had been here that the dark place wasn't really doing him a bit of good. He looked so saintly and awful. . . .

But—she was in fresh air now and her thoughts were soon ballooning outward again. She hadn't meant that at all—religion was really a great comfort to Bert. It was his whole life. She was just transferring her own jitters at him. At Christmas, he was especially spiritual (she supposed that acting queer was spiritual) and she was especially spiteful. One thing she had sworn she would never do was discourage Bert in his religion.

Without his annual spasm he might wind up as empty as Mrs. Forsythe, who found religion in the empty air.

She got her children into the supermarket somehow, carrying Kevin, dragging Rosemary and cajoling Betty, Jr., who was being lofty (St. Jude's often brought on spells of priggishness in Betty, Jr.), and was delighted to find a whole bevy of friends: well known clubwomen shunting up and down the alleys in a body, like a great fur engine run on talk.

Betty braced herself for an orgy of trivia. Manicured hands swooped as one at the cereals, the detergents, the vitamin-enriched bread; Bloodbury's finest tongues worked like stevedores to produce some of the most inessential statements of all time. Betty fairly hurled herself at it and felt instant relief. St. Jude's was OK if you liked opium dens.

It was good talking on Mondays. On Sundays, she supposed, they stayed home and read the magazines; anyway, the next day they were primed to the teeth with recipes, household hints and child-soaked anecdotes. Afterward nothing would remain but a small puddle. The girls would break up and go home glassy-eyed, relaxed and brassily lovable. She wondered what Bert did when he felt like this. But perhaps Bert never felt like this—he was so wise, really (yes he *was*), and well balanced, except at Christmastime, when he got spiritual.

She had a feeling this year was a bad one for Bert, anyway. She had a hunch he wanted to change his style, develop a little more depth; but with the cost of living and all, he kept putting it off from issue to issue. She was naturally optimistic and sure he would work it out; meanwhile, he was doing so much good. . . .

Already she was late for the doctor's, and didn't know where the time had gone.

2

Mrs. Forsythe was coming at them hot and heavy this month. To counteract any religion that might be going about, she had taken to sneaking over for midweek visits—forcing Bert out into the snow, or else keeping him in his study for marathon periods.

She came to visit on Tuesday. Bert from his study window could see her clambering out of her compact car with a great churning of bulbous knees, and then Betty trotting out to help her. He went skittering off down the back stairs and the back door slammed as the front door opened.

Mrs. Forsythe waded through the fluffy snow toward her daughter. Legs like tree trunks, summarizing the history of her race; a voluminous handbag full of ever-scattering thoughts, and that gravelly voice warning the other ships out of the way. A caricature, and proud of it, Bert, used to say. But other people said, "Your mother is a character," and, "Your mother is a wonderful person," and, "Honestly, I don't know where she gets all that energy," so you could take it either way.

"Greetings, my dear," said Mrs. Forsythe briskly. She lurched into the house, refusing assistance, and began to haul off her overshoes. "I thought the children might be amused by this." She disentangled from the wool in her bag a nineteenth century spinning top and gave it an absent tweak. Mrs. Forsythe always brought something. An odd strain of timidity sent her rummaging into the attic for an excuse to visit. The top came from her brother's collection, she said.

There was always awkwardness along the hall and into the kitchen. Mrs. Forsythe did not really think this was any way to live, but she tried manifestly to be tactful about it, averting her gaze from things and pursing her lips until they looked about ready to burst. Garish religious pictures sprang at her from both sides. She stepped cautiously over the roller skate and round the big rubber dolls into the kitchen.

"Bert's working, I suppose," she said. "I never get a chance to see Bert these days."

"I'll tell him you're here," Betty flapped. "I know he'd like to. . . ."

"No, we mustn't interrupt him when he's working."

The back door swung derisively in the cold wind. Down the steps ran his footprints, and they ran, too, not walked. Mrs. Forsythe knew the score.

"Well, Mother," said Betty. "It's nice to see you again."

"Yes, well, I thought I'd bring the top."

"Kevin will love it."

Conversation was slow at this time of year because the

political season was just over, and the transition period brought a slow deflation. Mrs. Forsythe was very big on politics, it was a kind of swollenness of brain and throat that came with autumn. Betty had long given up trying to follow her thought, but according to Bert, she believed that fluoridation and zoning were part of the separation of Church and State, and that birth control ought to be compulsory, and so, anyway, what could she say to the Flaxes at this time of year?

"Is that a new orange squeezer?" she asked.

"No, it's the same one we've always had."

"It looked new."

"It's a good orange squeezer."

Little Kevin came floundering in and grabbed Mrs. Forsythe's knees. She pulled her skirts down sharply and Kevin fell over backward. "Hello Kevin," said Mrs. Forsythe accusingly. "How's my favorite grandson?" Kevin began to whine and Betty hustled him back to the playroom. Her mother saw the children as a sociological disaster, and they made conversation all the more difficult.

By the time Betty got back, with three dirty handkerchiefs and a broken balloon, her mother had made some coffee and was ensconced like Dr. Johnson. That's who she looked like, Dr. Johnson, with her big black cane. "Betty, I wanted to talk to you seriously for a minute."

"Yes, Mother?"

"I know you'll think I'm being very tiresome. But I believe it's important."

Betty sat down and began to think about her mother. There was no special point in listening, because where would a new idea come from after all these years? But she liked to think about her mother, a gallantly foolish woman perhaps, and an incurable champion of trivial causes, but a comradely sort of mother and one hell of a committeewoman.

As long as Betty could remember, her mother had

been thundering along on the margin of things, "Let's be sensible, let's look at the facts," she used to say, but the facts were always privately printed, and there was something moonspun about the sense, too, when you unraveled it at night. Betty remembered shivering in draughty auditoriums looking at her mother's vast legs under the speaker's table. Thin nervous men in glasses stood next to her, trembling with excited talk; Mrs. Forsythe sat stone-still, listening to her own drum. Afterward there was much shaking of hands, solidarity under the bunting. But Betty felt nothing but the chill of the auditoriums which were draughty even in summer, weren't they? Her mother never had these people round to the house, or saw them between meetings. They were just props for a certain mood.

Betty went away to college where, like everyone else, she majored in condescension. Her mother's ideas were a joke from an anthropology textbook. All she really enjoyed was going to meetings and sitting on the platform and saying, "Let's look at the facts." Soft men went to the meetings to get away from tough wives, and tough women went there to get away from soft husbands, so that the inevitable alignments were resumed. Mr. Forsythe himself ran or perhaps sidled away during a meeting and was never heard from again, which led to more causes to fill the extra time: fluoridation, and school buses, and African students—a crazy *mélange* of fashionable interests.

Mrs. Forsythe never tried to foist any of these on Betty. And because they seemed so completely interchangeable, and because Mrs. Forsythe seemed so indomitably benign about them, Betty assumed that they were just a hobby. She said, "How was the meeting?" and her mother seemed to smile too as if she saw some kind of joke anyway, if not the best kind. They were good enough friends in those days, vastly tolerant and indifferent. Betty had analyzed her mother to death and had nothing to fear.

And then she had to go and get engaged to Bert Flax and

find out how seriously her mother really did take these hobbies of hers.

She remembered insinuating Bert into Bloodbury on the bus. New Jersey made him nervous and he twisted his hat shapeless and back while she said not to worry, her mother was nothing if not understanding. "Yes, but planned parenthood. And bingo," whimpered Bert. "And civil rights and sterilization and Spain." "I know," said Betty. "It doesn't matter. It's all in fun." So much was she sure of this that she had only written her note explaining Bert the week before, with her engagement already accomplished.

But Bert knew best. Her mother must have smelled something as he was coming up the drive, because by the time he reached the front door her face was like rocks. Bert did begin to look sort of Catholic, under Mrs. Forsythe's gaze. He almost tore his hat in two, and then he shook hands badly, hitting the tips of her fingers with his. Anyhow, they had engaged.

It was a funny sort of afternoon. Mrs. Forsythe suddenly whipped out a little stiff smile that Betty had never seen before and which her mother was to dedicate henceforth to Bert. It was the kind of smile that seemed meant to convey that the owner has false teeth, and wants you to know it; but gives away not much else.

She confirmed right off that he was a Catholic by probing into his schooling. And she pressed him to the point of embarrassment about his work. Writing. Yes, but what *kind* of writing? She looked at Betty while she nodded at Bert. All kinds of writing? Well, who do you publish with? All over the place? But name one—oh, I see.

After which she suddenly dropped the whole thing and became quite pleasant, in the special, constricted way she was always to take with Bert. A kind of obsequious irony ("What does Mr. *Flax* think?") was entwined with the smile, and it was all new to Betty, and very complicated. But she couldn't precisely say the meeting had gone badly.

After she had seen Bert out and reassured him to the point where he suddenly got quite cocky, she came back and found her mother bustling about more than usual—heavy somber dartings here and there. "He seems like a nice boy," she said in a brittle voice.

She held up the ashtray ostentatiously—boy smokes?—and looked thoughtfully at his glass—boy drinks—and headed for the kitchen with the evidence, meaningless since she disapproved of neither activity. Betty smiled uneasily and followed with Mrs. Forsythe's teacup.

The big woman was leaning across the sink. That seemed funny. The maid would do the dishes tomorrow. Betty touched her mother's shoulder diffidently, and Mrs. Forsythe looked around sharply. Her face seemed to be squeezed up like a prune. Betty thought for a moment she was going to cry. Horrible dry tears into the empty sink. But it wasn't tears, it was more like anger, a twisting, boiling rage. But too mobile to catch and name.

Mrs. Forsythe turned back and mauled a dish.

When she looked round again, it was with the same false-teeth smile she had given Bert. She was blessing their union, like a good committeewoman, which she had never really been before, even in committee.

3

Betty stopped being clever about her mother after that. It seemed sort of indecent, not to say pointless. Her mother was an inch or two deeper than her probe would go. And anyway, Bert had persuaded her to stop judging people. The big thing for the first year was to keep Bert and Mrs. Forsythe from coming to blows. She sometimes had dreams of them, rolling on the kitchen floor in grotesque embrace—a fight to the death over bingo, or Mrs. Roosevelt, or nuclear policy.

In waking life Mrs. Forsythe remained tensely polite with her son-in-law. They both veered demagnetized from dangerous topics and found little dull pockets of agreement.

In their rare arguments they used rubber clubs. Betty even began to wonder if they weren't a bit afraid of each other. Mrs. Forsythe made little mischievous forays when he wasn't there, and Bert could be pretty satirical in bed at night, but when they got together you could sense meekness coming from at least one of them.

Mrs. Forsythe showed on the surface an inflated enthusiasm for the marriage right away and bought them boxloads of household appliances and some improbable modern chairs. She also brought them antiques and dusty vases, and said things like "What good are possessions to an old lady?" which were disturbingly unlike her, and palpably insincere. "I always wanted you to have this candle snuffer when you got married," or snuffbox, or chafing dish, or birdcage. She had previously shown no interest whatever in her heirlooms, had stowed them away in the attic to rot, but now she was bringing them gleefully down again and driving over almost every day with some throbbing discovery.

Bert made a whole raft of jokes about this stuff, but it obviously made him nervous, especially when the kids got big enough to start smashing it. He put the vases out of reach in cupboard recesses, but the kids got to them somehow and there was always a new spray of china to be mopped up. The appliances got wrenched out of shape, until only the orange squeezer survived, which was probably why Mrs. Forsythe kept bringing it up. Bert ranted about the carnage out of all proportion to its importance. Mrs. Forsythe said nothing and brought more bric-a-brac out of her groaning attic.

The trouble, Betty decided shaky-jokingly, was that all the breakage stood in some obscure, anthropological way for fecundity. And you could tell just by looking at her what Mrs. Forsythe thought about fecundity. She had allowed with the greatest reluctance one child to inch its way through her loins. That was quite enough of that. You couldn't keep a decent house with children around. Look—

here's a vase, see how long it lasts. Bert was certain she set things up, actually putting them near the edges of tables, to prove her point. "What does she expect with kids," he railed—but it was Bert who spanked them so ferociously when something got broken, and it was Mrs. Forsythe who restored them to grace with a melancholy smile.

That was the little family game. Each of them would have had to admit, if asked, that it wasn't very important. Mrs. Forsythe would have denied its existence outright. It was only driving them slowly crazy, that was all. What they were really concerned about was things like the children's schooling. Betty yawned. "And while we're on that," said Mrs. Forsythe, "do you think the school lunches are nutritious enough?" the children's feeding, the children's phases. Mrs. Forsythe looked almost as bored as Betty, but first things first and that meant schools.

"How is Bert?" she asked next. "He always seems to get run down around Christmas."

"Bert is very well," said Betty. "Very well indeed."

"That's nice, I'm so glad." Mrs. Forsythe seemed restless though. She wanted to say something that wasn't in the rules. She said, "You've got to take care of that husband of yours." She played with her coffee spoon. Kevin came stumbling in because somebody had let him out of the playroom, and flung himself once more at her knees. She gave a startled push that tipped him back on to his padded backside.

"Kevin!"

"I'm so sorry," said Mrs. Forsythe. "I didn't see him coming. Granny is very clumsy," she explained to Kevin. "Will you forgive Granny, Kevin?"

She leaned forward and her face must have looked very big, because Kevin began to shriek. In his hands, which he shook convulsively at her, were two pieces of broken top. Oh dear, thought Betty, another one of those days. Kevin handed Mrs. Forsythe the pieces in an unexpected gesture, and she sat there holding them foolishly. They looked at each other blankly for a moment, grandmother and grandson, until Betty tucked Kevin under her arm and bundled him upstairs again.

When she got back, Mrs. Forsythe was standing by the sink looking distractedly at the orange squeezer. "Listen Betty, there really is something I think I should tell you." She would have sounded confidential only her voice was so loud.

"Yes, Mother. How about some more coffee?"

"It's about Bert."

"Oh, yes." Betty attempted to stiffen perceptibly.

"Now wait a minute. You don't even know what I'm going to say, Betty. I'm not going to talk against him. I've grown very fond of Bert, whether you know it or not."

"Yes, Mother. You've told me about that."

"We don't always see eye to eye, but he's a fine man. A fine *young* man," she added vaguely. "But, Betty, I think he's unhappy."

"You do!"

"Yes, I do. Betty—"

"Well, I don't. I think he's very happy. I think he's very, very happy." She closed her eyes, but Mrs. Forsythe didn't dissolve. Might as well have left them open.

"It's not just my opinion," her mother said firmly. "I got it from a friend of his."

"What sort of friend?" She almost said, "Bert hasn't any friends—in that sense," and was startled by the discovery of what this would have involved, had she quite thought it. Actually, Bert must have lots of friends.

"A charming young man I met at the Ethical Society. He said he was an old friend of Bert's. He said . . ." Mrs. Forsythe's voice rose like thunder, to overtake Betty's retreating attention and her eyes did a little crazy dance with

Betty's, catching at them, "that he saw Bert just the other night, and that Bert was talking very queerly, and he was really quite concerned. The friend, that is."

All these societies she belonged to were bound to catch up with you eventually, thought Betty. On the face of it, it seemed absurd that she should have met an old friend of Bert's anywhere. But the whole world passed through those societies, if you gave it time.

"What was the name of this friend?"

"It was an Irish name. Murphy or something. O'Brien . . . I don't know. He said that Bert was talking quite wildly."

"It's not like you to believe an Irishman."

Her mother smiled thinly. "He said, and these were his words, that Bert was sort of blaspheming the Church. He was talking against the Catholic Church."

"Was this friend a Catholic?"

"No, I don't think so. Not at the Ethical Society."

"Then he must have been glad to hear Bert sort of blaspheming."

"No, he seemed a good bit disturbed by it."

"That's funny," said Betty. "He must have tender feelings. What about you, though? You must have been pleased?"

Her mother suddenly looked indecisive. "No, not really. I mean, it's his livelihood and everything, isn't it? And I've always heard that Catholics go all to pieces when they lose their faith. Pious ones, especially." She seemed almost agitated at the thought. "They have nothing else, you know."

"I'm sure that Bert won't go all to pieces," said Betty pleasantly, "and I'm sure that he isn't losing his faith either. He may have said some wild things with his Irish friend. . . ."

"You think they were drinking?" asked Mrs. Forsythe quickly.

"Yes, very likely. Why shouldn't they be? But I know that Bert's faith is solid, even if he was pulling his friend's leg about it, and he wouldn't do that if he wasn't basically sure, would he? and strong and deep—why, Bert's faith *is* Bert." She suddenly felt the breathless warmth in her own throat and heard the rush of comfort which she couldn't wait to let out. Did she really care so much?

Apparently her mother did anyway. Mrs. Forsythe seemed to be subsiding, to be settling into her capacious clothes, as Betty reassured her. Betty, and Mrs. Forsythe, and Bert's friend, all wanted Bert to keep his faith for one reason or other. (We haven't got faith but Bert has.) It was a settled sort of thing. Bert without his faith would be unthinkable.

"I expect his friend had it all mixed up," said Mrs. Forsythe. "He, his friend that is, was probably a bit drunk."

"He was probably a lapsed Catholic too," said Betty lightly. "He'd gone all to pieces."

The back door, which still hadn't been shut properly, which in fact could never be shut properly, shook fretfully in the cold wind. It was getting dark and anyway Bert's footprints had disappeared under drifts.

4

Mrs. Forsythe made a noisy departure, churning her knees back into the car like a movie of her arrival being run backward. Bert didn't exactly spring out from behind a tree, but he did turn up very soon after she'd gone. "I was visiting Fred Mullin," he said. "Wasn't that your mother I just saw driving off?"

"I think you're really afraid of her," smiled Betty.

"Well, wouldn't you be? I know, I know, she's really very insecure." Bert snicked his overshoes open. "But what good does that do me? Being insecure is what makes her so savage."

Small talk, but Betty kissed him remorsefully anyway.

She knew he couldn't work with her mother barking downstairs. He joked a lot about being a professional inspirationist, but she knew that his inspiration was really a very delicate affair. He sweated horribly to catch the right note of tranquillity; and each time he feared once again that he wouldn't get it, that he had lost it for good. She knew all this by watching him—he never mentioned it himself. She really must do something about her mother.

"I've tried to keep her away on weekdays, but you know what she's like at Christmas."

"It has something to do with the moon," said Bert. "She's a very sensitive woman."

"How's the poem coming?"

"No poem," he spread his hands, which looked frostbitten, as if he really had been waiting in the snow after all. "No poem at all."

"That's too bad. Still, it always comes, doesn't it?"

"Yes, yes."

"I'll take Mother down to the cellar tomorrow." She hugged him and snow fell out of his coat. Hoarse cries of "Daddy" began to circulate upstairs, and then the incredible Kevin came waddling down at him and the Family Hour was on.

Bert played with them gloomily, trotting slowly from room to room as they bayed at his heels. Betty went to the kitchen and cooked. They were expecting a guest for dinner, Father Chubb himself, and she had a queer feeling that you had to have vast, pagan banquets whenever priests came. She felt that Bert expected her to, too, although he always denied it with much show of amusement.

The kitchen got all steamy, and Bert came scampering through and pretended to hide behind her, while everyone squealed, and then he scampered off again. Father Chubb liked to see all the children, so she had to keep them up till he came—which wasn't bad because he used to silence them with his hearty affection, and they went to bed quite quietly after a few minutes of Father Chubb. She had perhaps conveyed to them some of her own uncertainty in face of the clergy.

At half past six the doorbell gave a hearty ping (no, it couldn't really be any heartier than usual) and Father Chubb stood smiling behind it. She saw him through the little window next to the front door, beaming like Jack Frost or somebody, although he hadn't caught sight of anyone yet. Bert came along the hall to answer the door, and he was already smiling too. It was a curious tableau. She supposed it was a business thing.

"Good evening, Father," said Bert, thrusting out his hand. "Come in, you must be frozen."

To Betty he always seemed very big and clean. He took up the whole front hall in a massive kind of way, but it didn't matter because he was so clean. He took off his hat, disclosing white, short, wavy hair. He unwound his white silk scarf. He unbuttoned his coat. All this was extraordinarily interesting to her.

He held out his hand and said, "Betty, it's good to see you."

"Here, let me take your coat," she and Bert collided behind him.

He strode ahead into the living room looking for children. By all odds they should be running out to meet him by now. He was, as far as the eye could see, good with children, and there was nothing about him that they obviously shouldn't like. Yet they hung back and Betty had to rally them. "Look who's here," she said.

Father Chubb didn't seem to mind. He sat on the sofa and riffled a passing head and said, "And how's the world been treating you, Bert?"

"Fine, I guess."

"That's good. Hasn't it been cold though?"

Betty started another pair of children toward him and

headed back for the kitchen. They would talk some weather and then get down to business. She looked into the drink cupboard and was dismayed to find it empty, except for a jug of California sherry. It left one sort of defenseless.

Standing by the stove she could hear their voices, the voices which had bored her so as a child, and which truth to tell still bored her a little—good-natured, punctilious, passionless. It was a best-behavior kind of voice with Bert, as if he wasn't quite at ease with Father Chubb either; with Father Chubb it was a tactful, men-of-the-parish voice. Slowly the children began to trickle out one by one, subdued and asking to go to bed.

That took a while because, subdued or not, they all had their idiosyncrasies about retiring. Various dolls and animals had to be foraged for before they felt safe to face the night. Kevin insisted on brushing his Teddy bear's teeth. And all the time they could hear the voices droning downstairs. How dull it all was growing up, and sitting still, and talking. No more toys or colors. Betty indulged the children as long as she could, but they really did want to get to bed, and at quarter to eight she reluctantly straightened up from the last wet kiss of the day.

They lived in a rattletrappy house, by Bloodbury standards (her mother thought it was better than not living in Bloodbury at all, but only just), and you could catch what was said in the living room all the way up to the attic. Betty could hear them clearly before she reached the top of the stairs, but their voices were still so dead and empty that she didn't bother to listen till halfway down.

"I see your problem, Bert. It's never been great art, I suppose, but there's still time for that. You're a young man."

"That isn't the way it works, Father."

"And meanwhile think of the good you've done with it."

"I can't make it anymore, Father. But I've got to keep trying, haven't I?"

"Make it? Of course you can make it. Just take a month or two. You have a great gift, Bert, when you don't strain it. Naturally, you can't feel inspired all the time. . . ." What a silly thing to say, thought Betty.

"I can't afford a month or two," said Bert.

She realized that she had stopped outside the door and was now, technically, eavesdropping. She touched the handle, as if that made it all right, and stood there for another moment. That was really a terribly silly thing that Father Chubb had said—although heaven knew she had said it often enough herself. But when someone like Father Chubb said it. . . . Was this what went on in those dull voices? Perhaps very tense, strange things were hidden there. "Can't you?" said Father Chubb. "You don't mean to say this is your only source of income?"

Bert seemed to be controlling himself primly, but she felt a choke of excitement at what he would say next. "Of course not, Father," he resumed in oh such a dull, *dull* voice. "I have several projects going. It's just that, you know. . . ."

Whoof, so that was all. Projects going. She should have guessed, nothing interesting ever got said in those voices. The sad thing about grown-up life was that even eavesdropping you never heard anything really much. There were no big scenes, no climaxes, only people being patient with each other and practical with each other—so bored they didn't know they *were* bored anymore.

She pushed in and they stood up. Father Chubb was not the least romantic or frightening now. Big, clean and crisp, Chairman of the Board, as American as apple pie. Bert wasn't about to make a big gesture, either. He was just going to ask about the dinner. (My God, the dinner! she would have to say.) She belonged upstairs with the children, Bert had often told her so.

Well, it was all a great relief, really. Bert wasn't going to blow up. Father Chubb wasn't going to do anything sinister. Life would go on. It was thoroughly immature (her mother's pet word) to feel a shadow of disappointment. Still, she felt it. She had wanted something piratical to happen, and it hadn't, and there was this shadow.

And meanwhile, she had probably burned the dinner, and was quite vexed about everything.

5

She didn't want to get angry at Bert, but his face looked so silly. His ears stuck out even farther than usual when Father Chubb talked, and got red and, for all she knew, furry. The long face was very solemn and he nodded and said, "Yes, Father," until she was ready to scream.

It was frightening when Bert began to look silly. She was afraid he would never stop, although up to now he always had at the last minute. The first time had been especially awkward: right over the altar rail, before their marriage in the St. Jude's sacristy. He was wearing his rented tails, but that wasn't it. It was something about his face—a kind of gloomy reverence, waxy and artificial and almost clownish. Satirical piety, a new thing.

She got the shakes and couldn't look at him again. Perhaps the sacrament of marriage made people look funny, her too. The new face seemed to take over so completely with Bert that she couldn't remember what he had looked like before, yet when she glanced back a few minutes later, it was gone, leaving no trace. He was just looking sensitive again.

What she could never make out was whether it was something that happened to him or to her. She had felt so funny being in church anyway, with the banks of white flowers and the sinuous candles and a man beside her who believed that something went on here, a sorcerous thing which racked his face. And later, with the liturgical years, the same strange feelings came and went in her like the tides; and Bert's face changed to the same rhythm. So she never knew which of them was causing the trouble.

She looked at Father Chubb instead. He ate very daintily, dabbing his mouth with a corner of the napkin. There was nothing wrong with that, of course. Sometimes Betty found herself looking critically like this right into people's pores, as if she had very strong glasses on. Long ago in the stories she wrote for *Prospect III*, the college magazine, she had become notorious for dwelling on things like, oh, how people ate, and how they breathed and where they twitched. (It wound up as a joke in the yearbook.) She really hadn't had much to say, she supposed. But there were times when she really did hear more breathing, and eating, than other people seemed to.

Stop looking at Father Chubb go at it. Big pink hands, though, scrubbed, groomed. Spatulate fingers ("Miss Forsythe, you have *five* characters in here with spatulate fingers. What are spatulate fingers, anyway?") ("Oh, you know"). Very quiet chewer. Big, catlike jaws. You could make anyone sound disgusting this way. Dab, dab, Father Chubb patted his soft cheeks. His breath filtered through hairy nostrils. . . .

What was the matter with Bert? He was ahead of schedule this year, already looking mournful, churchy for Christmas; it would reach a climax, explode on Christmas Eve, and he would be comparatively peaceful at Midnight Mass. Religious experience worked like that, bringing a great deal of pain and then taking it away again, in some ghostly harmony.

Mrs. Forsythe had warned her just once about this and then kept her peace, except for oblique sorties. One night before the wedding, this was. Mrs. Forsythe had taken her daughter aside, Victorian-style, to tell her the facts of sectarian life. "Catholics are not like you and me. The bad ones are very sloppy people indeed. The good ones go through all sorts of invisible torments; almost like someone with delirium tremens. . . ." "Then you *don't* want me to marry Bert." "No, no, I didn't say that"—much aggrieved—"I was just warning you."

Her mother must have known in her heart of hearts that none of this applied to Bert Flax. Even in her presence, where he was inclined to fidget and occasionally even giggle, he was transparently sane and well balanced. He made Mrs. Forsythe's enthusiasms seem a bit silly, too, although he never said a word against them; he nodded thoughtfully when she mentioned fluoridation, say, and she would look perplexed and soon drop it.

This was part of his appeal for Betty. After a zany childhood, she grew up with a crush on common sense. And Bert seemed to have it in spades. So, suppose he did have to go through these crazy exorcisms at Christmas and Easter, it was still worth it: he came out of them a lot saner than Mrs. Forsythe.

Even with Father Chubb: he would have a lot of sensible things to say about Father Chubb after he'd gone.

And why didn't he go? He was usually brisk and dependable in his leavings. But tonight he seemed to be "hanging about" in a loutish kind of way, as if waiting for an opening of some kind.

She tried leaving the room and Bert bounded after her with an offer to help with the dishes. Father Chubb chimed in sonorously and began hauling off his jacket. "Oh no, Father, you don't have to."

Bert strapped on an apron and she began feeling vexed again. It didn't make any sense at all to feel so annoyed with the back of his head. Which was beginning to go bald. Or with the brown silk on the back of his vest.

She left them and went and lay down. The living room was extremely annoying. There was a newspaper on the floor. And someone had thrown a ball of paper into the artificial fireplace. How could people go on living in such a pigsty? She recognized the mood wearily. Just physical and very tiresome. Bringing up five children was very tiresome and Christmas was very physical or vice versa.

When she woke up, Father Chubb was looming overhead in his big black coat. She had missed the intense interest of watching him put it on. Was it her imagination, or was he looking just a tiny bit ruffled? Not a hair out of place, and a smile from Blandsville, but somehow he struck her as ruffled.

"Good night, Betty," he said; "it's been delightful."

He turned a handle and began to go into the cupboard. That was Father Chubb's joke. He came out flapping his hands. "That darned closet," he said. But he seemed out of sorts somehow.

"Do come and see us again."

Bert stood behind her and grunted his agreement. He was breathing hard. Through spatulate nostrils. Betty smiled politely at Father Chubb. There was something curiously indecisive about him—had he forgotten to say something? He backed out of the right door, and she watched him through the side window turn awkwardly round and into the snow.

When Betty was angry at Bert she made a point of being as nice as she could to him (in a stiff kind of way because there was no choice about that), hoping he didn't notice. She didn't want him to get angry back—that would really be tiresome. And she didn't want him to sulk, because he might go on doing it indefinitely, long after she felt better.

So she took his arm and said, "I thought Father Chubb was awfully pleasant tonight."

Bert didn't say anything to that.

"I mean, he doesn't make you laugh or anything, after the first time. But he's very cheerful."

Bert sat down in the best armchair and touched his fingers to his forehead. Betty perched brightly on the arm.

"Of course, you know about me and priests," she said, trying not to sound too dreadfully merry about it. "But I do think Father Chubb is awfully nice."

Bert looked up at her slowly. His face was a funny brownish color. "Will you give Father Chubb a rest? He's a—— and I told him so tonight," he said.

"You did?" said Betty. "Oh no."

"And now I'm going to bed."

"Oh no," said Betty. "Oh no, no, you didn't." She heard her voice shake.

Bert looked at her for a moment and smiled a thin, pointed smile. "Well, perhaps I didn't. But I meant to."

He sometimes overdid candor to make up for overdoing piety.

She walked up stiffly to bed, in no mood for joking, not trusting herself to speak to him again.

6

There was a park near the Flaxes, kept green and elegant by the township, and spattered most of the year like a Breughel painting with children in red, brown and blue playsuits. But in winter, it was desiccated: there was nothing the township could do for it any more. The trees were spidery and dead. The swings dangled from their gibbets (the township always forgot to cut them down) and the sand piles were lost under vast clumps of gleaming snow.

Betty like to stroll in Wensley Park while the children studied or slept. Years ago, she had trudged with her mother through the same kind of snow, in hefty pursuit of exercise. Now she had the park to herself, and no need for excuses.

A gray crisp wilderness just outside the Bloodbury neatness and, for a few months anyway, untouched by it.

A loneliness, rich, sensuous and dead; it was hard for her to remember right now that she was in the center of her angry time. When she got home again, the words would scratch at her skin; the wintry silence to be ripped, gashed again and again, punctured horribly by voices. But here, there was deep harmony, luscious and slushy, a sinking into the snow, that she never felt when she was completely technically well.

The best thing would be to keep walking toward the middle of silence, wherever that might be, and leave the family bawling away outside. (Funny how family's voices combined to a discord. Hers and her mother's, only two voices, and Bert said they sounded like a chicken run.) But the park was really quite small and she kept reaching its spiky-hedged boundaries. And beyond that, there was house after house, and the rasping sounds of families.

"Good evening, Mrs. Flax." A big fuzzy fellow slowly defined himself in the winter afternoon grizzle. Mr. O'Malley, the man who took the money at Bert's church. In a brown woolen jacket, walking his dog. Just when she had this good silence going.

"I'm walking Red," he said, and the implied other half of that was, And what are *you* doing? Nobody ever went out without a purpose in Bloodbury, a self-evident purpose. "I'm taking my vacation," he explained. And, "We were hoping to go to Florida, but Ruth got sick." . . . Now do I have to repeat, Mrs. Flax, what are *you* doing here?

"That's too bad about Ruth."

"Oh, it's nothing really. Just a bug that's going around."

"Yes, we've had it too."

They stood toe to toe. Something more conclusive must be said before they could break cleanly.

"How's Bert these days?" asked Mr. O'Malley.

"Fine. He's fine."

"That's good, I see him in church, you know," he said and suddenly gave her a look of deep concern and tenderness, which made her jump. His eyes had gone a watery blue in the cold, and they seemed to swim toward her. Was there anything he could do. Don't hesitate to call on him. Mrs. O'Malley and he were always— He stepped bashfully away with his big red dog.

Betty plunged her hands deeply into her pockets. Funny man. Had Bert been holding back on his seat money? she wondered. She looked back, and sure enough, Mr. O'Malley was gazing at her. He bent over and chivied his dog, as if the dog was to blame for making him look round. She was reminded for some reason of those touching ads—would she like to make inquiries about the truths of the Catholic faith? Tactful concern, a plain envelope, no one need ever know. Bert's Catholic acquaintances often made her feel like that.

She turned at the hedge and began to walk along the inside run of the park. She didn't want to go home; and hear the noise, like all that breaking china, of children's voices and husband's voice, bleating wants and enthusiasms to a deaf world. She loved the sight of her children; if only they could move silent as ghosts through life, with no more whining and shrieks of laughter and face-bulging sobs of distress; if they were as quiet as the dead trees and the deep snow. . . .

She greeted as an old friend this languor in her bones, this craving to walk very slowly and softly by herself. She was really feeling very well, but only in this context. At home she would be thin and nervous and touchy. Out here she was quite all right, full and velvety. A feeling of great love: for the shapes of her children, still touchingly haphazard and inadequate; for all kinds of shapes, so long as they kept quiet. If she could just lie down and go to sleep in the snow, everything would be lovely. Put her arms around the globe and rock it. But then Mr. O'Malley would come along with his dog. . . .

Dreary me. Did Bert feel like this? Of course, that's what he went to church for. With the spells and incantations and Merlin gowns, he and his friends could summon up this feeling and better any time they wanted to. Mrs. Forsythe used to snort at that and say, "I go out on a hillside and worship the sunset, and that's *my* religion"—but how often did Mrs. Forsythe actually go out on a hillside? Not very often, to Betty's best knowledge. Bert went to church every week. And when Mrs. Forsythe did find herself on a hillside, she was always fretful about the candy wrappers people had left lying about, and how people were vandalizing the countryside in spite of all the notices. That was *her* religion: picking up candy wrappers; clucking over soil erosion. ("Look, Mother, look at the sunset." "Yes, dear, it's very nice." Pick, pick, pick at the candy wrappers.)

As Betty got near the exit again, near enough to hear the Bloodbury clock chime four, her feet began to drag in earnest. The snow seemed heavier, more intractable; the wind was mustering itself around the park, puffing away the enchantment. She didn't want to go home. She didn't want to be pleasant again, to be a good sport. Her footprints made a plaintive smudge as she swung her leaden feet against the drifts. She didn't want to feed the children. Or talk to Bert.

Or talk to Bert. Talk to Bert.

It was her angry time, and she didn't want to wake up into its fullness just yet.

Mr. O'Malley came at her once more. He had made the other half-circle of park, possibly by design. The dog looked listless, as if O'Malley had been keeping it out against its will.

"Why, hello again," he said in a hollow voice.

"Hello," Betty answered shortly. A free course in Catholic instruction on its way. Have you given any thought? and so forth. He looked all tensed up.

"I meant to ask after Bert."

"You already did," she said as kindly as she could.

"No, I mean, I've been a little bit worried about Bert, Mrs. Flax. He doesn't look too well. He stands by the door, to tell you the truth, and he doesn't look too well."

"He's been working very hard."

"Oh, I know that, Mrs. Flax. We all know that."

"Well, is that all? Is that all you're worried about?"

"We haven't seen him at the Holy Name recently," he said lamely.

"I told you he was working hard, Mr. O'Malley."

"Yes, yes, oh yes," he backed away in spirit and began to smile, as unaccountably as ever. "I'm so glad to hear he's all right, Mrs. Flax. It'll be a great relief to Ruth." Nothing could be as good as he suddenly made this seem. "I felt I ought to ask, you know? He means so much to us, with his work and everything." He took a deep breath. "We *need* him, Mrs. Flax."

And waddled happily off into the winter twilight.

7

It took so little to satisfy some people.

When she got home, Bert had gone to church and the once-a-week cleaning woman was doing her wistful best to rein in the children. Jam was creeping up the walls, toys were bent and twisted. Everyone was crying in desolation. She was glad Bert was out anyway.

Five weeks to Christmas, and Bert was haunting St. Jude's, sucking up inspiration like oxygen for the December issues. (Where did he go when he said he was going to Holy Name meetings, she wondered.) The cleaning woman had put an illegible note by the telephone and couldn't remember what it said, but they finally worked out together that Mrs. Flax had called and was coming to visit at some quite unfathomable time.

Betty had a sudden ominous certainty that Mrs. Flax and Mrs. Forsythe would arrive together. Crunch! These things happened toward Christmas. The two mothers got fidgety, chafed by heaven knew what memories, and then they got careless and inevitably found themselves in the same living room, breathing polite defiance.

No use worrying about that now. The big thing was getting through the next hour or two. Kevin had a soggy diaper oozing between his knees; Betty, Jr., was primly informing on one of her mates—which meant an inquiry and some sort of rough justice, wearily arrived at. Betty clapped her hands vivaciously, not because she felt it, but because she had learned from Father Chubb's example that this kind of thing had a depressing effect on her young. "Come along, children," she said, rather meaninglessly. "Come along now."

She herded them around confusingly and gave them random things to do. But Chubb's magic could not be duplicated. Betty, Jr., was to tidy her room, but she said that Rosemary had made the mess, and Rosemary lisped when she was accused of things, so it was hard to make out her side of it. Kevin's diaper continued to droop. The cleaning woman got in the way. Life moiled and churned at knee level.

"I think we'd better get their supper, Martha. I know it's early."

Martha mumbled acceptance and began shuffling about with the cottage cheese. Oh, dear—cottage cheese. In a few minutes, it would be scattered over their clothes and in their hair and all over Kevin's high chair. There was no way of covering everything. Betty rested her head against her forearm. The noise came in dismal waves, yesterday, today, forever.

At six-thirty Bert came back, just in time to start kissing

good night. "I've been to church," he said, reaching for Kevin. "Benediction, and then I sat around thinking."

Betty did her best to appear interested.

"It's a wonderful place for thinking, a church," said Bert. The face? she didn't dare look.

"Yes, I'm sure it must be. Look, Bert, do you mind helping with the children?"

He set to mechanically. Bert had always been very good with the children. (Was it part of the unspoken bargain in mixed marriages?)

He did it in a military way, turning them over smartly, snapping their pins, dismissing them; whenever there was a cry in the night, he sat up smartly himself and marched into the offending room. It was a great help.

Before they were married, Bert told her he wanted to have lots of children. It was a disconcerting thing for a man to say, and she thought at first he must be playing up to her. Women were supposed to have these primal urges; men, not knowing what the words meant, went along with them. It was part of courtship.

"I do too, of course," she said, "but to tell you the truth, I'm a bit afraid." It was a funny thing to be talking about in the antiseptic Forsythe living room, an antifertility chapel, garlanded often as not with birth-control pamphlets.

"Oh, I know it's frightening. Anything worthwhile is frightening. But it's beautiful too, the most beautiful thing there is."

He looked so sincere. "*You're* frightening," she said, and that was all for the time being. They nuzzled on her mother's leather sofa and left the consequences to another day. She still thought he was kidding, in a sincere kind of way, making poetry, his poor, dear, bad poetry.

A year later she was trembling along the corridor at St. Martin's, still unbelieving. Did her husband really consider this beautiful?—not the words anymore, the thing. Stomach and hospital. Bert held her elbow and looked determined. "I'm very proud of you," he said again and again.

Fat, comfortable nuns, thin, beady-eyed nuns, swam by in a dream. Mrs. Forsythe had a subscribing interest in planned parenthood, and Betty had been reading broadsides and magazines on it since she was nine. Its propounders considered childbirth beautiful, of course. But in so many cases, children figured as the enemy, and they carried an odor of sulfur about them. Mother living in poverty, father out of work and, my God, comes a baby. Mother sickly, father away, and, oh no, another baby, grinding its ruthless way down. Deathwatch beetles, maggots, yes, death. Betty's fear of it was quasi-Biblical. Women must suffer with birth, the fundamentalists and Mrs. Forsythe agreed. It was like Bert's magazines on sex—beautiful in theory, but ugly in almost every conceivable instance.

In the death-white nightmare corridors, she gave it all over to Bert. He believed in what she was doing, so he could look after her. In her bits of conversation she was probably sharp and querulous with him (she couldn't remember) but inside she felt a desperate love. She closed her eyes in pain: images clashed and spun, but Bert's remained fairly steady. Long, serious jaw, unwavering green gaze. When she looked again, his eyes were shining: he really did see beauty somewhere in all this.

As long as Bert saw some point, well, as she said, she would leave it to him. And thus relaxed, in woeful pain, she began to see some point herself. She was conscious of the first gurgles between her legs, was deeply happy, and the next day was prepared to give Bert credit for preternatural wisdom. Her mother's point of view had never seemed pawkier.

Whatever the effects of childbirth on her (she wasn't aware of any, just a few tantrums and ecstasies, nothing important), they were very good on Bert. He expanded, became very funny and tender in a way she hadn't seen before. She had often been puzzled by a slight constraint, even artificiality, in his previous bedside manner. Now he was tired, but very much himself.

"We put you through a terrible thing, we men," he said. "I hadn't realized."

"Never mind," she said, hugging him into her bed jacket. "It was fine. I feel more grateful than anything." Sweet, natural reversal of roles. It made them laugh.

He clowned and courted around the stiff hospital bed, and knocked over her water jug, and when a benevolent nun in white came stumping up smiling, Bert wasn't embarrassed, but charming and obviously just right for a nun. He brought flowers and forbidden fruit and piles of magazines which she left contentedly strewn, unread. He steered her along the corridor every afternoon to make faces through the glass—at Bert, Jr.

How much of this was Bert and how much of this was just herself again she couldn't remember for long. But whatever it was, she had a crazy idea soon after she got home that she wanted more of it. Bert, she began to fancy, was getting polite with her as he used to before Bert, Jr., was born. He was conscientious about things like sterilizing bottles, but that was hardly the same thing. He had been such hectic fun in the hospital. Now he was acting all responsible. Well, you could hardly blame him, he was doing what was supposed to be right. But she missed the drowsy, rubber bliss of hospital and was quite glad to get pregnant again. Her new attitude delighted Bert, and naturally he took it to be permanent. It was one in the eye for Mrs. Forsythe, her daughter wanting children, and he made the most of it.

The second one started out even more comradely. She felt the same surge of affection for Bert, deep and inscrutable. But she was no longer lost or frightened. They joked all the way to St. Martin's and past the receptionist, who was pretty funny too, when you looked at her closely. Bert timed the contractions before she left the house, making a noise like a cuckoo clock every five minutes and then every four. And pretended to put silly things in her overnight bag. His dinner jacket was it? She remembered it all backwards, because that was the only possible way.

They had both minimized the painful part in remembering, and when it came storming back, she greeted it with a feeling of outrage and dismay. No, no, it wasn't like this at all. They had had such fun last time.

Betty, Jr., was a trickier proposition anyhow. She was facing the wrong way and she was an awkward shape. At first Betty smiled between spasms, to show that she still saw the joke, but they just went on and on and she couldn't smile at all of them, and slowly she groaned and sweated away all pleasure in childbearing.

The next day when Bert came round, she was not specially glad to see him. His good humor seemed forced. His tenderness was anxious. Not his fault, but her stitches hurt, and the new baby seemed a bit plain, oh well, you couldn't have perfection every time. On a lower key, they passed an amiable enough few days and went home to what already seemed a crowded house.

But Betty was now and for ever the girl who wanted to have lots of children. Bert seemed to depend on it; and besides, any change of policy would give comfort to Mrs. Forsythe. Which annoyed her a little.

So back to St. Martin's they went again and yet again. Bert still said it was beautiful, when she brought it up, but with a deprecating smile: well, it *is* beautiful but I know about the other side too, was what he meant. It was all part of being sensible, and she found it more than faintly depressing.

No longer did his image seem firmer than the rest. It floated, got pulled out of shape, even once took the form of a question mark. Was he really so wise, did he really know what he was doing? Nervous question, there was no actual change in him. She had just reverted, she supposed, to the planned parenthood subscription days. The babies hurt terribly as a matter of course and of right, making more and more reluctant and derisive entrances, and Bert said she was a saint to want to go on having children. But never asked her if she actually did.

He took Kevin by the hand to his room, very gently and courteously. A tall man in last year's brown suit. He paid too for his desire to have children, and never complained. She only wished he enjoyed them more. But perhaps he did, in some deep cavern of his mind.

When he got downstairs again he was smiling oafishly and inviting her to ask why. A disconcerting about-face.

"You're looking every pleased with yourself. Why is that?" she said.

"It came," he said in a funny singsong, "it came, it came, it came."

"What came? Not the Christmas poem." She was still clearing her mind of children.

"What do you mean, not the Christmas poem?" he took her shoulders and danced her around. It was a dance of infinite melancholy. "I was over to church saying a word of thanks," he said, and his ears looked just like a donkey's, a pious donkey's.

8

After a lag, winter began to move again. December, which Bert had held back while he finished his poem, started to rush by. Betty's black mood rolled silently away —that very night, as a matter of fact. She got peevish over dinner and told him he was hopeless. Because he made such a fuss over his silly poem and hadn't cleaned the cellar either. He was quite meek about it, but stayed up late poking about in his study which was a sure sign of distress. During a long waking sleeping mumph, she thought she heard the forlorn rustle of paper and muffled taps on the typewriter; typewriter trying to get in; the wind blew across her bed, and somebody kissed her on the eyelids she rather supposed and the next day she woke up feeling as good as new.

Mrs. Flax came to visit with Bert's young brother Walt, a quiet lad with pimples on his pimples, who went to school in Jersey City and said Father McManus stank on ice and Father Dennis was for the birds, boy, but Father Rafferty was pretty neat, while Mrs. Flax laughed comfortably either way it went. By great luck, she didn't coincide with Mrs. Forsythe. Both of them had their radar working better this year, she hoped. Everyone's cold went away and the shops filled up with quality goods, polished wood salad bowls, yakskin lampshades and such, and the parochial school had a moth-eaten pageant at which Betty, Jr.'s, angel wings came apart.

Everything was shaping up but Bert. He still seemed a bit tense, what there was of him. He had a lot of talks to give early in December, and meetings to attend, and when he was home he was mostly locked in his study—reading, it must be, from the silence—or tidying up the cellar with aggrieved overemphasis. Of course, he would get jolly when the time came, but he wasn't much help right now.

Father Chubb came over a couple of times and had that same look, that one hair on his wrist was out of place and everything had gone wrong because of it, but he was very hearty with the children and you had to be thankful for that. The second time, he clashed with Mrs. Forsythe in the drive, and she recoiled visibly. Betty had a wild notion that her mother was going to *cross* herself, to ward him away.

"Good afternoon, Mrs. Forsythe." "Good afternoon." She couldn't very well call him "Mr." and she was damned if she would call him anything else.

Still the number one joke—still diverting, in a way. But there had been nothing diverting about Bert a few minutes before. His hands were trembling as he came out of the study with Father Chubb. Chubb whisked himself off without the usual rigmarole. Bert stood rooted at the study door, so Betty had to follow the priest downstairs. Father Chubb was polite but hasty. He had a train to catch or a bus. He didn't step humorously into the cupboard. Betty suddenly realized he hadn't taken off his overcoat. It looked as if he had dripped snow all the way upstairs and down again, keeping it on his coat while he talked to Bert.

The study door was shut again when she got back to it. It looked very wooden and dismal. She examined the grains of wood, stabbing downward to the floor. Should she knock? It was against the rules, but Bert was breathing so quietly. No question of premonitions or anything, but—"Bert, are you all right?"

He grunted; then presumably not hearing the floorboards creaking her away, said, "Yes, dear, I'm fine," in a go-away voice.

There was nothing to do but back off and get on with Christmas and her mother. It rather took the heart out of things, just when life had begun to go a little better. Of course, she knew what had happened. Father Chubb had brought the poem back, or the articles, or both, for more work. Discouraging. And Bert would be up there worrying about the Christmas money all over again. Father Chubb's check was the one that put them over the top every year.

It was no use telling him again that she didn't care about money. He always acted disgruntled when she said that, as if she was somehow implying that he *did* care about money. What made it all so tantalizing was that Mrs. Forsythe was fairly panting to finance them and Bert wouldn't let her. Oh, well.

He stayed in his study till dinnertime, and she asked him if he wanted a tray or what and he said no thanks. He wouldn't talk about the money, so she had no idea how bad it was. The children were variously disposed of, so she ate by herself in the kitchen; very aware of herself eating, the sound of the fork hitting the plate, the succotash slowly diminishing. She would have supposed that he was working, but she hadn't yet heard the typewriter in this acoustical monstrosity of a house. The study was right overhead, and she could catch what sounded like a much heavier body than Bert lumbering from chair to chair.

After dinner she felt cold. The heat clanked off and the house had a clammy, cold quietness about it. She opened *War and Peace* at page 312, which was a new low in pointlessness, and shut it at page 314 and turned on the television. A family comedy. Oh my. She had never realized the full psychic horror of canned laughter. Embalmed gaiety. She turned off the television.

It was silly to get so jittery, this sort of thing had happened before, hadn't it? Yes of course, it must have. If only the house wasn't so cold and quiet. Her mother had foisted a wall-to-wall carpet on their living room and it seemed to be purring soundlessly.

The logical thing was to ask Bert to go down to the cellar (she had no head for thermostats), but something told her to keep well away from the study. Instead she went to the phone in the hall and began dialing for Father Chubb.

A woman's voice of rare surliness answered the phone and did its utmost to discourage her. Father Chubb was working . . . he mightn't even be in . . . was it important? . . . business calls were taken at his office. It made things that much edgier; Betty felt irrationally that she must get through to Father Chubb at all costs.

"Yes, yes, Father Chubb?"

"Who's this? Who's calling?" It sounded as if the woman had mysteriously turned into Father Chubb. Perhaps he had been playing one of his boisterous jokes, pretending to be the woman.

"It is I, me, Mrs. Flax, Betty Flax."

"Oh yes, Mrs. Flax."

He sounded as if he might be in his dressing gown. Or anyway, had his collar off—a state she always found vaguely disturbing in priests. Priests were supposed to keep their collars on.

"I'm sorry to disturb you, Father."

"That's all right, Betty. What can I do for you?"

"Well, it's really nothing important, Father. I feel silly calling you." Did he have a dressing gown with flowers on? Or would it be something like a vestment? "It's just about Bert. I wondered. . . ."

"Yes, Betty."

"I wondered if you, if you told him something that might have worried him this afternoon." There was such a long pause that she thought she'd better keep going. "I mean I wondered, you know. . . ."

"Yes, Betty. I know. I suppose I did, in a way."

"What was it about? The poem?"

"The poem *and* the article. I'm afraid we felt they didn't quite come off. There were good things in them, of course, excellent things—but not up to Bert's high standards. . . ."

"Oh yes, yes."

"We feel, my associates feel, felt, that Bert may have been straining a bit too hard. Usually as you know, his work has a delightful ease to it—I'm sure if he rests for a while. . . ."

"Well, he can do it again, can't he? Get it right?"

The telephone began to bumble at that. Deadlines too late . . . we really think it would be wise . . . always interested. She held the phone away from her: a torrent of icy discretion came pouring through on to her hand.

It died down at last. She steadied the receiver back against her ear and said, "I see. What you're telling me is that my husband's work is too good for your magazine."

Pause. "Well, perhaps that's it. You see, we have a certain kind of reader . . . a certain kind of format . . . and bumble, bumble, oh, bumble. We've been concerned about this for some time. . . ." She left him exegeting into a dead phone.

Two at a time up the stairs. Bert was standing in the doorway with the light behind him. His dark face was nodding slowly.

He turned and she followed him into the study. He had put his chair next to the window so he could sit looking out over the snow. The window was up, so that the cold air had been blasting against his face. He sat there now, with his back toward her, his shoulders hunched.

"Dear you'll catch cold—you should put on your jacket."

"Do you know what he told *me?*" His voice was not, at least, sad; there were no vestigial tears around the throat. "Do you know what that so-and-so told me?"

"What?"

"He said I wasn't sincere enough. Me, the master. Mr. Sincerity."

"Oh, but that's silly."

"Yes, isn't it? But even that isn't what strikes me as the most funny. What really tickles me every time I think about it is that here I am, a leading spiritual hack—"

"You're not a hack." She reached forward to comfort him, but couldn't seem to reach him.

"The hell I'm not. You don't think I could do good stuff now, do you? After years of peddling crap—anyway that's beside the point. What was I saying?"

Betty shrugged—she really had no idea. The wind was eating him alive, and she wanted to get at the window, then talk.

"That's it, a dedicated hack, a really good hack, and suddenly I can't make the *Catholic Passenger*. Christ, I couldn't have aimed much lower, could I?"

"You're too good for them, dear."

"Yeah, too good."

"You can start again, aiming higher."

"Oh, sure. Aim higher. Onward and upward." He seemed bemused now, inattentive. The crisis was all but over. She took a stealthy step toward the window. Poor, tired Bert—he'd be back at his poems tomorrow. Disgust was a writer's fuel, even a bad writer's.

"You know," he suddenly said, in quite a contemplative

way, "I sometimes think I've just about had this lousy Church."

"What? What, Bert?"

"Yeah, I've just about had it."

"But what? I mean, you can't blame the Church for Father Chubb. You can't blame the Church for what's happened."

"You know—that's the funny thing—I can." He turned around and looked at her. His face was curiously gleeful and dead. She didn't want to hear what he would say next. Bert, no, please, no.

"The Catholic Church is a——" She stuffed her fingers in her ears, but she couldn't keep out the feel of the words: black, foul poisons that must have been secreted in every corner of his body. Stop, please, please, stop. His mouth worked in strange configurations. She watched new and wild patterns of face, and only slowly realized that the words had stopped and that Bert seemed to be crying. She put her arms around him and took him to her. But his body remained quite rigid, repelling her with outthrust nerves. It was as if he was saying, "No, it didn't work."

And, for the first time, she began to understand the *kind* of thing he meant about being a hack.

Part Three

"The American cult of success is something at which the Christian can afford to smile gently."

FLAX. *Thoughts.*

1

Mrs. Flax, Sr., lived in Englewood with her son Walter. Mr. Flax had gradually withered away some years ago, leaving her with seven children—Bertram the oldest and Walter the youngest. The ones in between had spread in all directions. Beatrice was a missionary nun in Africa, Cuthbert a professional naval man, the others had settled in places like Toronto and Phoenix. Mrs. Flax hoped that Walter would investigate the priesthood close by; but he talked about buying a ranch in the Northwest. The Flaxes went in enthusiastically for things which were almost exotic.

At Christmastime, Bert was representative for the Flax diaspora and came in for a lot of wistful attention. His mother found occasion to consult him about family problems, although they were long since out of her hands: she talked about raising money for Beatrice's order, and foiling Wilma's chest colds. Once settled in the kitchen, she talked a lot about the old days too, the apartment on Amsterdam Avenue and the allegedly festive trips to Bronxville. If it was a Saturday, Walter would sit across from her aggravating his pimples. "Geez, Ma, we know all about that." His idea of a good time was to herd cattle across Montana with a clear skin and a red frosty nose; the past was uncles and aunts in stuffy sitting rooms and older brothers and sisters trickling away one by one.

"Maybe we'll all be living close together again," said Mrs. Flax, on the second Saturday of December. "Wilma's husband might find a job in New York." "Sure, trapping furs," whined Walter. "And Cuthbert could get a land job." "In a pig's eye." "Well, he might, you never can tell." "Oh, sure." Living close together, cheezt! said Walter's face.

It was the kind of conversation that had done so much to scatter the Flaxes: and perhaps Mrs. Flax was just beginning to realize that. Anyway, she shifted the subject over to Bert, who had just come up, clapping circulation into his hands, from the draughty cellar.

"I haven't seen your poem in the *Passenger* yet," she said.

"I didn't do one this year."

"Oh," she said. And after a moment, "You didn't?"

"No, not this year."

"Oh." She looked at Walter, for no very obvious reason. "They're beautiful things. Aren't they, Walter?"

"What? Oh. Sure." He hung his head sheepishly. "They're great."

Walter's embarrassment was contagious. A boy of his tastes would take no special interest in uplift poetry, that was all right. But the density of his embarrassment was something special. It suggested boys gangling up after school and saying, "Hey, this your brother, Walt? No kidding, Walt?" Heads shaking in fake wonder. "Geez, I don't know, Walt," and then, "What do you mean, Walt? I didn't say nothin', I just said I don't know." It meant beyond that, the one dry outspoken priest who had told them in class about "pious rubbish," and had liberated them all—all except Walt—from their burden of politeness and hypocrisy.

"I just didn't feel in the mood this year," said Bert.

"Oh dear, I suppose that must be a problem." Mrs. Flax clouded over. "You've been doing it for so long now, haven't you? Do you remember when you first started them? You had such a flair. . . ."

Walter released, like a skunk, a new barrage of embarrassment. How did a normal guy get started on stuff like that, he might be wondering. It was like your mother brought you up in dresses until you were fifteen or so. No, Walter wouldn't be going that far: it was just the thing with his friends. And the dry priest.

"What do you *really* think of my stuff, Walter? Be honest," asked Bert.

"I think it's great."

"Well, if you can't be honest, be funny."

Embarrassment lay too deep for wisecracks. "I think it's great."

He got up and shuffled out, looking suffocated. Mrs. Flax smiled conspiratorially at Bert and touched his hand. It was unsettling, as if she had understood about Walter's confusion and was telling him not to worry.

"I thought you were going to become a priest when I saw your first poem in the *Passenger*."

Or a nun. He remembered, too, the first poem. It came just like that after a game of stickball on a hot August evening. Geez yes, hot. The cars came grousing along the street every few minutes interrupting the game; the other guys were tired and itchy, but they wouldn't let anyone goof off for a single minute. It was spontaneous sadism, the kind of aimless thing that brewed up sometimes on a hot day. His feet still hurt to think about it; and his ears from the shrill cries of, "Get with it, Flax, get the lead out, Flax."

Afterward, he limped into church on bulbous sneakers. Father Murphy said something kind at the door and it was very cool inside. No shouting, or discipline, or guys twitching for action. No toughness or hardness. He plumped down in front of a friendly looking statue and yes, just that, the poem came. "Our Lady Queen of Peace," full of words like dark and soft and cool. It was a lot better way than sitting in front of a typewriter.

He ran home, tired feet and all, and wrote it down. He wasn't ashamed of it, it was just one of those things a guy did, but just to be on the safe side, he hid it between the mattress and the springs.

The next day his mother found it, etc., etc., but that wasn't what he wanted to think about now. What he wanted was the whole feel of that time, when it really came naturally. Maybe he should go back to the statue—that's what he would have done in one of his stories, and the statue would have spoken, and he would have smelled roses in the distance.

But it *was* a real thing. He had felt all kinds of good juices. Fatigue had dripped away, from his hands and his feet. That's right, his feet hadn't hurt at all as he ran home. He remembered perfectly: the feeling had been absolutely good.

If only he hadn't dragged it around for so long, like a dead cat. . . .

"Look, Bert, if you need any money for Christmas, I have some extra—"

"No, Mother, that's all right. I don't need any money."

"You're sure, now?" Mrs. Flax rambled a bit. "I'm worried about poor Betty, she's looking so thin. I'd hate her to have a worrying Christmas," and so on.

"No, that's all right. Betty's on a diet. We have money."

Mrs. Flax leaned forward. "I think it's hateful of them not to take your poem. I'm sure it was perfectly fine."

"Who said they didn't take it? I never said that."

"Oh, didn't you? I'm sorry, dear. I didn't mean to make

you angry." She was patently afraid of losing another Flax. "All your poems are good, I think," she said judiciously. "I should know better than to think anyone would turn one down."

How could he get that good feeling again? Perhaps he *should* take his dried-up soul elsewhere, North Dakota or the Zambezi. Mrs. Flax, by so eagerly not wanting him to, always put him in mind of the possibility. Right now he remembered the feeling so well he could touch it. But what could you do in New Jersey? The statues in St. Jude's never spoke, even in stories. There was too much shuffling and coughing and daylight; and rooting in handbags for money.

Maybe he should try a mountainside, with Mrs. Forsythe. One thing was sure, if he didn't get the feeling back soon, he was out of work. And the only thing between him and a bleak winter was Mrs. Flax, with her tiny savings, and Mrs. Forsythe, the patrician on the left.

And Mrs. Flax's savings were only a gesture, at that, a kindly limp gesture. The little Flaxes would eat through them like termites.

Mrs. Forsythe was unthinkable.

Which left looking for a job, of course. He knew this choice was critical, but he dismissed it quickly. With five children, a mortgage, no training and not much inclination, a job wouldn't answer half his problems. And what a triumph it would be for you know who.

The truth was, he needed that feeling. Funny, if you wanted a funny side, that the good feeling he had known that day should have become his bread and butter. It would never have occurred to him at the time. The pleasant ease of the church, the sweat turning cool on his face—that that in turn should become a kind of agony, was funny. God, to feel the ease again. And to be able to pay his bills with it.

Well at least he wasn't so far gone he couldn't see the funny side.

2

Betty was *looking thin, he thought idly. The lei*sure of unemployment would allow him time to look into things like that. She couldn't be undernourished yet, could she? They seemed to be eating the same sort of food as always—big-family food, the sort you got in institutions. Why, now really, come on, why did he have to have so many—no, he would never get his touch back asking questions like that.

She was thinner than he wanted her to be. She had always been on the slight side, more genuinely ethereal than any of the true believers at St. Jude's. The way she looked, on dates and things, was the way people ought to look on their way back from Communion.

Dates and things. Funny, now that he had given his tongue its freedom, it fell back on euphemisms. He couldn't control the damn thing at all. The way she looked *then*, during—he couldn't shape the words, even though they weren't really sacrilegious. (No, Christian in a very real sense, said the Archbishop of Canterbury.) What a box the old indoctrination got you into though.

Anyway, what he meant was that she wasn't just ethereal now, but fretful and sallow. Was she getting old? He noticed changes like that in the neighbors' wives regular as the seasons. Their knees suddenly got bony one summer, in their Bermuda shorts. Something went wrong with their eyes the next winter, the pupils became small and nervous. Their mouths got that skeletal look. But Betty was immune to all that. To begin with she had the only real complexion in Bloodbury, two tones, a regular bloom. And her eyes actually saw things. You could almost feel them making contact. And why was he thinking so much about Betty?

Because he had nothing else to do? Most of the husbands of Bloodbury, upon finding themselves incomprehensibly, inconceivably out of work, would have gone down to the basement to saw pieces of wood; they would have remodeled the game room, or something. He had always been supercilious about those hearty little hobbies of theirs; he had his intellectual interests, his philosophy books, his books on Napoleon; but now he wondered whether he really had them after all. Did he *really* care about Napoleon? (I mean, did anyone?) And how about St. Thomas, and the intellectual discipline of reading him in Latin?

All good enough when things were going well. A few minutes with St. Thomas and Napoleon, little touches that rounded a man off. Oh yes, Bert Flax has interests all right. Something for the questionnaires. "Bert Flax loathes exercise. Bert Flax likes nothing better than. . . ." OK, OK, make up your mind, tongue, how we're going to play it. But the fact was, he hadn't read a whole book in years and his Latin had gone all to hell.

He shifted uneasily. Where was Betty all this time? He had seen his mother to the door and had been standing there ever since, ruminating, juxtaposing the change in his trouser pocket. The half dollar between the two quarters, with the penny roaming at large. He realized that he had also been looking through the glass panel for Betty.

If she didn't come back soon, he would have to give the children their supper. He could already sense them beginning to circle behind him, wheeling hungrily and snarling up the cleaning woman. It was nice to have the extra time to spend with his children, mmm yes. Something very depressing about looking at snow through a glass panel and watching it get dark and waiting for someone to come. "A Christian need never be bored"—in a pig's eye he needn't.

Oh no! when something finally happened in the deadness, it was Mrs. Forsythe's Chevrolet again. Christmas was really a nightmare, wasn't it? The two mothers were orbiting closer and closer. Tomorrow he would be whisking one mother out the back while Betty stalled desperately with the other at the front. By the end of the week, they would surely collide, with that sickening grinding noise, because they really wanted to all along.

The glass panel was rapidly filling up with Mrs. Forsythe. It would be dreadful if she pressed her eyeball against it and encountered his. He backed away a few steps, to make it look as if he was actually coming out of the living room. He couldn't just run out altogether, because one of his children would answer the door and he would be trapped somewhere in the back, tiptoeing among the other children.

Mrs. Forsythe fumbled around for the bell. He stood frozen, listening to the clash of packages; then took a step backward, as he imagined the thumb swarming over the door. This would have been a silly way for him to behave

—only of course it was a joke. In the Benchley tradition. Humiliation in daily life, fear of cats, dogs, maids. He gave a rather startled chuckle and the door began to move in with a fat knee behind it.

"Good evening, Bert," the usual, odd formality.

"Good evening, Mrs. Forsythe. I'm afraid Betty isn't in."

"I know. I saw her just now. She didn't see me."

"Oh, no?"

"No." She paused, "I've brought some things."

"Oh, of course. Let me take them. Here." He wrestled them away from her. He felt like Harpo Marx wrestling with Mrs. Rittenhouse—he couldn't tell whether she was trying to hang on to the packages or trying to hand them over. Humor, with a touch of fever. Used to enjoy it more a few years ago.

"How are the children?" she panted.

"Oh, fine. They're fine."

He backed into the living room and she followed, pulling off her gloves.

"You've got your tree already."

"Yes. We've got it."

"Betty always loved a Christmas tree."

"Yes. She still does."

They sat down and looked around wildly for objects to talk about. "You've got a lot of cards." "Not as many as last year." There were things he would really have liked to talk to her about. Nosy, painful questions, but they would have interested her, too. But they were condemned to endless inventory.

It occurred to him that he might as well ask what Betty was doing in town. Mrs. Forsythe was being awkwardly discreet about it, after having brought it up. There weren't any very shameful places in Bloodbury were there?

Mrs. Forsythe looked discomfited. Perhaps she had been all along, he hadn't really looked above her knees yet.

"I'm worried about Betty, she's looking thin," she said.

"I hope she's getting enough to eat. Having so many children must be an awful strain. At times." She volleyed at random. "I mean, I hope you're looking after her properly, Bert."

It was rather amusing to hear her rattling on. It wasn't like Mrs. Forsythe to cover her gibe about large families with a lot of undirected chatter. If she meant a taunt to take effect, she always underlined it carefully with a few moments of heavy silence.

"Where did you see Betty?" he asked.

"Well, you'll never guess, I'm sure."

"What, the beauty parlor? Hennesy's Bar? Where was it, Mrs. Forsythe?"

"Oh no, nothing like that."

"We haven't got a pool room in Bloodbury." She liked humor, theoretically.

"You're joking, Bert." She had begun to scuffle with the brocade on her dress, plucking severely around her knee. "It isn't really anything, I suppose. I mean the big thing is for Betty to be happy, isn't it?"

"Yes, I suppose so. I mean, how?"

A shade of almost-comic melancholy crawled down her face. "It looks as if you've won, Bert," she said suddenly and dramatically.

"Won what?"

"It looks as if you've won, but I don't mind so long as it's what Betty wants."

She was certainly taking defeat graciously. But what defeat? There was something massively noble about her, as of a great ship going down. "What are you talking about, Mother? Mrs. Forsythe?"

"I saw Betty," pause, and the hulk seemed to shiver, "going into the Catholic church. By herself. With one of your black books."

There was a bad moment as Bert began abortively, and with a spasm like panic, to laugh.

3

"I'm very sorry, Mrs. Forsythe. I didn't mean to."

She looked quite wounded and baffled, shot by mistake. Had she been what these people considered funny? They must have their own caricatures of persons like her—had she outlined herself foolishly against one? He had never seen her look so dismal.

"I wasn't laughing at you, Mrs. Forsythe. I'm just relieved that it wasn't anything worse."

"It seems rather a serious thing to me," she sniffed, and he was afraid she might be going to fight after all.

"Oh, it would be serious, if it meant what you thought it meant, but what it means is that she might have been going in about almost anything. She often goes to St. Jude's to talk about the children. Or, you know, the school play."

"With one of your black books?"

A symbol. A black book with a gold cross on it. The Christian life was known by its symbols. He shrugged. "I don't know. She might have been returning it, or something. You never know."

"Returning it from where?"

"I don't know. The children. . . ."

"It strikes me as very fishy."

She seemed almost to want it to happen. She knew the power of darkness would get Betty in the end and was half-glad to have the struggle over with.

He began to feel excited about it. Seeing Mrs. Forsythe crushed wasn't half as pleasant as he might have hoped; more disconcerting than anything; some instinct kept him from enjoying her pain. But the crazy long-shot notion of Betty's moving toward the Church gave him a wild crackle of joy, of a kind he had almost forgotten.

Conversion was one of the few things that still relieved religion of its flatness. However dull it was in church, and desperate at his desk, he was still delighted to see his side doing well. Delighted to root another soul in.

Especially Betty, my God yes, Betty. A strange wild throb on his skin at the news.

"I'm sure it doesn't mean anything, Mrs. Forsythe."

"*I'm* sure it does."

The logical thing would have been to ask Betty. But they both knew that she would tell them the truth if they asked her, and they weren't ready for that. Their eyes met with a kind of understanding. For a moment, he felt he could almost love this woman. This big, fat, pagan woman. And she equally-almost nodded agreement to this: the skin under her chin fluttered. "I have to go now. I just dropped by to bring these things."

"They look very nice. It was very kind of you." They

were still in their boxes, as they would have been if Benchley had just finished thanking his mother-in-law for some absolutely perfect presents. He got her quickly to the door and she didn't seem inclined to dawdle. He expected to see Betty wading wraithlike through the snow to cut them off, but she wasn't in sight. Mrs. Forsythe made good her rather breathless escape, and Bert withdrew to savor his meaningless excitement: it might mean a way out of his difficulty.

It was the closest thing to *the* feeling he had had in a long time. The house became radiant with it, even the children looked good. Surely there was at least a casual essay in it. Careful with the feeling now, don't think about it too much: reflection would quickly tie him up in a neat little useless ball. Just let the geniality expand like yeast.

Mrs. Forsythe presented a pleasant posterior vision. She had her silly side, no doubt, but then perhaps he had made too much of that, too. There was nothing intrinsically wrong with believing in causes. As a Catholic, he was accustomed to sneering at other people's effort, other people's committees. But if they didn't have a Holy Name to go to. . . .

He felt unmistakably buoyant. Through the wintry crusts, a flower had upthrust itself. Through winter's snowy mantle, no, no. But he opened the door and stepped out. There was a violet light filtering up from the dapper stores and gas stations of Bloodbury. Through the fragile branches, no, the wispy, no, the spidery, whatever became of spidery, branches: the snow irradiated, iridescent, all right luminous, with a heavenly light. His tongue was working along the right groove at last. He trembled with his new possession, the bird under the cloak.

"Mr. Flax, oh Mr. Flax." The cleaning woman Martha's face, raddled with confusion, appeared at the door. "The children are getting hungry."

"Not now, Martha, I'm working."

"Well, all right." Caught again in an impossible squeeze, Martha withdrew. Bert smiled absently, tenderly. They never understood how you worked with your hands in your pockets.

The snow was not so damn radiant, it was gray, with only that slight violet tint. But this was no time for the New Criticism. He could look at the gray snow (the way he once looked at the Amsterdam Avenue slush) and write about white snow; look at the jagged wastes and write about downy blankets. That was what professionalism meant.

And who was yon kindly old man out betimes walking his dog? Oh for christsake, Mr. O'Malley from the St. Jude's box office. Foraging for the bishop's relief fund, or something. Bert crept back into the gloaming around his front door. O'Malley's dog stopped and sniffed at the snow. He must know that there's money about, thought Bert. O'Malley looked around him in airy innocence. Move it along O'Malley. Come *on*. Writing about the virgin snow was one thing; but with O'Malley's hound peeing on it. . . .

At last, they shambled off. O'Malley had apparently not seen him. God, these moods were fragile. Betty going into St. Jude's. Mrs. Feeley's advent wreath in the window across the street. Downy mantle. He walked off the porch and scooped up some snow. It drizzled away in his hands, leaving them mainly cold and wet. Now what exactly had he expected from snow?

Betty got home at last. She was in a funny mood. Rather gaunt and frowning at first, and then startlingly merry with the children, and once again rather dry with him over dinner. Looking at him with mild distaste. Great seethings must be going on within. He was indulgent and most elaborately avoided asking her where she'd been that afternoon.

"I'm going to bed right after we've eaten," she said curtly, "I'm awfully tired."

"That's fine. I'll do some work."

"Oh?"

"Yes. I think it's coming at last. Too late for Christmas. But it's good to know it's still there."

He smiled expectantly, but she just nodded and said, "That's nice for you." Funny, the parched skin that he had noticed seemed to go with a general dehydration of character. Perhaps this came on just before a conversion. (If she was expecting a conversion, maybe she should go somewhere and lie down . . . a remembered—or was it just remembered from a story, well anyway—feeling of cheerful awkwardness, of oafish helpfulness pinched pleasantly at his nerves.) "You go to bed and get a good rest," he said. She smiled thinly and left the table.

The paper was gleaming white under his gooseneck lamp, fleecy mantle of paper. He was going to write torrents tonight. He could feel it running, roaring, down both arms at once. The paper gurgled into his typewriter and rolled up all succulent on the other side. Hot damn, he had the words, the real good words.

The cool feeling in front of the statue. Hot spit. At thirty-two, he still had it. In a reverent sort of way, of course. Pow—the doubts and crap were just writer's block. He had been taking his literary troubles out on the Church. Don't worry about those things, son; just write your heart out, son. He flexed his fingers. Flax, flaxen, flaccid fingers. Leave that other stuff to the theologians, son son son. "Flax baby. Bert baby," he crooned talismanically.

And still, not a bloody word.

4

Bert had had a block like this years ago—a rushing through the bowels, and nothing to show for it. At eighteen, it had looked as if he was written out. He went in a squirming panic to Father Chubb, and Father Chubb was disconcertingly undismayed about it. "Writing isn't everything in life," he said. "Perhaps it's time for you to move on to something else." It wasn't like Chubb at all, usually the great encourager. But there was an odd strain in Chubb, a kind of sly listlessness that peeped through every now and then, when the complex game of being Father Chubb became briefly too much for him.

"But I want to write."

"Then I'm sure you will."

"But how?"

The puffs from the priest's pipe came as regular as snores. "Pray for guidance. To the Holy Ghost. He will help you."

"Yes, Father."

"I don't know what else to suggest. Be patient. Trusting in God."

"Yes, Father."

He shut the door on all that pipe smoke and brown leather and went home dispirited. He had expected some flurry of concern. Father Gonfallin of the *Tiny Messenger* had at least affected some gravity over Bert's problem. He hadn't much else to offer, seemed rather vague about the whole literary process, but did say, "You have a fine talent, Bertram. We can't afford to lose you." Father Chubb, on the other hand, acted as if he could fill his magazine with or without Bert. It was an unnerving thought.

The third of his patrons was Sister Melody, and he wrote to her that evening. Her answer came back by return post and went straight into his wallet. He pulled it out now, ragged from fourteen years of squatting in among draft cards and driver's licenses. He opened it with some embarrassment:

"Dear Bertram. Genuine poetic talents are rare." Skip skip. "They are also, thank God, sturdy." Skippety skip skip. "Fields lying fallow . . . life stirring . . . and at last, golden corn!" He flailed himself methodically. Golden corn, a most unfortunate flight. "I write this last paragraph with some diffidence and with the fervent hope that it will not be misunderstood. In the writing of poetry, I find that a pure heart is of the highest importance . . ." bingo, so to speak, that was it. "Not simply off-white, adequate, clean enough for everyday, but sparkling, radiantly pure."

Thus ended his first writers' block. He had pranced out in the street with a high heart—fourteen eternal years ago—lusting for purity. And he found for once a kind visiting priest who seemed to understand what he was babbling about, who smiled at him anonymously through the muzzy grill before disappearing for ever.

Now it was not so easy. He just held the letter, no high heart, no real lust for purity, but the same need to write something. If he wanted the old zing to return, he must make himself as a little child. He must go lisping to Father Terwilliger. Nothing else had ever worked. Even a hack—if that's what he was—had to believe in what he was doing. Bert had to get sincerity again, or the kids would be celebrating the Christian feast with turkey hash.

With a sigh, he pushed the letter back, making another small tear in the desiccated convent notepaper. His soul lay fallow and deep in weeds. Yea, Lord. No use tearing at them any longer with his bare hands. Best get to Terwilliger.

On the Saturday afternoon before Christmas, he was camped once more at the far end of Terwilliger's line. It would have been nice to go to Monsignor Flanagan, but the poor old fellow would have been so bewildered by everything. Father Terwilliger was in some ways a fellow soul—dried out from years of anxious religion, bitter from strain. He, like Bert, tried to force life in a barren field. There might now be a compassionate sweetness in him, at finding death in someone else.

Not bloody likely. "What do you mean, you have trouble with your faith? Are you a trained theologian or something?" was what he had got last time. Terwilliger's astringency would actually be part of the medicine. It didn't do you any good if you didn't get chewed out and grossly misunderstood.

The line gave a twitch, like a conga line, and everyone moved up a place. Bert gazed at a gaudy station of the cross. Shook his head slightly. Went back to his rambling conjectures. You lost your faith if you didn't go to the sacraments, everyone agreed on that. But once you didn't have it, how could you go to the sacraments? Then again, if you didn't have it, why did you bother to go to the sacraments? Et cetera, et cetera—all that was left to him of the great intellectual tradition was a certain arid ingenuity.

Father Terwilliger was ingenious too, when Bert finally made the box. "You wouldn't be here at all if you didn't believe." Neither would you, Terwilliger. Bert could tell that the priest had used the same hopeful logic on himself. I wouldn't be a priest if I didn't believe—therefore I believe, quick next question.

"Did you study theology in college?"

"No, Father."

"Have you talked to a priest about your difficulties?"

"No, not really."

What was there to talk about? Terwilliger probably thought he was having trouble with doctrine. Terwilliger in the same boat would be having trouble with doctrine. Or would think he was.

How could he explain to a man who had snipped off his sensibilities here, here and here, how it was just something that happened to his mind and inner tongue when he walked inside a church? How a clamp of boredom was placed on his skull? And how every word from the pulpit turned to acid in his own mouth, a sour spew of irony? Bert wasn't worried about the substance of religion, because there wasn't any, anymore, just words.

How did you phrase this particular problem?

OK, never mind about his own twist of life—look at what they had done to his friends, Flynn and Gilhouley. Flynn unmanned. Snip, ouch, and another set of sensibilities gone for ever. A convent-parlor face, two empty, patient eyes, but no feeling on the skin. No movement in the brain. And then, the best part, having smashed up old Flynn, degutted him, dehumanized him, they told him he was sitting pretty because he had the gift of faith. (That was Gilhouley's argument, of course, you wouldn't catch Bert Flax using an argument like that.)

And Gilhouley . . . they were just as much to blame for Gilhouley. A tenth-rate man-about-town. Solemnly doing all the things he had heard denounced, just because he had heard them denounced. The other side of the coin, just as dead as Flynn.

It was up-hill work purifying your soul. He became slowly aware that things were going wrong, that some devil was shrieking inside him. And, of course, the harder he tried to be sincere, the louder old Beelzebub shrieked and whistled. This might be the real meaning of sacrilege—to come to confession with a sneaky heart and have it turn to worms while you wait. He had come for selfish reasons and not because he felt sorry for anything. He had come to help himself write better—but his writing was a form of worship—shriek, shriek, that's a good one, Flax, worship. . . . No, seriously, he knew that you couldn't blame the Church for everything, for Flynn, for Gilhouley, for Flax. People got just as messed up outside, if not more so. (Look at the Peabodys, psychoanalyzing their own children, for petesake. Look at Mrs. Forsythe.) What the Church did for people like Flynn was to make the most of them, give them *something*. . . .

He was so tired of arguing. His brain had come loose somewhere, allowing him to take both sides for ever and ever. He listened instead to Father Terwilliger.

"You've been setting yourself up as a big man, trying to solve these problems on your own."

"Yes, Father."

"Can you tell me more precisely what these problems are?"

He shrugged in the dark. "I guess not." He wondered if the priest recognized his voice. For a lucid moment he saw himself jumping on his typewriter as a form of contrition.

His sin had something to do with a typewriter. Not all that easy to explain.

"You seem to be a very confused man," said Father Terwilliger severely. "I don't see how you expect to keep your faith if you stay away from the sacraments. Faith is a gift, you know. You have no right to trail it in the mud of indifference. And if you have any real difficulties, take them to a priest, a trained man."

"Yes, Father."

There was no point arguing. If Bert was going to get back on the tracks, he had to give humility one more whirl.

"Now for your penance. . . ." There was a great crowd waiting outside, because of the holiday season, and a good deal of what Terwilliger said was automatic. He was really a very conscientious man, doing his best with what must have sounded like a half-witted penitent. Of course it was useless. A priest without perception was about as helpful as a blind traffic cop. You couldn't blame him for being querulous, really, for shouting "stop, everybody stop." Bert made a stab at contrition and thanked Father Terwilliger as humbly as he could.

The people outside looked up curiously as he stumbled out. He had been in there a long time, and those who had hit a peak of sincerity too soon were, he imagined, a bit resentful.

He didn't wait to say his penance, but got out quickly before the interior shrieking could start up again.

5

Bloodbury didn't have Santa Clauses with scraggy beards and melancholy bells. What else? It didn't have boys' choirs that sang badly, or priests gleaming feverish from overwork and goodwill, or blighted trees shedding scruff over the snowy pavements (deep breath) trailing along behind small boys in navy-blue wool hats, mittens, sagging knickers. Anger, goddamnit, you missed the anger.

The unwavering blandness clashed with his mood. There ought to be purple traffic cops raging at Bloodbury's corners. But Officer Scanlon looked well rested. He smiled at the drivers and the drivers smiled (very small smiles) back. You didn't see hands white with frustration at the steering wheels, or creased, fanatical faces over scraping, dirging tire chains.

He didn't know whether that kind of confession counted, or whether anything he did now counted. It certainly hadn't brought "Instant Peace," the way it used to.

The stores were open late this Saturday. He peered into Howell's Gift Shoppe. Bloodbury's beste giftes. No anger in there. The handful of customers were never flung snarling and cursing on top of one another, the way they were in the good old days. Thin lips, the mark of the season, beady, frosted eyes—everyone was so damn polite around Bloodbury. You felt a long distance from Ohrbach's and Klein's when you walked pinging and chiming into Howell's.

An intelligent-looking woman with gray hair was on to him in a twinkling. "I'm just looking," he said quickly. "Go right ahead," she warned. In a few minutes she would wheel back to ask, "Was there anything special?"—and there'd better be something special.

Ashtrays made of Ubangi lip, inlaid nutcrackers. What does it profit "the man who has everything" if he suffers the loss of his own soul? What he actually wanted was something for Betty—something expensive and careless. He fingered some chic coffee tables, one inside the other. Seventy-five dollars a set and the kids would tear them to ribbons by New Year. The mahogany lampstand was more promising, but the shade looked a bit arty. Some thin women pushed quietly past. How much did *they* cost? "Have you seen anything you like?" The overseer had maneuvered in front of him again and was urging him to buy with all deliberate speed.

"Not yet," he said rather grumpily.

"This lamp is charming."

"Yes. I don't care for it." Some of the old Ohrbach's spirit. But since she just continued to stand there, he wilted. "I like those tables, though." His own anger was just private; he was surprised at the can't-we-be-friends note in his voice.

She must have somehow hovered it out of him. He hadn't meant to say anything about the tables. The rest followed like a dream. She told him they came from Denmark and ran her finger coaxingly along the grain. He swung around quickly to find a diversion, but everything else in the store was hopelessly irrelevant. The fertility ashtray clattered to the floor as he swung back, utterly clinching the deal.

"Very popular," she consoled him. "This is our last set. Denmark is the home of fine furniture." She tested the legs to demonstrate the craftsmanship. He bent over, very awkward in his winter coat, to pick up the fallen Ubangi.

"I'll have to pay with a check."

"That's perfectly all right. Perfectly." Her ballpoint was already poised over the pink receipt.

She gift-wrapped the tables and helped him to bundle them out to the Studebaker. That was Christmas shopping for you. Mrs. Howell's glasses glinted triumph at him from the door. Shooting fish in a barrel, was what it was for her. "Call again," she said. Chump.

He smuggled them past Betty into the cellar, where they could squat anonymously until Christmas among the excessive toys he had to buy every year for the children. Seventy-five dollars, was he crazy or what? The checkbook stub looked so stubby and torn, he felt a moment of blinding serious confusion. He had made a bad confession, so they had taken away his money. Out of work, and he had to tangle with one of Mrs. Howell's *svelte* things. Oh, well, Christmas.

He ran upstairs, looking for Betty. She was strewing tinsel on the tree and he kissed her heartily.

"How is it going?"

"All right."

"Can I do something?"

"If you like." She silently handed him a box of silver balls.

"It's looking very nice."

She concentrated narrowly on her tinsel and didn't answer. She didn't know that he had just bought her some finely wrought white elephants from Denmark. When she found out, she'd be more affectionate. She'd say what a wonderful husband he was. He only wished she'd say it now, to take the blight off that damn check stub.

"St. Jude's is beginning to look quite nice," he said.

"You're putting too many near the bottom, dear. Spread them out."

"I was over this afternoon to confession, and, honestly, it isn't half bad this year. Father Terwilliger must be getting some taste in his old age."

She stepped back and deliberated about the tree, then plunged back with fresh fistfuls of tinsel.

"Of course, I wouldn't want your mother to see it. The taste isn't that good. There are still those awful statues. But I guess any church begins to look good at this time of year. To me, anyway. Even the old ladies begin to look kind of sweet and the children become almost human. Look, Betty, I know it's cheating, but there's something down in the cellar I'd like to show you."

He hadn't said this all at once, but little by little, over about ten minutes. And with each word her face seemed to stiffen a bit more—or maybe it just failed to soften; the cheeks looked gaunter than gaunt, and the eyes that once lit on his with easy recognition now burned, if anywhere, inward. By the last phrase, he was quite anxious. She might be getting sick for Christmas, on top of his other worries.

She followed him mechanically towards the back stairs. Of course, he'd forgotten about the tentative conversion. That's why she was looking so funny. He took a step sideways and put his arm round her bony hips. People drifting toward The Church had always been a big thing in his life. Celebrities coming in, or rumored to be coming in. Friends making halting inquiries. Great shoals of Anglican parsons. The joy of his youth.

And now Betty perhaps. What he had wanted for so long. Family prayers. He only wished he felt more excited about it. Couple of days ago he had felt excited, for just that few minutes; but the joy must have been synthetic, because—well, nobody else would understand this—real joy would have shown in his work. Too eager, wait for it to ripen, you nut. He was really delighted about Betty, it was just what he needed to get back on the beam, "watchit, dear."

He flicked on the light in the musty basement. Children's clothes hung stiff from wall to wall, so that the parents had to bend their heads. The presents stood in a foolish heap, the table package awkward, prominent, like an overgrown boy. Bert seized it eagerly and began gashing the paper away: it fell in bright-colored strands on the wet, gray floor.

The tables emerged sheepishly from their cocoon. "These are for you," said Bert. "Your Christmas present."

He held them up for her. Smart, beautifully crafted tables. "From Denmark," he explained. "I got them just now."

It seemed silly holding them up like that: he put them down carefully and waited. After a moment, she came over and looked at them, ran her hand slowly along the grain. Something fluttered at the corner. Mrs. Howell, falling short of her usual efficiency, had left a price tag one one of the legs. Betty turned it up and read it. Without expression. Possibly a raised eyebrow in the basement murk.

Hard to tell anything by the light of a 25-watt bulb. At last she looked, almost reluctantly, at Bert and said, "They're very nice, Bert. You shouldn't have."

And went upstairs, leaving him to dispose of the gift wrapping.

The heat had gone off again and his study was Spartan as a monk's cell. It just needed a skull on the table—how about that for the man who has everything? His fingers were stiff as he took them out of the dressing-gown pockets. He hadn't got much mileage yet out of Betty's churchgoing or purity of heart. How about honest indignation? He hadn't tried that for a while.

It was too late for this Christmas, but it would do just as well for next. "The Commercialization of Christmas," he began to type: not the freshest theme in the world, but his wounds were fresh, anyway. "The merchants begin to salivate as the Christ-child draws near"—much too strong; "The babe who had nothing and the man who has everything"—better, less personal; righteous, noncontroversial anger. Nobody likes the man who has everything. "There is politeness in the air at Christmas, but it is not Christian politeness. It is a crafty, self-serving politeness. Rage would be a lot better." A row of *X*'s, "I almost think anger would be better."

He used to have such a sure touch, spirited but gentle; now he had to watch out for these meaningless spurts of rage; or, another time, Father Chubb would tell him he was laying the sincerity on too thick. Even as he hit the notes, his fingers would weaken and the hammer would land apologetically. He tried writing for himself, but the stuff always angled back toward one of his shrinking markets. "The expense of Christmas makes for tension, even in the best families . . ." could there be tension in the best families? Over money? He couldn't remember the simplest rules. . . . "A loving husband thinks that a wife has spent too much; a wife thinks, what does a wife think?" He wiped his forehead. He was bored sick with edification. If he could do just once the blackhearted merchants staring ferretlike from their shop doors; the black bile covered with purple spines; the fun of destroying a man for Christmas. . . .

He felt his jaw beginning to lock slightly. This had happened a few times before when he was writing. Not to get alarmed. He concentrated on the glass in the bookcase. It dilated slightly. There were little points of light on it. Concentrate on those. He was behind the glass himself, a small china jug. Nothing serious. His jaw unlocked and he found that he had typed, "Bishoprics are a prize for getting fat"; he laughed uneasily and unrolled the paper. Seriously though, not quite back on his form yet. Only two paragraphs. He knew what Chubb would say—he would say they were weak. That was what made his work so difficult. But he was getting back on the beam.

Part Four

"The art in our Churches may not always
be to the liking of our eggheads,
or even of our genuine intellectuals
(there is a very real distinction);
but if it brings one soul closer to God,
it has achieved a high purpose."

FLAX. *Thoughts.*

1

That evening, Bert played robustly with the children, ate his supper and went upstairs yet again to his study. Betty raced impatiently through the dishes and left them to drip; wrapped a green scarf round her jaws, catching a glimpse of high cheekbones in the hall mirror (Slavonic peasant, she thought), and opened the front door with furry stealth.

There was something very exciting about this secret burrowing-into-the-night. Padding through the snow in cloaks and shawls; Roman matron perhaps, dressed as servant, threading cautious way to catacombs. It was play-acting of course. She straightened up and walked more seriously.

St. Jude's was barely awake. A thin flame in front of the altar, and one man rumpled in prayer. Mr. O'Malley, of course, his tired, puffy face managing to organize a smile. God, how it pleased these people to see a pagan in church.

It's not what you think, Mr. O'Malley. Not a conversion, not a little voice in the ear. And, Dear God, not instructions in a plain wrapper.

The instructions might be written by someone like Bert. (Nothing wrong with that of course, but she knew what Bert had to say by now.) She took a seat near the garish crib.

Father Terwilliger was hard at work in and out of the shadows. Emptying the confessionals or something. Anything could happen in a Catholic church. That was the part of it that Mr. O'Malley wouldn't admit to; and perhaps commonsense Bert didn't know about it either, the craving to be a bit queer, now and then. It was what kept religion in business.

Her mother's meetings had done their best to supply the need when she was a child. But they never went far enough. The officers didn't wear magic gowns, or talk foreign. They didn't incant in the dark. They wore vests and spoke dead English; queer, all right, but not crazily, purgingly queer. (At that, the meetings were more like services than the ones they went to on Sundays: they had dogma, ritual and fanaticism, Canon Flood's three pet peeves.)

She had been doing this for about a week now. Really by elimination. To begin with, she had to get out of the house. The children were snowed in and hypertense, waiting for Christmas. Bert was probably embarrassed at having blown up like that about the Church; he never referred to it directly, but she got a feeling she was supposed to forget it as quickly as she could. He burrowed into his work as if nothing had happened; and at meals he talked about their five wonderful kids and their little house and how truly lucky they were . . . he always got a bit artificial at Christmastime, with the strain and everything.

So, out of the house it was. Unfortunately, the window displays were set for Christmas now, frozen wastes of gaiety, and in the other direction, the Park seemed to have got much colder since November. When she crouched on one of the two benches, the wind knifed her cruelly and kicked snow in her face. And when she walked she got dreadfully tired under her weight of bizarre worries. She felt like a child who had been told to stay out of the house for an hour, and could think of nothing better than getting back in. Genteel furniture from Mrs. Flax, mobiles and candle snuffers from Mrs. Forsythe and all, she wanted to be back in.

Bloodbury was deceptive. It had that friendly surface, but the doors were closed at night; just because people went shopping in their shorts didn't mean you could just drop in on them. (Unless it was a Meeting, she thought, between chattering teeth.) Or perhaps she'd got it wrong, you *could* drop in after all, but if you did you had to talk, talk b-b-b-brightly about the very things, husband, children, housework you were set on fleeing. And the men talked about how when they were boys they never heard of Little League, they played marbles and stickball and jacks; Mr. Skinner set beaver traps—you never saw kids setting beaver traps these days.

There was nowhere you could just go and sit and find quick, quick relief from the animated face and the metallic suburban tongue. Except, of course, church. You might get a famous rest in church—if they weren't holding pageants and raffles and exhibitions of child art at the time.

She tried her own first, All Souls. Just as she feared: Canon Flood intercepted her right off in the American-Gothic doorway, and they had a distraught chat. People didn't often come round in the evenings and he seemed anxious to make the most of her.

He was sort of uneasy though, as if he couldn't imagine

why she'd come. Mrs. Forsythe had given him a lot of trouble over the years from one flank (not enough social teaching, too much theology). Then Betty had gone and married a Catholic, so he hardly knew what to expect.

By the time she got to a pew she felt depressed and keyed up at the same time. Downtown Bloodbury had a mixed and shifting population and the canon had become famous for his ecumenical footwork; he was able to anticipate troubles she didn't feel and make dextrous concessions she didn't want—it was all so strenuous and trivial. She just wanted a place to sit quietly, get some of this opium of the people, and here she was met at the door by centuries of accumulated anxiety.

All Souls had never meant much to her, and still didn't. It seemed indecisive, as if it didn't quite know what sort of building it was supposed to be. Betty used to come here sometimes with her mother (vacant, Sunday-best eyes) and knew that any church her mother went to couldn't be right. Not right as a church, anyway. It had corners of queerness for the high-churchers, and an altar table that was neither one thing nor the other—Canon Flood would probably take it away altogether if she wanted, or put icons on it if she wanted. It was fearfully nondenominational. "This Sunday, Mrs. Forsythe, our guest preacher, will talk about the social gospel; next week, Bert Flax and his quote spiritual values. . . ." There was a stained-glass window at the back that looked a bit like Bert—a hack artist's idea of a saint.

Her mother had really ruined All Souls for her by so manifestly not taking it seriously. Betty was interested in religious experience and her mother said in effect, "Not in church, dear." She imagined it as a kind of whale's-belly feeling, sense of berserkness somewhere, waters swishing and sluicing, stillness somewhere else—it was pretty vague but religion was that or nothing. A church ought to know what it was doing.

Well, if that was what she wanted, she knew where to go

for it. A church where Mrs. Forsythes stayed outside like devils. The place where (in spite of the Fords they always seemed to be raffling in front) they kept the religion. She knew it was there because it made her so nervous at first. But later it got quite comfy, in a sinister kind of way. She didn't know how you went about believing in any of it, or how you would know it when you did. But religion was supposed to be a "felt need" these days, and she certainly felt the need of something. The art was unspeakable, but there was something correct about the atmosphere.

Was it something to do with windows being shut all year? She wondered. The air seemed thick and crowded, as if the Sunday congregations had left something behind. Their coughs and sneezes perhaps. It was something like warm breath that told you you were in St. Jude's and not All Souls. But in fact the church was quite cold and her toes kept going numb under the kneeler.

Father Terwilliger whisked around on his fusty errands, apparently making a point not to catch her eye. He seemed to enjoy puttering about inscrutably in his funny church. There really wasn't anything that needed doing—straightening tassels, adjusting pictures: he was just pleasuring himself, as she was, in the queer atmosphere.

"Good evening, Father." She wasn't afraid of him anymore: he looked so touching in his cassock and spectacles. Like a putty nose that he'd never got used to.

He smiled with embarrassment. She shouldn't have addressed him out loud, she supposed. But he came gliding up the aisle anyway, on invisible legs, and said in a very hoarse whisper, "Good evening, Mrs. Flax. How are the children?" Behind him, Mr. O'Malley was beaming approval. Well, one either liked this kind of scene or one didn't. At the moment, it seemed so insanely friendly that she felt like crying.

"That's good," said Father Terwilliger. "That's very good." Mr. O'Malley nodded and his lips moved. He was saying the words "that's good" unconsciously after Father.

2

The sincerity still wasn't coming too well. There was always some puny distraction—like money.

It was silly to go on brooding about the damned tables. But if Betty didn't like them, well, he had nothing else to give her. Maybe he could sneak down the back stairs and into Bloodbury again tomorrow—he needed that look of radiant surprise that she got every year. Even if it cost him his shirt, which it just about would. He looked at the check-book: five dollars and twenty-five cents left, cripes. And the same again in credit. There was an arch note ("Remember us?") from the telephone company on the left of the desk, and a less arch one from the gas company (why did the gas company always have to be so surly?). On his right were reams and reams of paper that he couldn't seem to fill.

Why weren't they taking his stuff anymore? It was just the same stuff he had always done. He read the carbons of his latest failures and compared them with last year's. They seemed no better and no worse. Somewhere along the line he had lost the knack of judging this stuff. It all seemed equally inspiring and childish, no child*like*, my son, a very different thing. According to our records, you are two payments behind on your new Electrolux, said the next item on the other pile. Remember the lilies of the field, Flax. Don't worry about a thing.

Why wouldn't they take his stuff? Because they knew he didn't believe any more? How could they possibly have spotted that? Where was he giving himself away? Anyway, apart from anything else, it wasn't true that he didn't believe; belief was an act of the will, and he was willing like crazy right now. And making headway, too. (Say the Creed with a lie detector someday and put a stop to these silly rumors.) He thought it was grand about Betty and the Church, for instance. Kneeling next to her at Midnight Mass. . . .

It made him feel a little bit sick, he couldn't exactly say why. Picture of Flax looking attentive, reading his missal; hiding his boredom. If he couldn't eliminate these negative thoughts, he was through. He made two new piles out of the bills. The situation wasn't all that desperate. It would be nice to talk to someone about it though, only it was rather hard to explain. If you tried telling Betty it might keep her out of the Church. If you tried telling Father Chubb you might never place another story in the *Passenger*. People expected Bert Flax to know what he was doing. Once, in the anonymity of the confessional, he had actually been recommended to look up an article by Bert Flax, on the subject of Faith: Flax was really the fellow he ought to talk to. If he could get through to him.

Come on now, just fill a couple of those pages, and fill

them right. "Heroic poem in praise of bingo." . . . The trouble with writing was that it still unloosed the same things that came loose in church: crazy words, things he didn't mean at all. He could be a perfectly good Catholic, if he could just give up writing and going to church. (When he was arguing with someone like Mrs. Forsythe, he felt like a great Catholic.)

Church and desk—that was where the devil could get at him. Wasn't always like that. One Christmas Eve on Amsterdam Avenue he did a poem that had the whole family in tears. Right in the living room, with everyone watching and chattering, he wrote it straight down. He could still hear Wilma sniffing. And Frank scuffing his huge feet. Oh God, why couldn't he do it like that now?

Nothing to get emotional about, now. Just let it come. Midnight Mass might do the job. Last year, coming back from Communion was like cool water. (He made a quick note, "cool water," work it in somewhere.) Where was he? This year. Could he go to Communion after confessing to Terwilliger? He hadn't made too much sense, had he? but at least he'd tried. He felt he'd left something out of his confession, though. Some sin so big that you couldn't even see it. So big they didn't have a name for it yet. But that was untheological nonsense. This of all years, with Betty interested in the Church, you couldn't miss Communion.

That isn't a very good motive, Bertram. Oh, don't you think so? He was talking out loud, as he often did when he wrote. Such a strain keeping it to yourself, you had to talk to someone. "Can I receive the sacrament just to help my wife, Mr. Flax?" "How do you know that that's your only motive, son? Just because you never go any other time doesn't mean. . . ." Flax knew the answers, all right. He could imitate any priest you cared to name. "My son," et cetera. The humble ones, the breezy ones. It was terrible to be a professional.

OK, if you're a professional, write something. He cranked some more paper into the machine and stared into the terrible white emptiness.

For so long, people said you did "lovely things," that you "wrote beautifully"—Bert had no idea what was good or what wasn't. Or whether he was even in the right game. A little bit of hypocrisy among the recent immigrants. If his name had been Sister Something, they'd be praising him still. He would be the grand old lady of Catholic letters. If only someone would tell him what he had done to displease the recent immigrants. . . .

Better write something, or Mrs. Forsythe would be round in the morning with a mink check. Not fair about the mink, but God, you couldn't give that woman satisfaction. You couldn't have her paying for children she didn't believe in. She had never had him in such a corner before; big, fat woman waiting for him to say uncle, waiting for him to admit that he lived like a pig . . . he'd write his way out, hell yes.

How about some free association to shake things loose all right clunk on the space Father Chubb a large prosperous banker talking, "You see we can't give him a loan because he doesn't believe in God anymore. It's beginning to show in his work. The stockholders are getting on to it." Not bad, banker talk. Anonymous editor fill him in later, "That's true perhaps but still there's this good that he does. His thing about Christmas past, children's faces, quite beautiful, some of it. 'And they didn't know that Daddy pays the bills' symbolism, God pays the bills for all of us, anyone can see what he's getting at there." "Yes, but this thing about God is rather important, we feel. Flax's position is becoming increasingly illogical. He seems to believe in the Church all right but not in God. Or is it the other way round? Bet *he* doesn't even know. Trying too hard of course, could believe in a twinkling if he didn't have to. We're seriously thinking of taking up a special second collection to make this possible." Ha, ha, pretty funny, Flax, what do you think you are, a new rectory? I mean high school, sorry.

Anonymous editor, with cardbord suitcase, beginning to see this guy a little better: "We think his heart is in the right place. He wants his wife to become a Catholic and that's good enough for us. The simple people, et cetera (retches expressively into suitcase). Unfortunately our policy does not permit payment. . . ." Chubb (bellowing), "But what does he actually stand for? What's inside him?" What happened to him, that he should wind up writing stuff like this like this like this no more free association, he was sweating on to the keys and, besides, the doorbell was ringing. He went along the landing to look out of the bedroom window: a mother-shaped bundle of fur below. He ducked into the bathroom and sloshed some water onto his face, avoiding the mirror, and did his best to compose his thoughts. It was normal enough to have wild thoughts, now and then; you were only in trouble when they began to show.

The banker had one last volley: "What does he think being a Catholic means?" "It means, never mind what it means."

Bert went down to answer the door.

3

Although she wasn't getting much out of it (after the first ten minutes she ran out of things to think about), Betty was reluctant to get up and go home. The trouble with Church therapy was that it didn't do what it was supposed to do. It wasn't making her a better wife and mother, on the contrary. She often got home quite crotchety from St. Jude's (maybe she wasn't doing it right); bored with the children, and bored a little with old Bert too. This afternoon his mooning tenderness had definitely got to her nerves. "Don't look like that, please," she wanted to say. "Stop being a model husband for just five minutes."

Instead of which he kept hanging about, handing her tinsel and smiling with his gallumphing, I-understand-everything gentleness. It was hateful of her to take it like this, and she turned sparks of annoyance back on herself—which didn't, she supposed, make her any better company. It couldn't be helped. You didn't want people around all the time. It was nice to wallow in velvety stillness like this—Bert knew that as well as anybody.

She wondered what Bert thought about in church. Suppose he was kneeling over *there*—how would he go about praying, how did he thrust the prayer *out?* He might be a bit of a hack in his writing (she just didn't know the field), but this assuredly he was good at. Did he look at the statues? Did he use those horrible flesh tints as a starting point? Bert said you mustn't be priggish, but honestly.

She half turned to avoid St. Joseph's popping blue eyes and the baby's stucco hair. Probably done like that to test the faithful. Where was she? For the first time in her life she didn't care *what* she was given for Christmas . . . still she really felt very bad about those Dutch tables or whatever they were. She had done all she could to raise the tiniest conventional enthusiasm, it didn't take much to satisfy Bert. But it lay in her stomach like a stone. She couldn't begin to describe how little she cared about the tables. And she knew Bert didn't care either, he did it only to please her. What he didn't know was that she was on a nonmaterialist kick, doing her bit to improve the nation's moral fiber for Time-Life.

Anyway here she was, back in church, breathing in the pea-soup silence, wondering if faith would come just by sitting here. How many people who came on Sundays really believed, and how many just liked the smell? She supposed what it was, was that they all came and aspired ardently and breathed it all out, and later ones came and sucked it up and passed on their own mixture, until the air was thick as stew with old prayers and hopes. But if God suddenly appeared, they'd all go charging down the aisle. . . .

She would, anyway. Her mother had imbued her with

Black Magic excitement over The Church. (It wasn't true, but watch it!) And she had seen Bert galvanized, twitched by it—miming her mother's predictions. Why did he get so tense over something that seemed to her so relaxing? His swearing the other evening fascinated her, as if the things he swore at were real. As if the room was full of devils, like a Dutch painting.

She had no system of thought for judging these things. Bert always answered her questions like a man in a plain wrapper, very wooden and correct. But she still had no feel for what it all meant, how you prayed and to what; how you went about loving, actually loving, an abstract God, or whether that was just a pious pretense. She began to feel the cold again and got up sadly to go.

On previous evenings, Father Terwilliger had punctiliously avoided serious talk with her. But tonight he had planted himself with a look of wretched determination in the doorway, and she knew that she would not get off so lightly again. She stopped at the magazines where Bert's pieties moldered (they didn't belong here, she suddenly thought, and wondered what she meant by that) and sensed the feet shifting gloomily under the cassock. This took great courage for a frightened, awkward man. He must have discovered by now that his timing was likely to be off, that he often approached people at just the wrong moment. She could imagine the rebuffs scalding his soft white skin. Nevertheless someone had to do it.

"I see you're looking at our pamphlets, Mrs. Flax."

"Yes, I am."

"We have quite a good selection, I think. They cover just about everything that's likely to arise, I mean."

"Yes, they seem to." Betty couldn't help smiling. "What to do on a date," "How much should I drink." Casuistry peeking into all the corners of life. But not hers.

"Of course, you may have questions that aren't dealt with in our pamphlets . . ."

"I can't imagine so."

". . . in which case you can always come to me." He opened his eyes and looked relieved that she hadn't gone.

"I don't think there's anything at the moment. But thanks, anyway." If he had done it well, she might have been annoyed. But to find a Catholic priest who didn't function efficiently was a joy in itself.

"I don't suppose there's much that Bert couldn't tell you," he wound up. "He's a remarkable man. But sometimes wives feel awkward. . . ."

He stood in the doorway, smiling farewell, and the incredible O'Malley came up behind him and smiled too.

When she reached the corner they could just be seen, talking to each other. About parish administration, or the war against smut, or her. Under the bright porch light, Terwilliger's face was pale, half-formed, studious. Curiously, from underneath, as he passed you in church, for instance, he looked rather brutal and jowly. It all depended on where you were stationed yourself.

When she got back, Bert was waiting for her in the hall. She could tell by his heavily comical face that the comical worst had happened. Also by two black hats, two commissar coats and two pairs of small rubber boots in the hall. The two mothers-in-law had collided at last, and the air rang with the grunt of battle.

4

Not really, of course. That was just the tired family joke, Bert's joke. They were both massively shy at first. Mrs. Flax was not a natural fighter: she had to be goaded. Mrs. Forsythe was usually ill at ease with strangers and people she hadn't seen for a while. Betty had watched her for years flinching at first contacts, then gathering confidence and finally steam-rollering.

They were talking children in fits and starts as she came in. Very slowly she took off the green scarf, watching her face in the mottled mirror and hearing the sounds of diffidence. "Getting to be very big, doing very well in school, Sister says . . ." new waves of discomfort at that—"Sister says"—was getting near the inflamed area.

It was amazing that people could live so long, pricking and parrying children, dealing with salesmen, bond drives, wrong numbers, and still be so awkward in elementary encounters.

Betty wondered if her own lifetime would leave her in the end thus tentative, vulnerable . . . one thought of oneself as constantly growing, developing, finding oneself, and this was what it all came to.

She turned the corner into the living-room and they both looked relieved to see her. Her mother beamed nondenominational season's greetings: "I came over with the thing to go with the packages." "And I brought one of my puddings," explained Mrs. Flax. Their combined bulk did somehow affect the atmosphere.

Bert came in from the kitchen with a tray of water glasses, squeezed her shoulders and went over and sat next to his mother. Mrs. Forsythe had given them some abstract chairs a year ago when the canvas got ripped in her wedding presents, but tonight she was anchoring the middle of Mrs. Flax's old gift sofa; she shuffled along to the end, leaving room for Betty. Which left the two families facing each other like doubles teams. Betty realized with a sudden twinkle of tension that the awkwardness of the two mothers might not be due to their declining self-mastery, but to a heightened sensitiveness.

"Well," said Mrs. Forsythe.

"Here we are," said Mrs. Flax.

One reason she hated to see them together was that each was sort of a satirical comment on the other, and what she had done and failed to do with the gift of life. Mrs. Flax looked slack and fuzzy, although she was easily the younger, and quite eerily ill defined in the presence of a worldly and decisive figure like Mrs. Forsythe. But Mrs. Forsythe might feel a bit shallow, heraldically barren and unaccomplished, next to a horn of plenty like Mrs. Flax. . . . Betty became aware that they expected her to say something. She wasn't supposed just to sit there and think about them.

"How do you like our tree?" she said, rather wildly. "Bert and I spent the afternoon fixing it."

They craned around to see it, although they must have seen it before, on the way in. "Very pretty, isn't it, Vera?" said Mrs. Forsythe. "Yes, it's lovely," said Mrs. Flax.

"It's begun to shed," said Bert. "The man swore it wouldn't."

Getting to be like Mrs. Bloom, thought Betty, or rather like the *Prospect III* contributor of college days: conversation was becoming more of a drag every day. While they went on about the tree, she watched their pores open and close and heard the breaths between the words. For most of the year they disapproved of each other triumphantly; each knew that the other lived a terrible, empty life. But there was no mistaking the little movements of uncertainty now: Mrs. Flax touching the wispy bun of hair—she knew she'd gone a bit vague and silly over the years. Still, it *was* right to give yourself up to your children, wasn't it? Even if the children grew up and found you at last to be vague and silly. . . .

A Dali painting of old cheese and open wounds. And touching the wounds with nervous gestures, Mrs. Forsythe's fingers wandered ceaselessly from her pearls to her mouth and back. Sharp, dry, brittle from too many paper-causes and nothing like enough life. (And she had talked such a good game about life is for living.) At least having children was *something*. It left you with something solid to point to, not just a shower of dead motions and petitions; passionate commitment was what they called all that at the time, but it was just a bray of dead voices, as she grew old and stiff and the globe took another satirical spin.

They were looking at Betty again. It had never occurred to her how much they depended on her to crank them up.

"I was saying," said Mrs. Forsythe at last, severely and then incredibly, something which Betty couldn't quite grip about fluoridation.

"But isn't it poisonous?" said Mrs. Flax timidly, but not all that timidly.

Oh well, so much for theories. Mrs. Forsythe's causes really were important, she supposed: it was only because they were Mrs. Forsythe's that she couldn't take them seriously. Bert had rather fed Betty's cruelty on this: she sacrificed her mother to give them a family joke. She wasn't seriously cruel, as she was as a girl, but comically, all-in-fun cruel.

Betty got up to make coffee. They would be at it awhile, now that they'd got a "topic," and they wouldn't need her help to keep going. Mrs. Forsythe would soon produce the pamphlets. Mrs. Flax would gaze at them, sightless over the tops of her glasses, and put them down again, uncomprehending and unmoved.

Bert came out to the kitchen with Betty and began to forage absently in the refrigerator.

"God!" he said. He got butter on his fingers from groping. "They're incredible, aren't they?" She smiled slightly. He wanted so much to be friends. "Mind you, I think they do each other a world of good. My mother doesn't believe in arguments, but it does her wonders to have one now and then. And your mother gives her a dandy. Just within her capacities."

Betty really wanted to talk about religion or something with Bert but she was afraid he would think she was "being converted" and go all stiff. Maybe after Christmas. . . . He frowned, "Seriously, though, I think they're two wonderful women. I like to see them together."

"Really, Bert—" she would be glad when goodwill time was over and he went back to being himself.

"But not too often, I guess."

He was the only man she knew who still wore a waistcoat (he was a bit like an old family photograph, it was a wonder he didn't wear a stiff collar as well). She thought he was splendid but she couldn't talk to him about anything important, not now. He would "take an attitude" and spoil everything. "You're looking tired, Bert," she said. "You mustn't worry."

"What me—worry?" he said, striking his chest and coughing mock-consumptively. "What would I have to worry about?" There was no humor in it any more, but she smiled anyway. "Did I tell you, I got a letter today from a man that said, 'Does the Church push you around, Mr. Flax?' " . . . "We'd better be going back" . . . "And I wrote and said nobody pushed me around, nobody cared that much." "Bert that's not true." "No, I think it's a wonderful thing. The Church doesn't even know I exist." She couldn't see what was wonderful about that but he seemed awfully pleased; he put some cookies on a plate and said, "Yum."

It was only nine o'clock, and the two mothers with time hanging loose like skin would stay till twelve at least. Mrs. Forsythe prided herself on not needing much sleep. Mrs. Flax didn't pride herself on it, but Betty had been told how she used to sit up regularly waiting for her children to come home and go on to talk them groggy. (She felt they were more approachable at night.)

Hours and hours of muddled talk. Neither would understand a word the other was saying; both would feel vaguely "got at" by the end of the evening and would make a frosty departure. It was the worst thing the Flaxes had to go through to get to Christmas.

"The Twelve Days of a Flax Christmas"; "The jousting of the mothers-in-law"; "The descent of Father Chubb" (he should have been round by now—lucky he didn't pick tonight); "The feeding of Bert's brother, Walter"; and finally, sharp little climax like the burst of a photographic bulb, "Bert transmogrified at Midnight Mass."

She hadn't let herself go with this habit since she was in school Mother-Goosing people. Miss Muffett said it was immature, Miss Muffett with the tic. Slightly amused at the thought of Miss Muffett and several other thoughts, she drifted from the kitchen jiggling the tray of cookies. A Kipling-type story tonight with a mongoose and a cobra. (Miss Muffett said it was arch and irritating.) Tomorrow, what was it, partridges, speckled hens, tawny pipits: think of birds, bosomy feathers, and the time would fly.

5

Fluoridation didn't last long. There was so little to be said. Mrs. Forsythe handed over her pamphlet and Mrs. Flax, to everyone's amazement, handed over hers. She had never had a pamphlet before.

"Who is this Doctor Murphy?" Mrs. Forsythe asked dubiously.

"He's fully accredited," said Mrs. Flax.

It was a stalemate. If it came to credentials, Mrs. Forsythe's pamphleteers were probably just as marginal and, anyway, it seemed small-minded to quibble about things on that level.

"The ADA approves," said Mrs. Forsythe. "Of fluoridation, that is."

"Humph."

"And the AMA."

"I thought you didn't like the AMA," chimed in Bert. "Aren't they a special interest?"

"All the more reason . . ." they were running very dry. Fluoridation might be important, but no one could pretend it was interesting. It must lead soon to the Big Government question, or everyone would go to sleep. Betty was already beginning to slip down and away when her mother startled her by saying quite rudely, "Of course, Catholics have to be against progress, don't they? Every kind of progress."

Mrs. Flax blushed, presumably over the bad taste of bringing religion up "at this time." Now she would show, by pained mongoose silence, how to parry bad taste.

Bert said, "There are lots of Catholics in favor of fluoridation."

"Oh yes, of course, and Catholics in favor of integration, and Catholics in favor of social security. It all boils down to public relations, doesn't it?" She kept looking at Betty while she talked, with curiosity and urgency. "You know how to make your handful of Liberals go a long way."

"Like the happily married couples in Hollywood, you mean?" Betty found herself saying, not sure which side this was supposed to help.

"Yes," her mother's, apparently, "and some of my best friends are . . . er . . . flagpole sitters and all that. Your two or three Liberal Catholics will be taken out of the store window when the time comes. The real spirit of the Church is something quite different." The Madonna behind her mother's head had funny eyebrows that always seemed to be raised.

"I don't know how you can be so sure about the real spirit of the Church," said Bert. "It's hard enough for us to know, sometimes."

"Well, look at history. . . ."

She had, many times, and would again—H. G. Wells,

strained through an imperfect memory. What interested Betty was the way she was tackling Bert head-on tonight, rather than with hit-and-run irony. And she was directing it at Betty, emphasizing her best lines with little nods—you may have heard this before, but pay special attention all the same, truisms are often true.

And Bert seemed to be laboring rather heavily in the ripost. His usual way in an argument was to keep everything very lighthearted, so that when occasionally he did get cornered, he seemed not to have been trying; a professional had to save his fire. If Mrs. Forsythe or whoever it was continued to bear down too hard, his airy manner made her look humorless. His main defense was that he was so *sane*. (Which, in Betty's eyes, was a pretty good defense, against her mother, anyway.)

But tonight, he was finding it a bit harder to keep things light. Betty winked at him and he gave her a worried smile and an "isn't your mother a character?" look. But in a moment he was back on earnest defense. Mrs. Flax was forgotten, and beginning cautiously to open her mouth in sleep. Bert got so excited that he lost the thread at one point and began to shout.

"Of course, I can understand about corruption," interrupted Mrs. Forsythe. "Even in an institution that claims to be divine, we must expect to see signs of human nature at work. But don't your people lean just a little too heavily on that argument? I mean, when the crime rate among Catholics is actually higher. . . ."

"Oh, the crime rate, the crime rate"—to the tune of "On the Bowery." Betty would have gone to bed right there, only they seemed to need her, as umpire or tennis net or something. Bert would say, the crime rate is because they're poor, and Mother would say, and why are they poor, and he would either say, because they're Christians, and she would snort, or else, because they're immigrants, and she would snort. And then *she* would say, why are Catholic countries so poor in the first place, and *he* would talk about industry and natural resources and the slums of Liverpool or something. No, they had veered on to mental health and Bert was stammering that Catholics never went to psychiatrists. . . .

She could safely leave it to Bert; maybe even join Mrs. Flax in a snooze, if they would just look the other way. But why were they telling her all this? Bert affected (while they were undressing after his occasional, less direct encounters with Mother) to have been dreadfully bored and she agreed as pointedly as she could; why did he suppose that she might suddenly be interested now?

Good grief, somebody had seen her going into church, that was it. How ridiculously, exasperatingly funny! They thought, because she liked to rest in St. Jude's, that she wanted to hear all about papal supremacy and, oh, unbaptized animals and crime rates and potato famines, and all the things that seemed important to the cranks on both teams. As if these had anything to do with the smell and taste of St. Jude's anyway.

And what about Mrs. Flax—was she in on it too? Hard to tell as she dozed under furry brows. After a while, she shook herself awake and seemed to stare ferretlike through her rimless glasses. Sometimes she looked questioningly, anxiously at Bert. He had probably got the news to her somehow, and she was circling gravely around with the others to see what happened next.

It could have been annoying again—Mrs. Forsythe trying to talk her out of the Church, Bert trying to talk her in, Mrs. Flax probably saying rosaries about it under her breath—but again she was rather hysterically touched. It wasn't a big thing, like *Paradise Lost*, but more like, which sorority gets the new girl? They were all out beating the bushes for talent. Canon Flood and Father Terwilliger and Mr. O'Malley, with wooden swords and paper helmets.

ing embrace. "What a bore for you," he said tenderly; but he had been trying to win that argument, all the same.

"Knights of East Orange," said the notepaper on the bureau. "Dear Mr. Flax, we certainly enjoyed your talk on 'Communism and Communications,' and felt that it certainly helped us to 'know the enemy,' as it were, both within and outside. However, Monsignor feels that we should stress more doctrine in our talks, and next year, he plans to devote the whole series to 'scripture.' . . ."

Bert never got any interesting mail: it was hardly worth the twinge of guilt that went with snooping. She got into bed and snipped off the light, and listened to the tapping of Bert's silly old typewriter, slapping tapping, until, in the density of half-asleep, it sounded as weak and thin as a bird pecking at the window, thin, thinner, nothing.

6

The study was getting pretty disorderly. He didn't like people coming in here tidying; and he had most of the files out by now, with hopes of finding a retread. He had burned up plots and thoughts pretty fast once, because he could always find more, and his idea file was the slimmest of all. (Couldn't pinch any more from Chesterton, either, Chesterton was going out of style, too.)

He had to smile at this one. Mother Mulrooney playing professional basketball to raise money for the convent. Father Danny Mulloy used to box and play pro football for St. Albert's, and Mother Mulrooney was just a twist on that. But Father Chubb pointed out that women didn't play pro basketball. And gave Bert a funny look too.

That was the beginning of the trouble, maybe, the first sign he was losing touch. A year or so ago he had begun to run dry on Father Danny Mulloy and Father Danny had been a great breadwinner in his day. He had played every conceivable game, and helped to build five schools and a children's hospital as well as paying for Bert's Studebaker. Although even Father Gonfallin balked at having him turn up on the waterfront. (Bert had thought—only thought—of trying a waterfront nun after that, which showed how far you could go when you got desperate.)

Mulloy was admittedly the lighter side of his work. The stories were written for boys, to sell them on the priesthood, and Father Gonfallin said that they did more good than a thousand he forgot whats . . . but for the first time, Bert began to feel a bit silly about his work. He wondered what precisely he thought he was doing, writing up this overgrown boy scout. By then, Betty, Jr., was expected, so there was no turning back. But he felt silly. And a bit dishonest.

Father Danny was a lean, clear-eyed man, with a spring in his step and a great fund of natural humility. Bert had never met a priest the least bit like him. The priests Bert knew—he checked himself. He had once done a light piece, "some of the nicest guys are priests"; he would stick by that for the time being. (Talk about self-satisfied, though.)

The words kept jangling around in his mouth, but the screen remained blank. Every now and then, it would churn up that damned tropical beach, or a Spanish High Mass—he supposed it was Spanish, because nobody moved; if you could make these scenes just a little bit firmer, you could climb into them sometime and frig the telephone company. But they wavered away leaving nothing but a white sheet behind.

The statue of St. Jude stood on the windowsill as a paperweight. The papers flapped forlornly, like shirts. A pinch of night air was getting in under the frame. He ought to have that window fixed—about twenty-fifth on his list of priorities. St. Jude went back to the old days (he thought it was a good omen, finding a parish with the same name), when writing was as easy as sweating; when the family was told, "Ssh, Bert's working." A thin jet of bitterness squirted in his belly. He took it out on the typewriter:

"Propositions:

(1) Intellect. All right, if you happen to be called St. Thomas. Otherwise, better leave it alone.

(2) Emotion. Very, very bad. Untrustworthy—unless you happen to be somebody's dear old Irish grandmother, in which case your emotions are worth a hundred eminent theologians laid end to end.

(3) Will. Very, very good. But wait a minute, not the way you think. Not Nietzschean will, not willful will, good heavens no. The will to submit is the ticket, to obey. To avoid bad movies. . . ."

He was surprised at how fluent he could be in a destructive vein. That's quite enough of that, you know what it can lead to, crazy talk. He was just poking gentle fun. All right within the group. Constructive criticism, nobody's perfect. But mustn't give comfort to the enemy, to Mrs. Forsythe, so damn self-satisfied, and Dave Gilhouley. United front.

There were some wise guys who didn't understand this. It was easy for them to write, no discipline, no loyalty. He might jot down a few negative thoughts in private just to get rid of them. (But he *had* given comfort to the enemy, hadn't he? To Dave Gilhouley. As he remembered, he just wanted an argument, to settle his own mind. But it was a crazy thing to do, giving scandal like that. It was on his conscience terribly now. In the future keep your doubts to yourself, Jack. That was a bad phase he was going through then, he was practically back on the beam now.)

You wonderful Catholic writers are in a position of great

responsibility. Yours is a joyous privilege—don't mimic, now, Flax, there's some truth in it. Look at the harm these guys do. It's easy enough to sow the seed of doubt, don't mimic. (Talk about giving scandal, he had an idea he'd said something to Betty recently, too—but he couldn't remember, and it didn't seem to have done any harm so. . . .) The point is you decide whether to be a clever writer or whether to do some good. And then they don't want you anymore . . . well, that's their privilege, of course. He had done some good, he knew, he had the letters. Maybe Chubb didn't realize it, but there were still plenty of people. . . .

He wiped his mouth with the back of his hand. Working alone like this, you developed sloppy ways. Careful to restrict them to the study. "People look to you, Bert." He inserted some more paper.

"Mothers may seem a little tiresome sometimes, but it is only because they want us to be happy. . . ." They wouldn't take it. He knew there was something wrong but couldn't finger it. A bit stale, perhaps. Must modernize and keep up.

They used to ask him to take part in those symposiums on "The role of the Catholic writer," et cetera, but his ideas were a bit stale now, even by symposium standards. This could be attended to. He knew about clichés, boy, who better? Their cure and prevention.

"The Catholic mother"—he was so damned tired. He couldn't keep this going much longer. With five wonderful kids you needed so *much* money. If he could just drop the whole thing, tiptoe away. Stop trying to sustain this mood. But there were the bills, and there was pride. Mrs. Forsythe, with her smart-aleck arguments. Her psychiatrists and her social workers. She didn't see that it was the break-up of the family that was doing it. They never had any trouble on Amsterdam Avenue, oh sure, a few fights and things. Fruit stealing. But there was affection in those days, and discipline. (And there was the time he got stabbed by Benny Lenahan—he smiled thinly.)

Where was he, mothers, all he could think of was four fat legs, couldn't draw much of a moral from that. The watch said three twenty-five. Better put it to bed and give it another crack in the morning. Betty would certainly be sound asleep, which was good, because with the bank balance and everything— He didn't finish the thought, but punched the wall on the way out and got a spray of blood on his knuckles.

7

She looked at the door handle and it assumed the features of Jacob Marley, by George, and then lost them again. Still working at her joke, rather desperately by now. The telephone, suppose Scrooge had had a telephone, the ghosts ringing up, "I have a call for you from Christmas past," that's enough said Miss Muffett. The phone didn't ring at all that day, which was perhaps the closest thing to ominous in Bloodbury. The sort of people who used to call up on days like this had somehow dropped away or perhaps never existed. The logical friends from the parish, fellow parents and such, were uncomfortable with her, or Bert didn't like them. His work was too lonely to provide new friends. As to *her* old friends and Bert—well, that was an old story. Perhaps, if they all tried again, Bert wouldn't get so overanimated, or whatever it was. Anyway, the phone was silent.

No omens, then, for Christmas. Just an attritional day with the children. Keeping them away from the presents in the cellar, and the younger ones from barreling into the Christmas tree; trying to make them all see the point of postponing their pleasure for two days; trying to teach them about boredom.

The Sage of Bloodbury was up in the study all day. A few more attempts to make contact with him over breakfast—probably not such a hot time to try to make contact—died stillborn. She knew if she brought up the mothers, he would make some hearty jokes and then add quickly, "But, kidding aside, they're two grand women" (don't make them like that anymore); if religion came up, he would do the deep, steady voice, "Your mother is really a Catholic and doesn't know it." So she just said, "Darling, give it up for Christmas, join the family," and he gave her a small smile and said, "I have an idea that might play."

After dinner, which he ate upstairs again, she sat in the living room, wondering whether to go to church, wondering whether Bert was really staying out of the way to allow her discreetly to do so, when the telephone made her jump by finally ringing, after all. Paralysis for a moment while the ugly black thing prang-pranged at her, and then she picked it up quickly.

"Hello, is that Mrs. Flax?" said a muffled voice.

"Yes, yes. This is she."

"You don't know us," said the voice, awkwardly, as if there were two people improvising on the other end. Practical jokers, "Are you the woman who washes?" or something like that. "You don't know us, we're friends of Bert's."

"Oh, yes. Where are you?"

"We're just down the street. In a booth."

"I see. In a booth." She had never noticed a booth.

"Yes, we were just passing through Bloodbury and we thought we'd like to say hello to Bert."

"Yes, well I'll get him, shall I?"

She had a distinct sense of someone nodding at the other end, and a less distinct sense of someone saying, "Yes, please." Very amusing, for an omen. Two stuffed owls, for the eleventh day of Christmas.

"Bert, there are two drunks on the phone who want to speak to you"—but Bert already had the upstairs extension and seemed to be nodding rather grimly over it. "Yes, yes. All right, come on over. No, that's all right. Right, yes, just turn left and keep going. Number twenty-nine, holly wreath—" He looked at the receiver; obviously one of the clowns had suddenly caused it to go dead, with a spastic flourish.

"Who on earth are they? Have they been to a party, or what?" She was glad to have silly friends calling up Bert; it was right for Christmas. But Bert himself seemed rather harassed by it.

"They're not drunk," he ran his hand through the thin hair. "Just embarrassed."

"Who? Why?"

"Matty Flynn and Dave Gilhouley. That was Matty you were talking to."

"Yes, but why were they embarrassed?"

He paused. "I can't imagine." But since she stood still gazing at him, he said, "Passing through Bloodbury. Nobody passes *through* Bloodbury. I don't know why they're here at all." With the light behind him, he looked like one of those hunted men in the movies who has been run down at last in the anonymous boardinghouse. The Big Swede. But as he passed her in the doorway, buttoning down his sleeves, he looked nothing much worse than peevish. Apparently his idea hadn't played after all: she *wished* he could give it up for a while.

She watched him answering the doorbell. The two friends certainly did look either embarrassed or drunk, extraordinarily disorganized for only two people. The smaller of them began pumping Bert's hand distractedly; the other stood back delicately in the shadows. "Hello, Matty, Dave, come on in." There *was* surely something hunted in Bert's voice. "Betty, I'd like you to meet. . . ." Flynn was awfully glad to meet her; Gilhouley a touch more suave. Certainly, they didn't seem much to be nervous about.

"I'll make some coffee. Or would you like a drink?"

"Just coffee please, Mrs. . . . Betty," said Flynn.

"Just coffee for me," said Gilhouley.

She felt that Bert wanted her out of there. There was clearly some mutual embarrassment here, some bit of shared past which rubbed back and forth. A trifle that could matter only to them anyway. She trotted toward the kitchen.

To her amazement, Matty Flynn came out and joined her a few minutes later. "Let me help you," he said and began clumsily really trying to. He was a very odd-looking fellow, wizened and melancholy—possibly just for the occasion, though. Was this the kind of friend that Bert went in for?

With his back half-turned, and hunched over, he suddenly said, "How is everything, Mrs. Flax?"

"Why, all right. What sort of thing did you mean?" She was taken off guard by the gnomish question.

"I mean Bert. Is he all right?"

"Yes, I suppose so." Everybody seemed to be worried about Bert, as if it was important to keep him well. An old friend had a right to a thoughtful answer, but she couldn't think of one. "He's pretty fair, I guess."

"That's fine," said Matty. "Fine." He had taken down some very big coffee cups, the ones they used for breakfast, and was trying to get them on to a small tray. "To tell you the truth, Mrs. Flax, Betty, Dave and I were a bit worried about Bert."

"Oh, you *were*."

"Yes, Dave and I."

She was ready to belabor him automatically, as she had Father Chubb when he turned down Bert's poem. Why, she wondered, had she developed this reflex of loyalty? Well she had a mother, poignantly open to jokes—jokes she used to make herself, and plant in other people's faces; and she had Bert, whom she wanted so much to admire, to think "all right." . . . She had to be loyal, she supposed, because instinctively she was very cruel.

"He came round to my place a few months ago, I guess it was, and acted very strange."

"I suppose you were all quite drunk," said Betty sharply.

"Yes, I expect so," Matty admitted meekly. "But believe me, Mrs. Flax, I know drunks. . . ."

"Yes, I imagine."

"And I know Bert. And, he was acting very strange. I mean, swearing and blaspheming."

She put a hand to her throat and said, "Was he, now?"

"Well, that's about it. My sister-in-law was there and she was quite upset. And then, to top it all, she couldn't find his regular Christmas poem in any of the magazines."

"He didn't do one."

"So? Well, anyway, Dave and I got together, he came over to my place, you know, one evening, and we began to talk it over. . . ."

"You began to talk over Bert," she said with heavy vexation.

"I know we had no business doing it like that, behind his back, but we were really quite worried. Dave, you know, said it was still on his mind. Dave was really shocked."

"Shocked by a little swearing?"

"And blasphemy, yes, It was funny about Dave. He was pretty irreverent himself, once upon a time. But hearing it come from Bert like that. . . . I don't know, Bert—"

"Why shouldn't it come from Bert?"

"I don't know, Bert always seemed different at school and

all. He wasn't goody-goody or anything. But you felt the language and everything could be hurting him. Dave used to make dirty jokes and things just to shock him. So—hearing him go on like that, I don't know. It made Dave change his mind about a lot of things."

"Well, that's nice for Dave." All the sarcasm she could still muster. "Perhaps my husband was just doing it to help Dave."

"Yes, well I didn't mean to go on about Dave. But what we both felt, Mrs. Flax, was that here was a guy who really knew what the words meant—I can't explain how we both felt about this."

He didn't have to. She could see the freakish, exceptionally pure kind of boy Bert must have been. (It was an accident of birth, or something, you didn't have to be religious. There were even people like that in her mother's circle.) Then you didn't see this pure fellow for a while, and he suddenly turned up again, with mud on his cassock—no wonder Dave and Matty felt so funny about it.

"We don't know what went wrong, Mrs. Flax. But if there is anything. . . ."

What went wrong, indeed. Bert might be having a rough winter but he was still the sanest man she knew.

"I think we can do very well without your help," she began to say primly.

But by this time, the sound of voices in the living room had become insistent, slightly strident, slightly off tune: giving some weight to Matty's theories and making further argument pointless.

She picked up the overloaded tray, and with Flynn carrying the fourth enormous cup, moved into the eye of the latest teapot storm.

Part Five

"Evil is very real. And it may wear the face and habiliments of a friend."

FLAX. *Thoughts.*

1

So now Gilhouley knew what he did for a living. It was painful, of course—especially after the way he had denied it; and especially now that he wasn't even doing very well at it. For a brief moment he realized that he had never been so afraid of anything as of Gilhouley finding out. But he saw that this must be a mistake, it was so petty. Gilhouley very kindly didn't sneer: he was quite grave and delicate about it, as if you shouldn't laugh at somebody's leprosy—not in front of him, anyway.

Then surprisingly, came some of the pseudointellectual guff you were always getting in letters: *why* did he do it? did he really think it helped? et cetera. A professional just had to learn to live with this crap, or go off his head. Pretty funny coming from Dave Gilhouley, though; old Dave suddenly coming down with a tender conscience. Old Dave worrying about intellectual integrity.

Painful, boring, hard to follow at the end of a day's sweat at the typewriter (pseudointellectuals didn't know about the sweat part); but then Dave said something that wasn't funny at all, and wasn't just personal either. It was suddenly something to get your righteous anger into—the rage that kept spilling out over nothing had a target at last—especially in view of the part Gilhouley had played in his own life.

How did that go again? While Gilhouley was hesitantly speaking his piece (he'd become so damn tactful, *no* one could follow him), Bert reviewed the case against him. To begin with, it was Dave that first gave him the funny feeling about church. . . .

He remembered the sunbeams raising pillars of dust in the Bishop Mahoney chapel, the memory of a memory by now, and Dave Gilhouley poking Matty Flynn tirelessly in the rump with his ruler; and Flynn's attitude was that this was all right when you were fourteen, but at fifteen, cheezt! Then at sixteen, Gilhouley got the point and stopped fooling around, and Bert, from his observation post down the aisle, found himself with mixed feelings about it. Sometimes he did get a little bored in church, and the action amused him. He wouldn't have done it himself, of course, but he didn't mind watching. So the point was, Dave had put him on to the blasphemous pleasure of irreverence—he had even fooled around when they were serving Mass together. And conned Bert into fooling back. When Dave lost interest in that, Bert was stuck with it. Unless someone was horsing around, church always seemed a little flat.

Outside of church, it was the same. With his private TV set and his brother in the navy, Gilhouley led the march on puberty for Matty and Bert—Matty dragging his feet but getting there all the same. The ever-wet hair and the comb in the breast pocket—these were Gilhouley innovations; along with the vast inventory of girls' names, just names, to be ticked off at regular intervals. "Rose, yeah she's pretty nice. Ruth, you know Ruth? I didn't know you knew Ruth." The cold, bright football weather coming round for the last time and they watched silently while Dave made the phone calls and fingered his ever-present laundry; as if he would need every bit of it if the calls worked out. "Ruth? Remember me? I'm Dave Gilhouley. Yeah, Gilhouley. I met you over at Betty's last summer. Yeah, Betty Sims. That's right. *That's* right." And later casually, "Well, Bert, I got you a date for Saturday."

Nothing very bad about that, but he'd come to something in a moment. Gilhouley making phone calls—what happened after that? (Memory was slow and foolish. . . .) He made a few phone calls on his own, he remembered, tremulous but reasonably successful calls. Flynn could never bring himself to do even this: he was always saying, "I don't feel like going, I gotta lot of work," and everything had to be arranged for him, or he didn't go. He didn't much care for Dave anyway. Bert was his friend, and that largely because Mrs. Flynn was a friend of Mrs. Flax. Dave just went with the package.

When they left Mahoney's they slid off in all different directions. Flynn went to Holy Cross, Gilhouley saddened his religion teacher by going to Columbia, and Bert stayed home too and went to St. Pat's in the Bronx. They used to get together in bars or at Gilhouley's frat house—God, what a den that was! And what a switch from playing ping-pong at St. Pat's . . . better not go into that perhaps. Anyway Matty Flynn found a girl from Marymount, whom he wasn't scared to telephone, and as she didn't see much point in sitting in bars all evening, Flynn dropped out of the group by inches. Bert hung on ambiguously right through college, not condoning or taking part, of course, and then made a sharp, temporarily invigorating break the year after graduation.

He decided he couldn't very well spend the kind of evenings Gilhouley liked to spend, and write chaste poetry the next day. Once Sister Melody had put him wise to purity of heart, several changes had to be made. He stopped frugeling around with old Dave and company and tried to cultivate a few Catholic friends to fill the gaps. His buddies at St. Pat's lived mostly out of town and were soon knee-deep in children. But he took in some parish dances, he made the scene at the Holy Name, he joined some groups around town—not social apostle groups, which he poked gentle fun at in his writing, for being too intense and humorless: sanity was always one of his big things—but transitory coffee-and-cake discussion groups.

And he did succeed in meeting a lot of nice people that way, but they were never quite his idea of friends. The years with Gilhouley had planted a restlessness in his chest. He found he missed things like Dave's antics in front of the television set, the bawdy, relaxed talk—you couldn't be wholesome from morning to night: or at least, he found he couldn't.

This was the point about Gilhouley. Sort of an evil genius in his way. *In absentia* he became a bright red symbol of what a good man had to give up.

His new acquaintances seemed awfully mild by comparison. You just knew that they weren't going to swear or carry on. Well, that was all right, purity of heart and all that, but they were mild in other ways. He felt no sudden floods of friendship with them. They went home early, without reluctance: no fire in the mouth to be talked out slowly. They had responsibilities, they were good people, and he suddenly found them making him awfully nervous. He invited them round to his place on Horatio Street and they either couldn't come or they couldn't stay long: the slight tug of responsibilities was forever twitching them homeward. There could be no friendship with people like that, because there was never quite time to clinch it. They had to get back to the children or the sick wife or the lonely mother.

These, of course, were the very people he was writing for and about, the sane, low-pressure heroes of the common life, and he approved of them wholeheartedly; but they droned at his souped-up nerves, all the same. At the pi gam frat house, he had felt like a Christian among pagans: but was this what the other Christians were like? Wonder what old Dave's doing tonight, anyway? he used to think; and then, look, just forget the useless crud for five minutes. Pay attention to this guy with the sallow face and the wistful voice. "Oh, so you're thinking of chartering a plane to Fatima? Grand!" Wonder what Gilhouley would say to that? He began a habit of his own, quite harmless at first, of making sardonic comments to himself out of the past, to relieve the pious tension and drain off some of the hot fluid. The kind of comments they used to make. . . .

Harmless. At first he only did it during the last half hour of Holy Name meetings. Then during the whole meeting. Then in church. Then writing. The habit roared like a fire, even though he braced his will hard against it. He could actually see Dave Gilhouley mouthing the cracks, the obsession almost terrified him.

Then, of course, he met Betty Forsythe, and another cool stretch of memory began—things like picnics, on clean grass: none of the grime and greaseproof wastepaper of the parish outings; drives to Connecticut. Purity became temporarily vivid and interesting, with Betty.

But back to Gilhouley for a moment. Leaving New York meant leaving people like that. Sly, corrupt people who got at you a thousand ways. It meant leaving the war against smutty entertainment which raged up and down 42nd Street, and which featured people one remove from Gilhouley slugging it out with exasperated monsignors, while innocent bystanders (named Flax) imperceptibly writhed. . . . It was perhaps a bit farfetched, bringing Dave into the war against smut—but he was the *type*. Bert had written some paragraphs about pornography and found it useful to use Gilhouley as a kind of tailor's dummy, to help personify the evil—not such a bad choice either. Try writing lyric poetry in this filthy, throbbing town, he wrote. Try keeping a pure heart, pumping purely. He wondered how he had kept it up so long. New York was a Babylon, he concluded, but Father Chubb turned the poem down.

The joke came a bit later and, appropriately, in installments. (And perhaps tonight's was the final one, with Gilhouley perched on the armchair like carrion.) Little by little, the old restlessness had come creeping back. Bloodbury was so *dull*, St. Jude's was so dull too, compared with the excitement he had known as a boy. Finally—on some pretext which he couldn't even remember—he had gone looking for Gilhouley again, hadn't he? Gone groping back behind the boredom and fever, to a clearer time; when evil lived in one small, dark apartment (like a confessional gone wrong) with a stack of wicked magazines and a brother in the navy. . . .

During the few months he was engaged to Betty, though, he really thought he had the Gilhouley cancer licked. As soon as he decided to leave New York, his mild Catholic friends began to seem very purposeful and sound. They knew about love, but it was sane, well ordered love. And responsibility was its badge. He had been saying this all along in his articles, of course, but it was good to feel it as well. He thought that maturity had arrived at last; that he too was entering the ranks of the mild and purposeful.

It was one of those incandescent bits of life, a memory of a time when things went right. All sorts of things. The Holy Namers suddenly brightened and gave him a party; and they proved to be wonderful fellows. (One of them got high and called him "Bert, you old son-of-a-bitch!") His writing became, apart from that one outburst, very ardent and easy, and Father Gonfallin sent him a special note about it. It was all oddly illumined now, an incredible scrap of happiness, possibly a mistake in the Divine Plan.

He knew even then that it couldn't last, of course—maturity wasn't all roses. But he imagined that that period would always be his touchstone of happiness; anything like that was the real thing.

Instead of which, the good time seemed now incredibly painful and bitter; a series of fictions that laughed in his head like a tunnel of horrors. The notion that maturity had suddenly come upon him like a thief in the night—that brief spell of bubbling childishness, maturity!—and that Bloodbury would bring peace. . . . Bloodbury with its rich mutton-headed Catholics and its smarty-pants sophisticates, its stinking landscape gardening, back to Gilhouley then. Got the goods there, I think. Gilhouley had just committed possibly the worst sin imaginable—why not write about Gilhouley, might make a good next assignment, and call him by his right name.

Betty was coming in with the coffee, and he strove to impose order, to get the right phrases lined up. This might be a heaven- (or hell-) sent chance, to get flowing again. Just remember these points: Gilhouley is only a tailor's dummy of evil, not the real thing, so don't overstate your case. Betty is outside all this and must follow her quiet way to church. No need to frighten her—make the thing firm, pleasant, instructive. He was so excited that he got a little confused.

Man makes his own kind of house, furnishes it his own way, gives it his personal benediction; smiles at his mother-in-law's presents, reunites himself with stuff from his mother's house—that was the kind of thing he stood for, whatever his fuzziness in other areas. The Home, the Christian Family. He almost wished he had a pencil. But Gilhouley made it another kind of house: a pad, a shack, cheapening everything with his breath and his hands. This could be dealt with quite calmly.

He shut his eyes and heard the venomous, protracted swish of the coffee in the vast cups. Gilhouley took four lumps. Flynn had given up sugar for Lent one year and never resumed the practice; he sat next to Dave in the left-hand court. Betty sat next to Bert. Flynn began diffidently to serve Bert.

2

"Nice place you got here, very nice," said Matty.

"Yes," and so on. Gilhouley wouldn't let Bert catch his eye—not after what had happened between them a few minutes before. He was looking into his cup, and then suddenly past Bert to the Christmas cards on the mantelpiece. Big red face. "Lots of cards," he said, when he finally had to say something. Which wasn't especially true, there weren't so many cards. But Bert wasn't going to be suckered into changing the subject. He felt some slight difficulty with his mouth and wanted to stick to what he had prepared.

"You doing anything special for Christmas, Bert?" asked Matty, helpfully.

"No."

"I mean, are you having your folks over?"

"My Mother. Father died."

"Yes, I remember. That was too bad."

Dave seemed to be using all his guile, learned in a lower cause, to keep his conversation going with Betty. Good God—he wasn't taking *baby* pictures out of his wallet? Nieces and nephews, he could pretend they were.

"You get those photos at Woolworth's, don't you, Dave?" Bert shouted over genially. "Great little icebreakers."

Dave smiled slightly and went on chattering to Betty in a low voice.

"How's your mother?" pursued the relentless Matty. "I haven't seen her in a long time."

"She's all right."

"That's good. Your mother's a great woman, you know that, Bert? Does she still get around the way she used to?"

"She still gets around."

"Boy," Matty shook his head and gave a startled laugh, "what energy!"

"I don't suppose you want to see pictures of the young Flaxes?" Betty was saying. Did his mother get *around*, for godsake?

"*Sure* I do," said Dave.

"I'll go upstairs and get them." And now, the unmitigated hypocrisy of this man, pretending to be interested in babies. . . . Dave jumped up too and said that he would get them. So Bert jumped up and actually did get them. He knew that when he got back—why the hell didn't Betty make the kids get their toys off the stairs at least? He kicked savagely and hurt his toe—there would be much banter about who looked like Bert and who didn't.

He selected just two pictures, covering all five kids, and threaded his way down again. They couldn't go on long about two pictures.

But, of course, he should have known it—Matty had his

damn pictures out by now and was making Betty gurgle over them. A collection too big for any normal wallet was scattered across the red and yellow stripes of the sofa.

"Before we proceed with the children's hour," Bert said, in as pleasant a voice as he could make it, "I would just like to finish what I was saying about Dave."

They stopped talking, and their eyes looked huge. Must phrase this just right now. Humor and sanity, the wonderful strain of humor that Father Gonfallin had praised a hundred years ago.

"I should preface my remarks by saying that I've known old Dave for a long time. And I think I can really say that I *know* Dave, too." The ticking of the hall clock reminded him, because it seemed to come from Dave's face, of his last tilt with Gilhouley. He must do what he could to keep it under control this time, keep it good-humored. Watch out for sudden swells of anger, however justified. His mouth was bothering him quite a bit. "I've seen Dave pull some stunts in my time that you wouldn't believe. OK, I'm not judging, that's Dave, and that's Dave's business. If I didn't approve, I shouldn't have hung around him, I guess."

He could hear them breathing and see their eyes. Bert was distracted and slipped off on a tangent. "Mind you, I've paid plenty for hanging around with Dave. I said some terrible things recently at Matty Flynn's house—that was under Dave's influence, of course"—good chance here to get the record straight about that—"You think you can be around that stuff, you know, evil, and as long as you keep still and don't do anything—but I was just fooling myself there. It really gets into your bones, doesn't it?" They were looking concerned, they didn't see what he was driving at. Never mind, they would in a moment. And meanwhile, there was unexpected relief in this tangent. "Yes, I played with evil, and one day I realized—"

"Dave was never that evil," Matty interposed lamely.

"What do you mean, *that* evil?" Bert's voice went up.

"You and your stinking hair-splitting. He who is not with me is against me. Dave was against—look, it wasn't *what* he did, he didn't *do* anything so terrible. It was his intention, his festering intention. And that was always clear enough, wasn't it?"

Matty obviously didn't want to answer. But under pressure, he said, "That isn't fair, Bert. It was just a joke, Dave's attitude, just in fun."

"Just a joke? Dear Mother of God. Was it really just a joke, Dave? Did I miss the point or something? All that God-mocking stuff was a joke?"

Gilhouley was terribly embarrassed. This sickly smooth tolerance of his had left him unfit to face anything. He was weak and soft—but sly, too. Play him carefully.

"All right, well I don't want to dig up the past. I just wanted to say that while I was trying to be a good Catholic and live an upright life and all, I was fouling myself up at Gilhouley's nest, and I paid for this, and it's still with me, something to be fought, as I discovered at Matty's house the other night. And a few other times. That's all. But I don't blame Dave for this. I assume the entire responsibility." Perhaps a little pompous, but it was the only language he knew for this sort of thing. And anyway, it was the right language, really, wasn't it? Kidding aside, he believed it was right.

"Or perhaps we'll just say, along with Matty, that boys will be boys and that it was all in fun. I may have picked up this evil that I feel in me, someplace else. I was going to say 'thorn in the flesh' but of course it's nothing as serious as that. I believe I'm getting on top of it now." He hadn't felt so articulate in months; he paused to savor the taste of it. His case was so wonderfully *strong*. And you so seldom had a chance to say things like this these days.

"Do go on," said Betty in a sudden anxious voice. "Tell us what's troubling you."

That was very annoying, her trying to mother him. She

was, after all, quite new to these things. People these days thought that anyone who spoke with passion must be out of his mind. "What I'm getting at is just this. I've seen old Dave up to lots of tricks, and I've never said a word to him about it. But this evening he pulled something that I cannot forgive."

Everyone looked at Gilhouley, who seemed just bewildered and unhappy. Evil found out was nothing but confusion, thought Bert.

"In your own house, do what you like, Dave," he went on gently. "But don't come to my house—"

"What is he trying to say?" asked Betty.

"He isn't well," Matty explained. "He's been working. . . ." Hot damn, he was really flowing. What was that Matty said?

"Hah. That's pretty funny, Matty. Working! No, please listen, I feel perfectly well. Just let me tell you what Gilhouley did. But maybe you won't see what's wrong with it, because in this age certain things have been lost sight of. That's why I went on like that about, you know, evil."

"He's not well," said Matty.

"This evil man told me, told me, mind, that he's begun practicing his religion again. This blaspheming man."

He waited, but of course they didn't see the point. "Let me explain again. This is the man who led us all into corruption. This is the man who has, for me, absolutely personified evil. There were always some things you couldn't be sure of, but Dave was absolutely certain. . . ."

Gilhouley looked at him for the first time, as if the worst was over at last. "A lot of things have changed, Bert," he said.

"Well may*be*, may*be*. But not you, Dave. No, really, you couldn't change. I suppose I shouldn't say this, folks, but I have always comforted myself when things were going badly with me, that I'm not as bad as old Dave. I suppose that's very wicked, isn't it?"

"Yes," said Matty diffidently.

"Well, and why should he suddenly start going to church then? We don't want him. The last time I saw him he was doing very well, up to his old tricks. . . ."

"Jane went back to her mother."

"Jane and Ruth and Irma," he chanted, and then changed his mind. "No, it wasn't the girls. It was the other part, the blasphemy, the horrible, horrible blasphemy." A hot sword passed scraping across his tongue, and he looked around him and saw they were all about to pounce. Well, not really, but they were watching him like men with a net. "I just wanted to say that," he stumbled, his mouth quite constricted, "so that you'd see where I stand. You thought I'd be glad to hear about your conversion, Dave. That's a terrible thing to do. Pretending a thing like that, for human motives. But I'll pray to the Heavenly Babe for you, and to dear St. Jude"—he was crying, he couldn't help it, real, cooling tears. He had his fluency back, he had the "feeling"; he couldn't wait to get it down on paper.

He heard them through a mist shuffling out, whispering good nights like people in church, the door closing softly and lights switching out, and then Betty, dear old Betty, dropping down next to him and breathing concern on to his wet cheek. It was all very cool and restful, he had made his point, quite like the old days; and if Father Chubb didn't take the piece, he was crazy, and Bert wouldn't be responsible.

Part Six

"Christmas, as Chesterton once put it . . ."

FLAX. *Thoughts.*

1

She watched him sleep like a baby, and his deep, even breathing seemed in itself out of line. A wispy strand of hair stood up, lay down, stood up, lay down on his forehead, as the breeze puffed across him. By five, she still hadn't dozed off, and she was fidgety from watching. She had really been frightened this time. But he was sleeping splendidly now, not groaning or twisting the bedclothes, and she began in the icy darkness to wonder if he wasn't going to be all right after all.

A nervous breakdown, was that possible, for someone as sane as Bert? Of course, everyone had them these days. She could picture the men arriving from the hospital (especially chosen for their large, soft hands), and the children lining the stairs in stricken curiosity; Bert, pale, delirious, being passed swiftly down among them; and then the explanations of why Christmas wasn't as much fun as promised, and the awful lunch with Mrs. Flax and Mrs. Forsythe, who would need explanations too, but wouldn't believe them.

But watching Bert's lips puttering contentedly, a worse thought worked its way into five o'clock coherence. Suppose he just woke up the same as usual, as if nothing had happened? He was beginning to look dreadfully like it. . . .

For some reason, this seemed even more frightening than a breakdown (breakdown was just a word anyway; she hardly knew what it meant). He'd done this two, three times now. Was it just part of his hackwork? staging scenes to see what he thought, or to force emotions he could use later on in his writing? One day denouncing the Church, the next day defending it, it made no sense; it was too late at night to make sense. She had believed in his agony at the time. Better leave it at that.

He rolled over with a merry sigh and snuggled irritatingly into himself. When would he do it again? Sometime in front of the kids maybe. . . . She lay there with bristling nerves while he caressed himself carefully—she knew she shouldn't think about it any more. But the evening's horror had congealed in her mind, Bert sitting in the living room like the prophet Jeremiah, denouncing his old friend. Talking about some mysterious evil he had found in himself and blaming it on someone he knew in school. Had there always been hatred and spite in Bert's religion? No, she was sure not, this was new, he wasn't well. And Gilhouley evil, how absurd, big polite man.

A cold fog crept over her thoughts. Bert the hack has writer's block or writer the Bert has hacker's block, Berter's hack. Hasn't had a new feeling he can use in years. What to do? Stage little dramas. The night Chubb turned his poem down. Drama of blasphemy, but no good at that either;

if he wrote atheist pamphlets like the ex-priests they'd be sincerely insincere and awful, hack is a hack is a hack. . . . Or like—ah ha, what her mother had told her about the Irishman and the Scotsman, phwah, a real yawn thank heaven, no about the Irishmen who said that Bert was swearing—why, that would have been Gilhouley, stopping off at the Ethical Society on his way back to the Church. Fancy Gilhouley getting religion because he heard Bert swear. It was every bit as mad as Mummy always said.

She was getting too light-headed to last, and with dawn about to crack, and the first child, Kevin, soon to embark on his first exploratory scream, she was fading out at last. Her last thought was that if Bert woke up in the pink, she would take a very dim view of it, very dim view. Dim-a-dim.

(In a big, empty church, a man went up to receive Communion, and the priest handed him a bill for four Danish tables.)

Betty seemed to have put in a full morning with the children before Bert finally got up at nine-fifteen. Through haggard, imprecise eyes, she watched him over his breakfast. He read the paper very carefully, news, sports, the modest funnies of the *Herald Tribune*, Lippmann, David Lawrence, had three cups of coffee and an extra piece of toast, was pale and unshaven but not much more so than usual. He read the letter that said, "3,000 words on your favorite saint . . . no payment," without comment. She found she was watching him with clenched hands, the thumb clamped inside the fingers. He wiped his mouth, tossed the napkin away, yawned, scratched his ear—she must have noted at least twenty-five items by now, but no sign of remorse or explanation. She asked how he felt and he said, "Fine." He got up and said, "I guess I'll do some work, I think the juice may be on today." He smiled, about six inches to the left of his wife. "Dear, tell me—" she began, and saw that it was hopeless; his smile was made of best candle wax.

She took his stuff out to the kitchen and washed it fiercely. . . . Bert followed her out and tilted his ashtray over the garbage can; and gave her a quizzical look, to make sure everything was going smoothly. She looked as wooden as she could until she heard his slippers shuffling out; then went on looking wooden anyway, because she didn't trust herself to look anything else.

The children, driven half-crazy by restraint, made it almost possible for her not to think for the rest of the morning. There was nothing to do but get on with Christmas. She didn't even want to go to St. Jude's about it; St. Jude's was part of it, part of the fear. Only the most ordinary activities were safe.

Mopping the kitchen floor, with children at ear level, was an admirable way not to think. Then into Bloodbury to get a whole new lot of colored lights, to be strung in inaccessible spots. (She thought for a moment she saw Bert with a face like death, outside the shop window. But it was Mr. Faversham from the Real Estate office. Must be having a bad Christmas, too.) She bought tinsel and angel hair and stars. It might not be a good Christmas, but it would be a gaudy, feverish one. There would never be another like it. After lunch, the children took their naps, and she tried, feeling a bit shaky by now, to start dusting the living room. But the task suddenly seemed quite pointless and she tottered over to the sofa and collapsed, face down.

Suppose, just suppose, she ever wanted to leave Bert? Of course she never would, she loved him didn't she, and children needed a father, especially boy children. It was just a game of suppose. To calm the jitters. Her mother would support them of course. They would need thus and so much a year. . . . Sad to have to admit to her mother that she had failed—and yet not so sad, since her mother had failed too. There would be no recriminations, only a great two-way rush of understanding. (She *knew* hack pamphleteers from the old days and Bert *wasn't* like them; get on with the game.)

Mother's house was quite big enough. They could put up swings in the garden and still have room for, oh, various games. She could see the children romping vaguely in sunshine. Turning hoses on each other, perhaps. Having a father wasn't everything.

Old friendships, suppressed for so long; people who talked about, well, the theater, the arts. Didn't want to sound too priggish, it wasn't what they talked about, it was a whole view of life. Her game leaned to the cultural rather than the voluptuous, because she remembered just a bit too keenly how much there was of the other, and how glad she had been to get away from the endless lounging and the pointless drinking, the getting a tan every summer. The country-club people, with whom her mother paradoxically kept up "because they were there," and to whom Bert had seemed such a refreshing contrast. . . .

But a married matron making a clean start could presumably leave out all the dull parts and live a really very rich, interesting life. For activity, she might even join some of her mother's causes. Her snottiness about those had been very juvenile, hadn't it? An excuse to let her mind slide and her conscience sleep. She had picked up a certain kind of lazy Catholic cynicism about public issues—picked it up from you-know. Fix all that when she felt less sleepy.

Find out about the machinery from her mother, after lunch on Christmas Day. Mrs. Forsythe's Christmas present, a daughter. Not losing a son-in-law, gaining a daughter. Not likely. Free to doze now, with all that settled, she pressed her nose into the sofa cushion and let peace suffuse her from the peace center, somewhere in the top of the head it seemed to be, out to the sprawled extremities, and that's how she was when the doorbell rang.

Her mouth opened woozily and took in a stale taste of cushion. God, what was that? The Christmas partridge, left over from yesterday when all that seemed pretty funny. Nothing deader than dead whimsy. She struggled up, fishing for shoes, and went with an ill grace to answer the door.

Upstairs, Bert's fingers moved listlessly over the keys, scavenging for a miracle. From the little he could remember of it, his pep talk last night to Dave didn't seem worth writing down—he had been awfully tired and had overrated the importance of what he was saying, an occupational complaint. (Forget it, a Christian looks to the future. Areas of vague pain and embarrassment wash back into the past.)

"Commercial Christmas, fleece, sheep, shepherds, wool over our eyes," a row of dots, nothing in that. He crunched and threw: it rimmed the basket and joined two other near misses on the carpet. "The spirit of the cave, the spirit of Macy's . . ." better not mention Macy's by name. Shouldn't even be mentioning Abercrombie & Fitch. Tiffany's might be all right though, Tiffany's was above the battle, nothing anyone said could touch Tiffany's. Alabaster women in basic black dresses. Floorwalkers were they called? My sister was a floorwalker at Tiffany's. Ten fantastic illustrations. The commercial Christmas had been milked drier than dry, but another thought struck him.

"Memo," he typed. "The trouble with pagans is that they are essentially, and in a very real sense, undersexed. Check if Chubb's magazine takes this kind of talk." It was possible that the readers of the *Passenger*, although undoubtedly oversexed in a very real sense, would find this reminder a bit rich for their blood. And wasn't that Father Chubb now? He heard a deep, neutral voice seeping slowly through the defective architecture; heard backwards a doorbell ringing, a mumble, a silence, a fresh torrent of mumbles. Father Chubb must have been here for about twenty minutes, talking to Betty. Ask him the score then on undersexed pagans. (And hey, maybe he'd brought a check for old Bert.)

He paused at the head of the stairs, where he could see a

faint sliver of Chubb through the living-room door. And hear voices, clear as bells. He stood still for a few minutes, gripping the banister like frost. Chubb's voice came slow as the light from stars, and clear. Something had happened to Betty's voice too. It had split in three.

He didn't for once dare go down and show himself. This was serious—he had lost control of his face for a moment, and didn't know how to get it back. There was heat in his cheekbones and throat, more serious than anything he could remember writing about. It was like watching all the china break in your cabin. On a still day. In the South Pacific, where he'd never been. (What was all that about?)

He suddenly couldn't get angry any more; rage slipped out of place into confusion, Gilhouley Chubb the public OK, OK—but not Betty, not his protégée. He would be fine in a minute, but right now the blood was booming into his cheeks, making it impossible to concentrate. After a while, even the clear sounds became noises and he wandered back to the study. He honestly didn't know what to do next.

2

Father Chubb looked even more indecisive than Matty and Dave had; or perhaps he just seemed that way, because he usually knew his mind so conspicuously well. Shuffling his feet on the grate, he said, "I had a call to make in Bloodbury, and I thought I'd look in, is Bert around?"

"He's working."

"Oh, I don't want to disturb him." Father Chubb began to swivel on the grate. "Tell him—"

"No, come in, Father, I'd like to talk to you a minute."

He looked at his watch and came in (Betty knew that if she asked him the time, he would have to look at it again). He seemed awfully tired, and slumped in the armchair, he looked uncharacteristically rumpled and about a foot shorter than usual. "How are the children?" he asked.

"They're fine. Look, I'd like to talk about Bert for a moment," she said in a rush.

"Yes," said Father Chubb. "Of course."

"I suppose you know what I'm going to say? You ought to, you had a lot to do with it."

Chubb showed a surprisingly quick understanding—for a big man, she thought dimly. "Perhaps we did," he said. "We should have seen it coming."

"Yes, you should," said Betty, still rather cross and sleepy. And then, "Seen what coming? What are *you* talking about?"

Father Chubb leaned over and unclipped his briefcase. He pulled out a Manila folder and handed it to her. "I was going to give these back to Bert, but perhaps you ought to see them first."

She opened the folder. Bert's latest poems. Oh God, oh God—she had no idea. Father Chubb, blessedly unurbane, seemed to be nodding at her over the top of the paper. "You ought to be ashamed," she said at last, "letting him get like this." The piety she had tried so hard to admire was parodied here with a kind of vicious cynicism. Or so it seemed to her. Heavenly babes and ladies in blue juxtaposed without rhyme or reason, forcing pain even in an unbeliever.

"We turned down the last lot, as you know," said Father Chubb judicially. "I think that may have made him a little overanxious. Anyway, here they are . . ." he made a move to get up. "Perhaps you can give them to him."

"Overanxious? Overanxious?" said Betty, not quite sure why this seemed so outrageous.

Father Chubb settled back with a sigh that was part him and part the chair. "We had noticed this, well, slightly overdone if you like quality in his work for some time, but we didn't know exactly what to do about it. I mean he had a family to support. . . ."

"That sounds like a funny way to run a magazine."

"I suppose. But Bert has always been something of a special case. Offhand I don't know of anyone else who tries to make a living writing for the religious press—it's just not geared for that. Most of our writers are amateurs, more or less. We never thought Bert was going to go on with it, or take it so hard."

Betty felt itchy and grizzly, but she couldn't think of anything to say. It was such an awful kind of conversation to be woken up for. All she knew was that Bert was in trouble, and Chubb was to blame.

"A magazine like the *Passenger* simply isn't worth a man's lifework," he explained. "It's not a literary magazine, or anything like that. In fairness to us, I tried to put this to Bert some years ago."

"In fairness to you," chimed Betty, "in fairness to you."

"Our readers are simple people. They like to be given some little thing to think about—the kind of thing Bert used to do so well as a youth—maybe a warm chuckle or two. . . ."

"A warm chuckle or two—Father, honestly, aren't you ashamed?" A warm, moist object called a chuckle. Bert slowly drowning in them.

She had no idea whether he was ashamed or not. She assumed he was a subtle man, under that smooth finish. His superiors had divined that he would be good at literary work and had put him on to this parody of it, as a punishment. He did his job with such impeccable mediocrity that it was impossible to tell what he really thought of it.

"It's humble work," he said stiffly, "but we think it serves a purpose."

"Keeping the uneducated uneducated you mean?"

"I wouldn't say that."

"Well, what *would* you say? No, I don't want to hear it." She realized that she was being dreadfully rude. She stopped talking and grizzled inwardly. Father Chubb might as well go away. She'd never get an honest answer out of him if she waited all day, and besides, Kevin would be waking up in half an hour or so.

"Well, it's debatable," said Father Chubb. "We may be wasting our time altogether. We think we're raising our people's standards a little bit. But we can't," he suddenly pointed at the folder, "raise them that way."

"What do you mean, that way?"

"Bert's way. False feeling, subjective theology and the like." This was strong talk coming from Father Chubb, and he scooted quickly across the ice. "Bert's out of date, Mrs. Flax. The Church in America is changing . . . er . . . on the campuses and so forth. All this gush he writes is out of place in the 1960's."

"But the *Passenger* has nothing to do with the 1960's."

The problem of manners kept coming up. They fell silent again, groping for politer methods.

"Bert was an awfully promising boy," attempted Father Chubb. "I'm sure he can start again."

"*Where* can he start again?"

"Well, anywhere," he waved his hand.

"For heavensake, Father, don't you understand anything? Who can Bert write for now? Who is going to buy his late Victorian junk now? You people bring a boy up on James Whitcomb Riley and Joyce Kilmer—"

"I doubt if anyone did that."

"And then you praise him by your own nutty standards until he doesn't know good from bad, up from down. And then, and *then*, you have to go and change your magazine, so that he hasn't got *any* place to write for. How dare you change your magazine like that? There must be lots of old ladies who liked it the way it was."

"Even old ladies can spot false sentiment, Betty."

"If they could, you'd all be out of business," Betty felt like saying. But there was no time for rudeness and slow retrenchment. It was getting closer to Kevin and she wanted to get at someone for what they had done to Bert, while she had the chance. "It isn't Bert's writing, so much, is it? It's what you've done to his whole character," she said. "Let me give you the latest on that."

And she did, very quickly, while Father Chubb nodded gravely and clucked his tongue metronomically and shifted this way and that in his chair. He frowned at the Gilhouley episode, but didn't say anything. She had started out trying to make it sound as bad as possible, then got qualms, and finished rather lamely. "But anyway, you can see why I have to question your policy of warm chuckles and little bitty thoughts. Just look, for godsake, look at what it's done to Bert."

"Yes," Chubb answered quite humbly. "It wasn't the thing for him, was it?" One more understatement, and she swore she was going to go over and muss his wavy white hair. "But then, I don't think that Bert ever had the faintest idea what the Church was really about, do you?"

"How would I know?" she said sharply. "He was the only Catholic I ever had to go on."

"True—but even you must have felt that the things that exercised him were pretty trivial for a grown man. Seat money and dirty movies, you say, and where angels go in the winter, such childish concerns—he seems to have had no sense of the sacramental, of sacred places and things, of liturgy and initiation into mystery."

"I never saw anything like that in the *Passenger*, either," was what Betty felt like saying to this: nor did these things seem much in Chubb's personal line. The things he had described as trivial sounded like the table of contents of his magazine. But Kevin was already overdue, and waiting for him to shriek was like waiting for a kettle to whistle, the silence around it was sucked in and nerve-wracking. "Yes, words, words," she said. "I really don't know whether he was a good Catholic, or a bad Catholic, Father, or a what kind of Catholic. All I know is that whatever it was wrecked him, and perhaps he ought to give it up for a while, if he still can."

"But Betty," he suddenly darted out a hand, although she was yards away. "It isn't the Church's fault—we aren't even an official publication, I mean."

"No, it's never the Church's fault, is it?" a cheap shot, felt cheap in the mouth, and Kevin sent down a first whine of disapproval. "The Church is all right for some people," she explained, "but not for Bert. He was a good man, Father. You've made him into something dreadful."

She had no idea what she meant by "the Church"—but somebody must be responsible. It was like arguing with the A & P.

Chubb seemed quite distraught and uncreased, as if he really, personally cared—although of course he couldn't commit his Company. "No you can't say that, you mustn't." There was no attempt at cleverness, only this incoherent flurry of concern. With Kevin suddenly in full wail upstairs, chaos had come upon them. "Why not?" Betty said more shakily. "Just tell me why not."

Father Chubb got a tentative grip on himself. "You don't know what you're saying, it's really much more complicated than that."

"I think I do."

Father Chubb was just trying to weasel out, saying that Bert didn't know about the *real* Church. If that was so, he might have brought it up with Bert, some years ago. Whatever Chubb said about it now would be massively beside the point.

"He would have to give up his writing, of course, and cultivate tranquillity. Let his mind and tongue rest. . . ." Chubb's editorials featured a sort of purring wisdom. She had never been able to finish one yet.

For some reason, her mind drifted back instead to her game of suppose. Leaving aside Bert for a moment, fancy thinking that going back to Mother was thinkable; that it would not mean all the hell it always had meant. Of course Mrs. Forsythe *would* act out "Mother was right" in spite of a lifetime of her own mistakes. It would be cruel to ask her not to. Between Bert in any form, and that. . . .

"You know," Father Chubb wound up forlornly, "the Church is so much more than you or I . . . but I have an idea what happened to Bert."

"I don't know, it might help." She couldn't decide whether to leave Kevin whistling for a few more minutes. Other voices were rising around his. It was all very distracting. "Please go ahead, Father, don't mind the noise, tell me your theories about Bert." Chubb tended to look at the ceiling as he talked, so you didn't have to listen; and his presence did make things seem a little more normal.

There were children's voices reverberating through the house, all right, a child-clangor, it was like being trapped in a bell tower or something, with dark confusion spreading on all sides (food and clothing, food and clothing, ding dong bell); but it also gave you something to concentrate on, something to do. Old Amsterdam Avenue discipline, you could do it if you had to. Wash the face, get a grip, hey hey. He was surprised to find that his face, which felt so disorganized, held up OK in the mirror. Discipline. He had just begun going through the bills again, because that was discipline too, the one chance of fighting through to clarity. Christian father. Keeps the worries to himself. Finds a way, pays his way, beholden to none, with charity to all, and a bill was something solid, not a tin whistle in your head. She might not take him seriously, but at least he went through his bills.

But a child was solid too. He decided to look into it.

3

"I don't suppose you'll understand what any of this means," Father Chubb began unpromisingly. "You have to know something about sacred things."

"Yes, I have my idea about those."

"You do? But surely you don't believe in them?" Christian hope again.

"No, not in your sense, no," she said hastily.

She didn't know what she meant, and mercifully he kept going. "It's a question of using sacred things right, rightly. Excuse me, I'm very tired," he trapped the yawn in his handkerchief. "I've been visiting some people."

People with problems, she thought. Even Father Chubb went a little bit pastoral at Christmastime.

"There are two or three ways of looking at this," he began again. "Now what do you suppose I meant by that?" He closed his eyes and sat absolutely still for a moment. She didn't know whether he had just given up. The children overhead had stopped crying and were banging furniture—except for Kevin, who was doing both. She was about to go up and organize when Father Chubb opened his eyes and said, "Look at it this way. Bert starts out at sixteen or so writing about sacred things, right? They are his subject and he has a real feeling for them. I know it sounds silly now, but we even thought he might become a priest, and we, at least I, were, was, much more interested in that than I, excuse me, *we*, were in his writing. He was a fine boy, Mrs. Flax"—Betty noted now she became "Mrs." in certain talking-to Mother contexts—"a boy of great purity and simplicity."

He shook his head desolately, as if at the wasteland of mistakes and misunderstandings inevitable in even an efficient man's life. "I suppose we should have told him to become a lawyer, like all the other boys, or an engineer. For myself, and maybe I shouldn't be saying this, I lost my enthusiasm for his writing, simply as writing, quite early on. But I encouraged him to go on with it, because I thought it was an authentic spiritual expression."

He seemed genuinely appalled by this and had to stop again. Encouraging bad writers to write wasn't a sin in anybody's religion. All the same. . . .

Hey, here's an idea for while Father Chubb's talking. Maybe after putting the most incompetent man in the order in charge of answering the telephone, they put the second most incompetent in charge of the magazine. No, silly. . . .

"Well then, there he was, writing about sacred things, but not by any means becoming a priest. What Dr. Jung has called a shadow I believe. . . ."

"I didn't know you went in for psychology, Father," she said sarcastically, "even hand-me-down psychology."

"What was that? No, heavens no. The point I'm trying to make is old-fashioned enough. And I know that you're going to think it's farfetched, even before I say it." The usual Christian defense, arms over the head. "It's just that if you use sacred things wrongly it's sacrilege, and you pay for it. These things aren't toys to play with. We believe in the objective seriousness of actions."

It was all so abstract that it somehow kept the spooks at bay. "That doesn't seem so unreasonable," she said—although she was willing to bet that nobody else had ever been punished for writing tripe in the *Passenger*.

(Of course if Chubb really *was* incompetent, then nobody was to blame. But a big smooth man like that couldn't be incompetent, could he?)

Kevin stopped crying and the furniture died down. Bert must have intervened. She could just hear his wistful footsteps and a murmur of negotiation. Would be bring them down? She must keep hurrying along to get what she could into, and out of, Father Chubb. She had never had such a feeling of rolling in fur: probably young diplomats got this feeling at their first international conference.

"Maybe you're right," she said. "It doesn't matter whether these things really *are* sacred: so long as he thinks they are, that would be enough to cast a first-class shadow, wouldn't it?"

"You think that would be enough? Perhaps, perhaps. We must never discount natural causes."

For a moment, she felt that perhaps she believed more than he did, and wanted to argue the other side. The queerness of St. Jude's, that was what he meant by sacred things. If you made the wrong move in St. Jude's, something funny could easily happen. Seven years bad luck. But it would take much too long to put her confused thoughts in order. A mother of five never had time for anything.

"I suppose," said Father Chubb, "that any poet who tries to force his emotions is in trouble anyway. So Bert was getting it two ways. And simony makes three," he added in a low private voice.

"Simony?"

"Yes, selling sacred things for cash."

"But everybody does that, don't they . . . ? I mean, it's a recognized industry."

"Yes, well, there are certain subtle distinctions."

"Of course. I was expecting those" (this sounded distressingly like her mother) "any minute."

"Life is not always simple, Mrs. Flax," he answered primly. "Anyway, the connection between Bert and simony is just one I make in my own mind. It may have no basis in objective fact. I shouldn't have brought it up."

He was stiffening again, resuming his uniform. Time was almost up. She didn't mean to keep attacking him like this. It was some waspish reflex. She wanted him to stay and talk coolly and remotely about the terror upstairs, until it just went away.

"I see what you mean, though," she said. "Thinking of Our Lady and such in terms of cash on the barrelhead."

Father Chubb kept on visibly traveling away, remorseless as a heavenly body. His patience for pastoral work was probably slight anyhow. "I mean that was why the commercial side of things worried him so much," she said. "He was in it so deep himself. Is that what you're trying to say?"

He was attractive enough as a human being and she wondered why he always went back to being Father Chubb. To save wear and tear on the nerves, perhaps.

"Yes, something like that," he said. "But remember, the simony is only a theory."

"But it's an enchanting theory. Like being carried off by pixies," said her mother. Go away, Mother.

"I can see I haven't explained it properly. Be that as it may, please remember this, in all fairness to Bert: he was doing it, selling himself, selling piety and goodwill, for you and the children."

"*Oh* no, he wasn't." This was a last, monstrous twist. "He was doing it for *you*."

"He stuck to a task that was lacerating him—don't you

suppose he would have given it up if he could have afforded to? If he was a single man? I never tried to detain him—though of course we were always more than glad—"

"Are you blaming me?" Betty almost shrieked. "Instead of yourself? And your stupid magazine?"

"No, no, of course not. It's just that, well, *you* know—much may be forgiven if one has loved much."

"But writing for the *Passenger* has nothing to do with love. It kills love, if anything. It kills every kind of feeling."

"No, that's too strong."

"A writer like Bert fakes love at four cents a word. It's part of his stock-in-trade. God is love. Bert is love. It's a living."

"You have no right to judge him like that."

"What do you mean, I have no right?" The issue suddenly became almost *too* clear. "If I don't judge him, how can I help him? It's all very well for you, not to judge him, not to help him. I've got to try. Anyway, I think after seven or eight years you sometimes *can* judge somebody. Pretty darn well."

"Nobody knows the secrets of the human heart," mumbled Father Chubb.

"That's just cant, and you know it. Catholic cant. I don't have to accept it. The old mystification of everything, God how I hate that."

"Do you?"

Did she? Or was it just her mother? She was beginning to feel as confused as Bert. She had no idea whether she hated mystification or not. "I don't want to talk about that. What were we talking about before?"

"About Bert, was it?" he picked up her frantic tempo. "I just wanted to say that, first of all, Bert defiled the temple—in his own mind, as you would say. And secondly, his understanding of the Church never advanced beyond grammar-school level anyway, because it couldn't afford to. If it did, he was out of work. You will say, perhaps, that love of his family had nothing to do with this, that it was all our fault. You may be right—although we have many contributors less good than Bert and they don't seem to worry about it. All I know is what a fine boy he was and what a sorry state I find him in now, and if I can be of any help. . . . Now I really must be going." There was something oddly formal about his leave-taking. He stooped over the hall table, in a bereaved way, and straightened up with a piece of paper in his hand. Chubb undoubtedly played many parts. But he really seemed to care about Bert, like an out-of-practice father, and the worry of it made him look very old as he tottered away over the snow.

"I'd hate to see who they have in charge of the telephone," she thought. No, that wasn't fair. Chubb's magazine had a good circulation and plenty of preposterous ads (statues that sing in the dark et cetera), so he must be a good editor. It was Bert who had lost touch.

Father Chubb seemed so humbly flustered to find a contributor who took his work seriously in a literary way: and astonished that anyone should actually need the money. (Lay people are usually fed by ravens.)

It occurred to her as she softly closed the door that the house was awfully quiet. Bert had stayed upstairs with the children after all. Perhaps he had heard Father Chubb's voice and wanted to avoid him. Perhaps he had heard Father Chubb's voice—oh dear, oh dear. If he had, would he *feel* anything? Would he throw a fake tantrum? Or frown, with great sad eyes? A prominent emotion manufacturer, whose stock is running low and out of fashion, might try almost anything. She climbed the stairs with a certain dread, remembering halfway up to look at the paper Father Chubb had written on; it was a check for five dollars.

4

Bert was on all fours with Bert, Jr., on his back and the others lined up informally waiting their turns. This was Bert's staple for entertaining the kids; he groaned and jiggled, and they clawed at his shirt to stay on.

"Hello dear." He grinned and shook his head. "These kids. . . ."

"Father Chubb was just here."

"He was? Why didn't you tell me?"

"I thought you were working."

"Giddyup," said Bert, Jr.

The same long thin face and sandy hair; Bert, Jr., was halfway to being his father already, but without the ravages and ironies yet. Was there any way of heading him off from those? He seemed to Betty to have the same fineness of quality that Bert was supposed to have had—which meant apparently just asking for trouble.

Next on the horse was Betty, Jr., who was supposed to look like her. Semisecular vagueness and frivolous ardors for her. People looking like people. There was a family picture on the wall (they were using it as a Christmas card this year) and everyone was grinning the same big family grin. As if it was just wonderful to be a Flax, this year and every year. And around it, bright crayon sunsets, boats on a curly blue sea, scarlet-faced shepherds—the surface had to be kept happy for the children, whatever went on underneath.

Bert was letting the kids get excited and the overflow began clamoring around her. Patricia and Kevin liked to play ring-around-the-rosy: they clapped hands and moved round in a circle, Kevin sedately, Patricia skipping impatiently. "One, two, three and we all fall down." Kevin sat down stiffly on his padded behind; Patricia sprawled. "Mommy, you have to fall down too." Betty lowered herself resignedly and in a moment they were ready to start again.

Bert had come round to Bert, Jr. again and hoisted him on to his shoulders. He went lunging about the room with great, stalking strides while his son shrieked his fright and pleasure. Bert stopped en route to kiss Betty, then pranced away to drop Bert, Jr., on the top bunk.

"Me, Daddy, me, Daddy."

"One, two, three, all fall down."

He seemed to be doing everything perfectly, right down to loving the children. You looked for the queerness that had begun to seep into his writing and you found nothing but ponderous sincerity. It was like expecting your face to look a certain way in the mirror and finding it looked quite different.

Still, the queerness was there, it must be. He had always

been able to put on a first-class show when he had to. All he was doing now was make the children happy, and that made him seem all right. But it didn't change anything.

He insinuated himself into the ring-around-the-rosy, with his great oafish strides. When the cry went up to fall down, he staggered dementedly about the room clutching at the furniture and finally tripping headfirst into Kevin's crib. The children were sick with laughter and looked to her for confirmation. She smiled and shook her head. "Isn't Daddy silly?" said Betty, Jr.

Ring-around, ring-around, Daddy had them all in the game by now, and all watching him like hawks to see what he would do. "All fall—" they stopped and just stood watching. Bert began to wheel and spin; the sick, exhausted laughter started up again. Daddy whirling like a dervish, bouncing off the walls, steadying himself against the mantelpiece—what was he going to do with the flowerpot? Oh no, how silly. But the children laughed on in a frenzy.

"That's enough," Betty found herself saying. "You're getting them too excited, dear."

They stopped and looked at her with sober disappointment. Patricia gave a last sniffle of laughter.

"All right," Bert confirmed, "that's enough, kids. Everybody downstairs."

Betty didn't know why she had stopped them: suddenly their excitement had seemed dangerous. They looked at her a little reproachfully, but Bert herded them out in a lump, making it his order as well as hers. "Snowsuits and look snappy." She heard them dinning down the stairs, starting a new batch of excitement for the garden.

She stayed behind in the nursery, picking up all that was left of last year's toys, a brokenhearted, hopeless collection by now. Without the children, the room was suddenly very dark; the toys had no color. It was a funny time of year to be festive.

The children took a long time getting into their galoshes

—it sounded as if all five were trying to get into the same pair. And Bert too. But at last the back door slammed and a little while after that she heard Bert's tread on the stairs.

She was holding a woolly lamb to her breast, as if it was wounded. It was, too, its little starter had come off. Bert smiled when he saw her, and she turned away. His face was a wet red.

"What did Father Chubb have to say? Anything?"

"He brought back your poems and things."

"Oh," she heard him grimace. "Did you get a chance to look at them? Pretty lousy, I guess. Boy, what a mess a few kids can make." He picked up a train engine and flipped it into Kevin's crib. "Kevin's talking pretty well, don't you think?" An awful waxworks of a doting father; it seemed absurdly melodramatic, but she walked past him with her head down and to one side.

He didn't follow her into their bedroom next door. She pulled down the crinkly covers and took off her shoes and lay down. Her eyes were quite dry and, she imagined, trancelike. It was no good trying to comfort each other by touch. He drew away like a frightened stag at this time of the month. Would there ever be more of Bert's foolishness in her womb, the question trailed off in drowsiness.

She heard his voice calling tactfully from the doorway. She must have been asleep for a while, because it was quite a bit darker outside. "That's it, dear," he said. "Have a good rest. We'll be up late tonight." What's on tonight? she wondered vaguely. "I'll give the kids their supper," he continued, "and put them to bed too."

"All right," she said, "you do that," and rolled on to her face.

The next thing she knew, the windows were black against the bedroom light and Bert was unbuttoning a clean shirt.

5

She had a funny feeling that St. Jude's was good for her and bad for Bert. It pleased her to think about it as she gurgled up through sleep-mist. Organ music and incense for Christmas, the two softest things of their kinds; then Monsignor Flanagan quaintly decked out in his girdled tunic and his red drapes; mismatched altar boys trickling hither and yon, all in their various ways touching, one for his thinness, another for his ineptness; Father Terwilliger in shaky command, pulling the foolish ones by the shoulder, and if worst came to worst jerking them awake, with resigned twitches. You were moved by the things they did well and moved again by the things they did badly. The actions must have been left over from an age when they made sense: the boys and Father Terwilliger worked at them in the twentieth century with grim incomprehension.

That was what she remembered from last year, when St. Jude's still frightened her, and she saw no reason for this year to be different. Christmas always seemed to take St. Jude's by surprise. It had no regular choir for the singing; the altar boys were not adaptable; they got through the ceremony somehow, Terwilliger finishing five minutes ahead of the field.

Bert stood in the hall in his scarf and earmuffs. "All set?" He shouldn't be going, though, it was bad for him. The wild poems, the denunciation of his friend—he needed a holiday from all that. Besides, he seemed to be more excitable at night. "Mrs. Pelotti's here," the quavering eighty-year-old baby-sitter. Couldn't very well call it off if Mrs. Pelotti was here—the effort of explaining to her that she wasn't wanted after all would be too exhausting.

They trudged to the car through silence and thick snow. The moonlight made a harsh glare underfoot. Bert cast a surprising shadow under the streetlight, heavy, swollen face above gigantic shoulders. The Studebaker looked shrunken and cold huddling in a snowbank. Which did the man say were the people who bought Studebakers? Salesmen in bow ties, she rather thought.

Then there was Bert's other shadow, the one Father Chubb had talked about, wonder what that one looked like. Catholics married and became one flesh, one shadow. She wished she could share Bert's malignancy, find out what was really bothering him and help him to bear it: but not while he was smiling like that, shiny jingle-bells smile with no life in it. As soon as she looked away it would disappear.

St. Jude's was too hot to be true, which made it a different kind of place. The heating had begun overnight to work with a vengeance, shooting pent-up steam up the walls and damping the wrinkled yellow ceiling. Mr. O'Malley, the poor man's Greek chorus, sat in the doorway and raked in the seat money with rosy, gleaming grins—a special holly-berry beam for Mrs. Flax, which seemed to open a new sweat duct in his cheek. O'Malley was an unfinished kind of man, in lots of ways, but on the other hand, he always had on his smart suit, his pearl-gray tie and his monogrammed handkerchief.

Bert used to rant about that more than anything. The parishioners at St. Jude's were altogether too well dressed for his taste. What he liked was a simple, working-man's parish—well not that perhaps, but not a *Ladies' Home Journal* sort of parish, anyway. Bert never *quite* knew what he wanted, perhaps because, as Father Chubb said, he couldn't afford to.

He said that St. Jude's parishioners were lace-curtain Irish, and worse than that, high-fidelity Irish. The Flaxes had tried long ago some reciprocal dining with the O'Malleys and the Wards, but Bert went on so about "worldly Catholics" afterward that it just didn't seem worth it. The O'Malleys didn't strike Betty as being so worldly, more interplanetary, really, but Bert explained: "These people come to Bloodbury with nothing else in mind but to pile up goods. And to them, a man who hasn't got goods is an abject failure. You've read about people like that haven't you? And OK, I'm human enough to admit that it bothers me a little to have people sniffing at our carpets and thinking 'poor things.' " "Oh, Bert"—she used to say, "Oh, Bert." "You go to O'Malley's, or Ward's," he went on, "and first thing you know, the guy claps you on the back and says, 'What'll it be, Skipper?' and you know that whatever you ask for, however farfetched, he'll come up with it. And then they try our place and all we can offer them is one lousy bottle of rye. We have to say, 'Would you like some rye?' " "But that doesn't really upset you does it, darling?" "And *another* thing, they always say,

'Glad to have you on board, Bert, old man,' and I could never say that." "But it doesn't really bother you," she persisted. "I mean your values are right and theirs are wrong, that's all." "No, it doesn't really *bother* me. It's just that I think we make them uncomfortable. We're not smooth enough for them."

She didn't think for one moment that they sniffed at her rugs. She thought they rather respected Bert, for his writing and his dedicated life, but again he said no: "They just think I'm some kind of goon, because I'm not out making money and piling up goods like the other boys. And staying home for lunch, my God, what sort of man does that? I just can't convey to you what people like that are like."

She never saw any sign of any of this, but she supposed in those days that he must know. He came from the same kind of background as these allegedly greedy ones and might even have invaded Bloodbury with the same objectives, if he hadn't been so dedicated to spiritual things.

By contrast to the O'Malleys, Bert used at first to cite his New York friends—plain, no-nonsense people, real Catholics in fact, who didn't give a rap for status. (Not poverty or pacifist cranks either—although she would rather have liked to meet some of those.) She suggested that he should invite a sampling over for dinner, and after some hesitation, he got hold of a couple called Tiernan and had them out for a hamburger barbecue.

Fran Tiernan, she remembered, latched on to her right away, and talked about pregnancy, which Betty was then in the middle of, and helped her to fix the salad. She seemed a nice enough girl, if a bit single-minded. Outside on the lawn, things weren't going so well. Why did you invite us, was it anything special? said Tiernan's face. Bert kept nodding and looking up toward the house.

Afterward the Tiernans said it was vital they get the nine-fifteen bus, because they had a dollar-an-hour baby-sitter, and even at that you couldn't be sure because she was only fifteen. Bert took them off, amid cries of, "Must come and see us," and, "Oh yes, after the baby, after the baby." No dates were mentioned. The Tiernans said, "It's been grand."

When Bert got back he said right off, "Joe's an awfully good fellow," and Betty said, "Yes, he seems very nice," and Bert said: "He doesn't shine at conversation. But he says some very acute things." "Yes, he looks as if he might." "And Fran. . . ." They said a few things, in the same vein, about Fran. The Tiernans were never mentioned again, nor were his good-as-gold New York friends.

Poor Bert, he didn't belong in this world. (Couldn't afford to according to Father Chubb.) She had tried very hard with her own old friends, too, and he had developed this awful animation with them—talking too fast and pumping his hands and sort of braying. He seemed to think that was how you talked with clever people. (Though she didn't think her friends were all that clever.) Or maybe he was still embarrassed about the singleton bottle of rye. Or maybe by being asked what magazines he wrote for, or heaven knew what.

After the MacIntyres, he said, "To be quite truthful, I didn't like them very much. A bit too glib . . . values . . . worldly, et cetera." After the Spodes, it was obvious that he couldn't say the same thing, he couldn't dislike everybody, so he said, "I like them a lot better," but Betty didn't think so. He hadn't talked so fast with the Spodes, but he hadn't been himself, either. He smoked like an exhaust pipe and got a little bit drunk. She hated to see him so uncomfortable: and since he wouldn't admit he *was* uncomfortable, they couldn't even discuss it.

Anyway, the Spodes did not invite them back for three months, by which time Bert was utterly overanimated again. The babies were beginning to impinge by then and life was getting more complicated by the minute. Bert seemed quite happy not to go out any more. He even made rather a thing of not being a "mixer," and so forth. He was conventionally satirical about togetherness, and wrote an article about true Christian togetherness, as opposed to the bogus trumped-up kind prevalent in certain suburbs.

All very easy to scoff at, she supposed. But what kept her from doing so was the knowledge that he had only to crook his finger at Mrs. Forsythe to make himself at once the perfect host. He could offer his guests Scotch, gin, crème de menthe, anything; he could drown in his own carpets —if he would just play ball with Mrs. Forsythe. And playing ball just meant admitting that he could use the money —it wouldn't keep him from laughing at her to his heart's desire.

She was not used to this kind of integrity. Most of her friends didn't have any at all, that you'd notice. Mrs. Forsythe was considered a monument of it around town, because she crusaded for progressive causes. But Mrs. Forsythe lived pretty well; you were served at the meetings by a maid with a white apron. Bert could have had that—and she was pretty sure that he wanted to have that, or at least to keep up with the O'Malleys—but with much sweat he kept the impulse down. (How could he have so much integrity in his life and so little in his work? Was that another Catholic thing? With her mother it was quite the other way.)

She peeped at him, expecting to catch the pious-donkey expression, the Christmas Eve special. But now that she expected it, he was looking sensitive enough to burst. It was weird how you couldn't call the turn, just once, on someone. Even on your own face in the mirror. She wondered more than ever how he prayed; longed, and was terrified, to ask him.

People kept shuffling along the aisle in twos and threes. Bert didn't look around as the seats filled up on both sides. The Franklins sat right next to them, and the Franklins and

Bert kept their eyes down exchanging no sign of recognition. Catholic discipline. Good example and all that. She wanted to smile at the Franklins, but it would have to wait.

Without warning, a high female voice at the back of the church began, like a great organ pipe, to exude the "*Adeste Fidelis.*" A man's voice, two octaves deeper, joined hesitantly in, straggled to a halt, tried again. Only two people, and they couldn't get started at the same time. Not very good for a *House and Garden* parish. Perhaps the smart clothes were just a blind; perhaps they were floundering like everybody else.

The two invisible songsters cranked somehow through the first verse, only to come to real grief with the chorus, where the voices have to get gradually louder. The man hadn't foreseen this and was already going much too loud: he fairly had to bellow the last line and his voice cracked. Drawing a fast, grinding breath, he launched himself at the third verse. The woman began, with audible severity, on the second.

You weren't supposed to be attracted by the inadequacy. Probably the only inefficient Catholic church in America, and she had to be stuck with it. She just couldn't help it. She was moved by all the wrong things, she just wasn't the religious type at all.

6

Mass began at last. Betty tried to concentrate on it. It made even less sense than usual, because she was so worried about Bert. On the other hand, it seemed like as good a way of getting in touch with what was "out there" as any. Monsignor Flanagan moved gravely to and from the big book. His hands worked with a kind of grace, although he obviously had difficulty with them. There was, in his stance and the slope of his shoulders, a tranquil certainty that it was all working well, whatever it was.

Bert was sweating horribly. He usually had a dry skin, but this was heat to suck sweat from a rock. It put a sort of glaze around Monsignor Flanagan, making him look like a mirage: a coptic priest drifting among tropical reds and yellows and greens, a cascade of flowers on the altar, a red vestment, and there went the little wizened priest moving knowingly from his book to his cruets; water splashing over his fingers, a desert mirage. He wiped them off with a fantastic little towel and returned to his doings, a million light years away from the Church Bert wrote about. (Which was the real one?)

A few minutes before, everything had seemed much more normal. Monsignor Flanagan had turned the pulpit light on, flushing it on his tired transparent cheeks, and said, "On behalf of Father Terwilliger and myself, I want to wish each and every one of you a holy and a happy Christmas." Bert smiled slightly at the formula. But now Bert looked more as if he might be going to faint. The sweat was fairly leaping out of him and his face underneath it was worried and sick. Was he composing something? When she looked inquiringly at him, he managed to smile and sit up straight and attend to his Missal, fidgeting with the ribbons.

The bell rang, and they were all kneeling again. Bert went crumpled immediately (it usually took several minutes), with his behind propped against the seat. But then Chester Franklin was having the same trouble. His large economy rear seemed to probe ceaselessly for the bench, moving slowly backward; but just as it was about to land, Chester would remember and straighten himself up. A moment later, and he was probing again.

She watched the consecration with her usual curiosity. Everybody bowed, seeming to share Monsignor Flanagan's stooped-shouldered conviction about it. She could see how you might quite instinctively join them one day, not because you shared their belief, but because it was the only thing to do. The consecration was "something," an event (though she could never believe it was what they thought it was), and you bowed to it. From the corner of her eye, Bert seemed to wince. But his face was still covered when she looked.

After that, everybody relaxed and began to cough up a fresh fog. The St. Jude's atmosphere. Was it a joke about faith? Did it just come and go? No, Bert said you had to co-operate. Was he praying now? Were the words getting out of his head? Self-consciously she tried a prayer herself. Well, not a prayer, but an aspiration of the human spirit.

In a minute, they would begin to go up to Communion and Bert would come back looking like a plaster saint. She hated that look. It was all stiff and cold and blind. It was like honoring your parents and respecting the clergy and submitting to your spouse. Beyond personality and above feeling. Bert called it a free choice, but it certainly didn't look that way with him. When Bert had that look, it meant he always felt exactly what he was supposed to feel, about parents, priests and spouses, spice, what was it? She had supposed it was a necessary part of religion, obedience and all that: but now she was beginning to wonder whether Chubb might be right and whether Bert hadn't got it wrong. (Bert wrong about religion was still hard to grasp, and she let it go.)

The anxious ones were already beginning to edge toward the aisle. Bert would not be one of those. Mrs. Franklin began to wriggle purposefully along the kneeler, followed reluctantly by Chester, who clearly preferred to wait a bit longer. Bert leaned back to let them pass, which they did with surprising dexterity, and knelt forward again with his head still in his hands.

Mrs. Franklin had opened the floodgates, and in a moment the aisles were flooded with communicants. Mr. O'Malley, looking very much the traffic cop, stood at the front trying to channel it up the middle and down the sides, but Monsignor Flanagan had forgotten to request this procedure and there was muzzy confusion as the silent people jostled each other and tried to make speechless arrangements. It was a curiosity of the Bloodbury parishioners, said Bert, that they never foresaw this.

They did very well, considering, and Monsignor Flanagan and Father Terwilliger went slippering along the altar rail at a great rate giving out Communions, and slowly the lines began to shorten. But Bert showed no sign of moving. He glanced up once and his lips were white and seemed to be moving in some kind of prayer; his eyes were red from where his hands had been and looked loose in their sockets. It always gave him a wild-eyed look to sit like that.

The tail of the line was sucked in shorter and shorter. The Franklins had long since come back and plunged into their thanksgiving. The last man in the line shuffled solemnly past the Flaxes' pew. Betty thought she felt Bert move, but when she looked around, he had just shifted his position. He was considerably more sitting than kneeling now, and staring blankly at his missal. He was not going to go up. He was not going to come back looking pious.

She was startled. All through Mass, he must have been trying to make this decision. It meant a lot to him. Christmas Communions, he had always said so; it gave him interior peace and such. In his articles he went so far as to say it made him one with the shepherds. The decision must have hurt plenty; twisting his face all up so he had to hide it.

Poor Bert. Her mother would have said it was just another of these silly pseudoproblems that he made up for his own bedevilment. "If the boy would worry about something *real* for a change. . . ." But it was real enough to Bert. (Unless he wasn't really worried and was just trying it on, to see how it felt. But that was too horrible to contemplate.)

His unexpected move, or failure to move, unsettled her. Afterwards he stood rather blankly in the doorway, flexing his fingers. She took his arm and he looked at her with swimming red eyes as if he wanted to explain what had happened. She felt a tweak on her sleeve and whispered, "Happy Christmas," to the radiant O'Malleys. "Are you all right?" she asked, and Bert said something about a touch of the grip. Her mother would have said, "Go to Communion if you're going, be still if you're not. It's nothing to get sick about." But then her mother would have said the same thing to Chester Franklin's bottom. "If you want to sit down, my good man, plant the damn thing and be done." No, that was improvising, her mother never said "damn."

Bert sat hunched at the wheel, still working at speech, his lips forming and unforming, while he sweated in the cold air. He was trying to look calm and sensible, and she said, "Are you sure there's nothing wrong, darling? Don't be ashamed. . . ."

For a moment she thought he would break. But he seemed to take courage from the cold bright air, the murmuring and exultation of the people who were Happy Christmasing out to their cars in twos and threes, and he said, "I love these occasions, you know?"

She gazed at him, unbelieving. He looked almost jolly and almost tender. He seemed to see that something more was called for, and he said, "I broke my fast. With a Life Saver."

She knew that he was lying (he would never make a mistake like that on Christmas Eve, and he never ate Life Savers either) and that she could do nothing for him tonight.

She heard him moving about in the study, a few doors away, and the idiot rustle of paper. Oh, no—not tonight. But she didn't quite dare ask him to come to bed.

She got into her nightgown and brushed her hair with harsh vigor, counting the strokes out loud. She thought she could hear Bert's voice calling, but it stopped after a moment and she got crisply into bed. She had changed the sheets in the manicness of the morning and they felt like fresh cellophane. A lovely cool-warmness. Religion might be true but it brought so much mischief with it; try to forget it in the modern American bedroom.

Bert's voice started up again. It sounded as if he might be talking on the telephone, pausing courteously and explaining patiently. He sometimes did this when he was writing—it was a family joke. Family jokes did not bear thinking about. She tried to catch what he was saying, couldn't quite make it. Probably something about the Heavenly Babe coming into our resisting hearts at Midnight Mass—poised and chattering on his terrible tightrope, piety one side and blasphemy the other. Poor Bert, must stop saying that, poor Bert. Religion must sometimes mean just keeping quiet, not trying to coin phrases, or drum up "thoughts"; Bert once wrote a thing about keeping quiet, about the silence of Christ, and it chimed with something she felt herself. She had said, "Yes, yes, that's it. He understands." But even that was just talk. He had no intention of imitating Christ's silence himself. All he had left was the words, and he was calling on them now for a final assault on the Christmas bills.

Maybe she should never have brought him to Bloodbury. He didn't belong in a nest of rising executives. He was used to going around in a windbreaker and meeting people in bars and drugstores and delicatessens. Sitting on doorsteps with Father Murphy, was that how it went? Swapping stories about Catholic sports favorites. He knew the Church in that context, not this one.

He would have said, "That's all right, they're tearing down the context anyway," and that was right. His old neighborhood had been demolished several years ago and one of the stupidest developments she'd ever seen had gone up on the ruins. All the same, a boy with a windbreaker and a missal. . . .

That was funny, too, the way he talked about evil last night. Only religious people got possessed by devils: it was the chance they took, she supposed. Since he behaved with a monotonous, almost nerve-racking, virtue his guilt must be altogether a thing of the mind. Maybe the smidgen of hell he should have been raising in school and college had just bloomed and bloomed in there; if he thought evil was so hot, maybe he should try it for a while. But he couldn't, of course, that was the whole point.

She had airily told Father Chubb she wanted to help him, so she had to go on with it. Perhaps, follow out this theory and then go to sleep, if Bert hadn't been so unnaturally good as a boy, if he had tooted around with an impure heart like the other fellows, he wouldn't be so plagued by all that now. If he hadn't tried writing old lady's poetry before he was ready for it. . . .

His voice went up a notch, waking her from seven-tenths asleep to five-eighths awake. God, it was much more tangled than that. He didn't have to talk that loud to write a story. And a good boy usually became a good man didn't he? Bert *was* a good man, and yet she suddenly felt he had done a terrible thing in lying like that about the Life Saver. He was so hell-bent on edification that truth had no claims on him any more. She almost formed the words "rotten with dishonesty," but you couldn't say that if he always did it for other people, could you?

He had been costing her a lot of sleep one way and another, but she was so dizzy now with all these zany changes of heart that she plunged suddenly and quite fiercely into sleep. At one point she thought she heard a child crying with alarm; and later she thought she heard Bert fairly shouting, a man possessed for sure. But it might all have been dreams, like going to her mother's house up the drive and through the dogwood, and Frieda, how silly, Frieda, the maid they used to have when she was a child, said that Mrs. Forsythe couldn't come down, she was having an attack of joy; she had locked herself in her room and was crying to beat the band. Frieda began to cry, too, which was pretty unnerving. Frieda was a big German girl and definitely wasn't supposed to cry, it wasn't one of her duties, and now she stood by the door looking so sad, and Betty suddenly realized that she had a gloomy paw on the handle and wasn't about to let anyone out. Betty had other worries too. She was afraid that the door upstairs would open and that her mother would suddenly appear, unrecognizable for tears—somebody was in fact sobbing near her feet. She turned on the bed lamp and caught a tiny ball of hair and flannel. Not her mother after all. Betty, Jr., had put her head on the bed and was sniffing to herself. "I couldn't sleep, I couldn't sleep. Is it Christmas yet?"

"What is it, Betty? What's wrong?"

Betty, Jr., didn't want to say; she buried her head for shame. Betty, Sr., comforted her, patting at every sniff, until the little girl was reasonably composed. "Now why don't we go back to your room and try again?"

They both looked at the empty bed where Bert was supposed to be. Betty felt a kind of dreadful understanding with her daughter. She nodded and Betty, Jr., clambered into Bert's bed, falling asleep on the way. Betty, Sr., kissed her cheek and pulled up the covers. She went to the cupboard and got out the slightly frayed red dressing gown that Bert was always promising to replace; it hung between the old suits and the old dresses that Bert didn't like her to say she didn't mind about. She moved quietly down the passage, steering by fitful moonlight.

The study door was shut. There was no more talk behind it, but a violent chink of light at the bottom. She was afraid to go in. It would be some terrible sight. Bert prostrate before a statue. Bert naked at the typewriter. In the middle of the night, she wasn't up to it.

She stood by the door, looking at the play of light on her nervously shifting slippers. If she went back to bed the memory of the study door would nag at her; she would have made another big mystery out of nothing. If she went in she would have to sort of sail in and tell him in a kind voice to stop his nonsense. Tell him he was frightening the children. If it weren't Christmas night, she would tell him—

oh, what a wretched Christmas night! She hadn't thought about it before. She grabbed at the handle and marched in, really upset over what was happening to Christmas.

He was sitting at the desk, looking quite ordinary in his Sunday suit. His back was turned, but over his shoulder she could see the family accounts which he had spread out all over the desk, and all kinds of old bills and receipts, things she thought had been thrown away years ago. The files were out at full stretch, so it was a wonder that the cabinets didn't fall over.

Poor, crazy Bert, worrying about his money on Christmas night. "Bert," she said gently, "come to bed, Bert." But he didn't look round, or answer. "Bert? It's me, Betty," she said, feeling that some identification was needed. In the typewriter she could see a routine memo—"The trouble with pagans is that they are essentially, and in a very real sense, undersexed—check if Chubb's magazine takes this kind of talk." She shivered. He took for granted her presence, and handed over his shoulder a receipt which was all of seven years old and said, "I don't remember paying that." It was for a pair of shoes. Everything was so normal, and gentle, not what she had expected at all. "Bert, stop it—" she said. "And what about this," a receipt for Danish tables, four days old, "and this," a basketball on Amsterdam Avenue, sixteen years ago. He talked as if he had something in his mouth. She took them and looked them over and handed them back. "I don't remember," she said.

There was something on his face, when she finally brought herself to look at it, some trace of the peace which should have come from Communion with God, but must have come to him through some mystic encounter with nothing. There was also something on it which probably only she could see, of sly triumph, as if he had found a perfectly brilliant solution.

He was quite tired and consented to come to bed with a gentle foolish clasp of the hand. She led him sleepily along the moon-shot passage, not so much frightened of him, no, not frightened at all, but fidgety over this latest and wildest stunt; not religion this time, but money, mad money. The things he thought up. He wasn't really trying to make himself break down, was he? (Like a child forcing himself to be sick?) So that he could just give up?

Perhaps the Bert-within had tried it before and it hadn't worked. Perhaps tonight, under the stimulus of the Sacrifice which he had trivialized for a living (a bare living), and with the sacred things reaching a peak in the sweltering church, he had tried again. But it was silly, you couldn't make yourself break down any more than you could make yourself go to sleep. Only a professional make-believer could make such a mistake. He would still be the same old Bert in the morning. He was incurably sane.

Part Seven

"When Father Danny reached the goal line,
he tucked down his head and just kept running.
And none of the boys at the orphanage
ever saw him again."

FLAX. *Father Danny's Last Game.*

1

It was the kind of Christmas night he used to write about, bright and still. Choirboys singing with aching sweetness over the snow wouldn't have surprised her one bit. But the silence was even better magic. Dense, cool silence you could touch, smell, keep time to. The department stores that sang "Silent Night" sang better than they knew.

Because of St. Jude's, the Catholic Church would always be the Church she associated with silence. When they talked, they could be as foolish as anybody; but when they kept quiet, they were pretty good. They knew it, they had confidence in their silence. They knew they weren't boring anybody. No need to keep singing and reciting and spinning out ingenuities, thinner and thinner and thinner—they could hold your attention without constant nervous grabs at it. Except for old Bert—he had to keep talking. Even in church, his epiglottis never stopped going.

Well, that was one theory. Anyway, Bert was quiet enough now, breathing gently on to her hand, which had been stroking his face for an infinite time. Was it possible that he might not wake up the same as before? His body was hunched foolishly, with just a slight fanatical clustering at the shoulders, as if he had carried his madness safely into sleep and would still have it tomorrow, and the next day. It wasn't like last night when he slept so soundly.

Silly to pretend she wasn't frightened, but she forced herself to think about it anyway. The only breakdown case she knew was Aunt Ernestine. They gave her shock treatment and she always seemed a bit slow after that. But that was in the early days of shock treatment. Bert, if he really had a breakdown, would come back again good as new once it was safe to, once his life had been made habitable. By others—he had given up trying to fix it himself. That was looking at it from its fantastic worst.

The alarm clock was still making an audible tick, even from the cupboard where she had put it for muffling purposes. Otherwise, it was just night, nothing but night.

What was it he had written? "At the moment of his life," something like that, "when Christ had his biggest and most attentive audience, when he could have done the most good to the most people, he perversely refused to speak. His final, greatest lesson was silence." Why didn't you listen to yourself, Bert? You had the whole thing right there, and you muffed it.

He was quiet now, poor lamb. Be himself in the morning, all bright and chirpy for Christmas. When she first knew him he was capable of a wild joy on the principal feasts—she had never seen such joy. . . .

Bert Flax has officially retired, and his last message to his fans is, Keep quiet! Bert Flax has inspired his last Irish grandmother. There will be no more well meaning chatter, Granny has had it.

Finally, he has agreed to accept his mother-in-law's help. (Too proud to ask for it, so he has to do this.) Silent Night. Christmas bringing him the only kind of peace he was still good for. A refusal to fight anymore. She shook herself awake again.

Bert, you don't have to. We can get money some other way, borrow it from friends or something, oh this is ridiculous. Things like this don't happen to Sanity Flax. It sounded reasonable enough when Bert said it about Aunt Ernestine; he said that someone who got as fouled up as Ernestine just had to be broken one way or another: it was like resetting a bone. It might be a mess for a while, but it was probably the will of God. Very comforting at the time. And OK for Aunt Ernestine who dyed her hair and lived in California—but not in your own house. . . .

What was left of the night lasted a long time; she supposed she ought to phone Dr. Romilly, just to make sure, to discuss symptoms and be reassured, but Mrs. Romilly always answered night calls with a voice like Death; and anyway, Bert was just sitting at his desk looking at his old bills, nothing wrong with that. Meanwhile she felt a kind of contact with him for the first time in so long. Madness was the ultimate in candor: perhaps she was going a bit mad herself, but tonight, Christmas night, seemed like the real religious thing, with her and her husband waiting quietly in the eye of God, as people were supposed to. Anyway, what *was* the normal thing to feel at a time like this?

Practical, she supposed. As dawn began at last to yellow up the sky, she realized that it was time to shake herself awake and do what had to be done. Anything you thought at four in the morning was a kind of dream. She fought against full, hundred-percent waking; the sky outside fought against light, lying heavy on top of it. Then the sky gave up, and Betty gave up too.

The kids would have terrible Christmas fever by now, clambering, clustering, bouncing, tugging. Bert would sleep late and, when the worst was over, come chuckling down the stairs, no more broken down than she was. He wouldn't refer to last night—these little eccentricities were already to be taken as part of his way of life—and she felt she was not expected to mention them either. It had something to do with being a "creative person." It was going to be all right.

They had gathered in the nursery, which was really the boys' bedroom, and when she opened the door they all tumbled out in a ball.

"I saw Santa Claus last night," said Bert, Jr. "It was Daddy wasn't it?"

"Of course it wasn't."

"It was a big shadow at first and I didn't know who it was. And then it tripped on the string and I knew it was Daddy."

"What string?"

"The string I put out to trip Santa Claus. And Daddy shouted—" he whispered in Betty's ear and nodded gravely.

They had to eat breakfast before opening the presents, an extra refinement of torture which the Amsterdam Avenue Flaxes had also practiced. Betty took the opportunity to fiddle with the turkey. The children roared through their breakfast, saving their saliva for the unknown future. Betty said they still had to wait for Kevin, which reduced them to wailing fury, because Kevin was dropping every spoonful on his chest today before eating it and then picking randomly at his bib, stuffing in a crumb here, a milk-coated finger there. It was just another day to Kevin.

The worst part of the tradition was always waiting for Daddy. Usually he arrived at the point of greatest tension, rubbing his eyes and asking what all the excitement was about. But today tension had begun to turn to sobbing apathy, and still he hadn't shown. At half-past nine, Betty went upstairs to investigate: his shoulders were still hunched in sleep. She thought of ringing Dr. Romilly, but she now realized that she would feel awfully silly describing Bert's symptoms to a conventional man like Romilly. Whatever she said, Romilly would whip out an antibiotic, and they'd sit on the bed arguing. . . . She pulled the covers up and went down again.

By ten, Betty, Jr., had begun to whine insupportably, from warmed-over curiosity and greed. "All right, then, we won't wait for Daddy," said Betty—but this wasn't quite right either. Daddy was supposed to be there. They *had* to have the presents by now, it was a fixation; but they trooped in forlornly to get them. It was just relief that they wanted; with Daddy clowning in the background, it would have been pleasure as well.

At least, this was the mood until they actually saw the presents. Then they hit the tree with a whoop. Red and blue paper began to swirl, and yelps of surprised satisfaction—Bert had surpassed himself this year, with electric trains and unpredictable bears and skittering monkeys. The room was alive with buzzing, shuffling life. "Fold up the paper, remember whose toys are which," said Betty, but the hum of life was too much for her, and she bathed herself in the Commercial Christmas.

"What have you got, Mommy?" asked Betty, Jr., about an hour later. Betty, Jr., was the only one who even pretended to care. Anything in wrapping paper excited Betty, Jr.

Well, there were the tables, of course. But because those had not gone down very well, Bert had apparently bought her something else as well. She tore at the red flowers on the wrapping. There was a gleam of blue silk underneath. She pulled it shivering out: a bright blue dressing gown with blinding brocade at the sleeves and throat. Well, that was really very sweet of him.

And there was something else, something like a second postscript jotted down desperately. She began to feel fresh twinges of alarm. He had never spent like this before, even in their comparatively good years. He must have used up every penny they had on this junk, which was already beginning to lie in listless heaps across the floor. How did he ever expect to face the New Year in this kind of shape?

It was a little jewel box, and she hardly dared open it. But Betty, Jr., wouldn't rest while anything remained unopened; she jumped from foot to foot, clamoring for action. Betty unsnapped the clasp reluctantly. (Was this the only way he knew to please her? Was the spiritual stuff simply a hoax?) Behind the sparkling stones, which she hardly saw, perched on the cool green velvet, was a smart-looking card. "To darling Betty," it said and underneath that "please forgive me." The unexpectedness and touchingly synthetic melodrama of it made her sniff, something between a tear and a giggle.

There was lots of "What is it, Mommy?" and "Why is Mommy laughing, crying?" and "Mommy isn't laughing, crying," but Betty, Jr., shushed them very sensibly and said in a hideous little voice, "If Mommy's crying she's crying for joy." Betty left the room through a reasonable hush, and when she was outside she could just faintly hear Betty, Jr., showing them the present that had caused the trouble.

She dried her eyes with a paper handkerchief and started up the stairs again. Her face was a skinny mess in the mirror at the top. She wished she would have looked just a little bit pretty for Bert's Christmas, but it was too late to think about that now.

She opened his door again. The bed was empty, except for a crazy sprawl of striped pajamas. She tried listening outside the bathroom, but couldn't hear so much as a drip or a breath. "Bert, where are you? Bert?"

She looked in the study. It was still a wasteland of old bills, notes, working papers, held down by ink bottles, or adrift on the floor. But no sign of Bert.

It seemed he had gone out.

2

He must have gone out very quietly. She saw footsteps leading from the back door and circling round to the front. Another of his sly escapes. It was no joke, of course; but she couldn't help thinking of one of those comic-strip husbands who was always tiptoeing down the back stairs, to freedom.

The footsteps passed close enough to the living room for him to have looked in, if he had felt like it, and taken in the euphoria. In front, they swung left away from Bloodbury and were distorted in drifts. There was slush in front of the Mullins', where Fred Mullin had been shoveling all day yesterday. The houses along the street had those dead fronts.

The trees made a dismal tunnel for the wind. It was no use asking if anybody had seen Bert go by: non-Catholics went to parties on Christmas Eve and lay low the next day. The Feeleys across the street were a childless Catholic family (wry jokes from Bert about that) and hadn't got up yet.

"Is Daddy getting up?" "Did Daddy go out?" The chorus didn't help any. Should she phone the police about it? It was weak-minded of her, but she decided to wait a bit. Calling up the police sounded so easy; but think of starting all that rumpus and then having it turn out that he was only taking a stroll. What would the police think? (Ironic smiles, most likely, "No trouble ma'am, that's what we're here for.")

She shepherded the children backward across the porch, where they had come to watch her, and said, "Yes, Daddy's taking a walk. Perhaps he went out to buy something."

There was uneasiness in the house after that. "When's Grandma getting here?" "Which grandma?" Any grandma would do. They wanted company—not just a mother who burst into ambiguous tears under the Christmas tree, but real, everyday people, large, grinning grandmas. Betty hoped that Mrs. Flax and Mrs. Forsythe wouldn't arrive before Bert got back. They were due at one o'clock, an hour and a bit away. She could spend the time trying to think of a plausible explanation for Bert's absence; or she could just wait.

Actually she had to spend most of the time in a distracted shuffle between the kitchen and the living room. Betty, Jr., kept pressing her new, incoherent understanding of things, with melting glances. When she saw her mother gazing out of the window, she came over and squeezed her hand and said, "Daddy will be back soon," in a sticky voice, but it didn't look like it. Everything was so gray and still, it didn't look as if anything were going to happen out there. Betty almost jumped when a branch cracked and fell on the roof of the car.

At twenty past twelve, a bundled-up figure went burrowing past, but it didn't seem to be Bert. It was involved with a dog, and might have been Mr. O'Malley, or might not. You couldn't tell under the wool hat and the fleecy coat.

She was just approaching the edges of panic. Her plan had been to phone the police at half-past twelve, but by then phoning seemed even more impossible than before. It would take the police a while to get here, if they were going to come, and they would probably make it just in time to question Mrs. Forsythe. The human frame could stand only so much embarrassment.

At twelve-forty the phone rang. She ran to it, past gaping, vaguely depressed children. "That Peggy?" said a drunken voice, "Hi, Peggy, happy, happy."

She explained that he was calling Bloodbury 2337. He thought he was calling Bloomfield 3227. "You can understand my mistake," he said solemnly.

He rang off, after playing this hell with her nerves. "Grandma always gets here early," said Bert, Jr., to no one special. "Which grandma?" Look, the one thing she knew for absolute sure was that Bert was sane. So stop worrying. He was planning some kind of silly surprise.

She should have been giving the children their lunch by now. She liked to have them in bed soon after Mrs. Forsythe got here because, for all her mother's shrill exclamations of delight, Mrs. Forsythe never really settled down with the children about.

She took them out to the kitchen and began capriciously shoving food at them, slivering the turkey, without defacing it for the grown-ups. She had barely reached the first impasse (Patricia and carrots), when the doorbell rang.

She walked quickly to the door, opened it and before Mrs. Forsythe could say anything, Betty said, "Bert went out and I don't know where and I don't know what's wrong with him or with me or with anything."

Being embraced by Mrs. Forsythe was a sobering experience. Mysterious pins and buckles pressed against you, bringing you to your senses, although she appeared to dress simply; and there was a sense of chilly encirclement that Betty had almost forgotten about, which made one draw back involuntarily, as one always had.

"My dear," said Mrs. Forsythe, with such a glinting tenderness that Betty just turned and led her in. "Well there it is," Betty said more briskly, "I didn't mean to put it quite like that." Mrs. Forsythe looked meek as she bent to pick up her bundles and her cane; Betty had made it quite clear years ago with those slight, deadly gestures, that her mother didn't react right to human situations. Mrs. Forsythe had made her usual game try, but was perfectly resigned to failure.

"The question is, what should we do?" she said more efficiently. "Have you called the police?"

"Not yet."

"Well, let me do that." However disastrous the circumstances, Mrs. Forsythe plucked joy from action.

"Very well," said Betty, and her mother was soon standing hand on hip waiting for her connection and saying, "What time did he leave? Hello, Patricia, Happy Christmas there, hello? Is that the police . . . ?" It was a kind of relief to see the old war-horse swinging along the old groove. Lately, Mrs. Forsythe had been groping, uncertain, hadn't she? But here she was splendidly herself again, massive, confident and presumably irresistible. Now watch Bert come leaping out of some cupboard and land by mistake on top of Mrs. Forsythe!

Patricia had come out to complain some more about her carrots, and Mrs. Forsythe had given her a sunnier greeting than she could possibly have managed had she had nothing else to think about. (Bert would leap out and shout, "Boo—oh it's you, er, Mother.") Betty took Patricia back to the kitchen and told her the point about carrots. She had forgotten how Mrs. Forsythe could express her love by phoning people for you.

By the time Mrs. Flax arrived at one-fifteen, Mrs. Forsythe had made crisp calls to everyone but the National Guard. She opened the door and said, "Oh it's you, Vera. I thought it was the police."

"The police? What police?"

"Your son has run away. We've phoned the police about him." An approach that should have put Mrs. Flax at a crushing disadvantage: but the old lady proved to have surprising resources. "I expect he had his reasons," she said, and anyway, "what do you mean, run away?"

They sat in deadlock waiting for something to happen. Betty realized now that bringing the police into a family affair had been an abject surrender to her mother's point of view: but she couldn't bring herself to call up and say, "We haven't found him, but it doesn't matter." An inspector arrived at last and asked if Bert had been drinking. Inspector Price wasn't surly, because no one in Bloodbury was surly (except the men who ran the cigar stores); but he conveyed impatience in his own oblique way. Husbands who wandered out into the snow and went to sleep a few feet away from their own houses were not all that uncommon at this time of year. Bert was probably sleeping it off somewhere in the bushes.

Mrs. Forsythe assumed that the police must have some sort of dragnet out. "No, not exactly, ma'am. But we're doing the best we can." He seemed to Betty to encompass so much more than Flaxes and Forsythes: he could have been Father Chubb's younger brother, the one who didn't quite make priest.

"Was he disturbed in his mind?" he asked.

Was he ever. "He'd been a little worried," Betty said.

"A lot of husbands worry at this time of year," said the inspector. "About paying for Christmas and all. But they always come back for more, you'll find." He gave a brief outline of what they were doing: it didn't sound much but he said it was enough. He explained about the difficulties of

Christmas, putting the Flax disappearance in civic perspective. He had known of Mrs. Forsythe for years and knew that she played a big part in local affairs: but Bloodbury was so full of important people that they cancelled each other out and there was no question of special attention.

"Thank you, Officer."

"That's all right, ma'am." You couldn't tell whether he was fronting for a very busy department, or a very idle one. Betty was so busy during and around his visit that it all rather blurred on her. Calls came in and went out. Her mother stood by the phone, a-buzz with plans. Mrs. Flax wound up mechanical bears for a few minutes and then helped put the children to bed.

Lunch was late and tasted of nothing. Betty knew she was expected to advance a theory or something, but was darned if she was going to talk about her husband like that. Mrs. Forsythe made a show of admiring the cranberries. Mrs. Flax said, "Mmm," in a constrained sort of way, still bristling a little over her welcome. Betty hoped for a wild moment that, since nobody knew how to begin, the meal might go all the way in silence.

But Mrs. Forsythe had no such ambition, and when she saw that nobody else was going to do it, she plunged in, distastefully, but in. "What do *you* think has happened—Vera? He's your son, you know him." As if Betty and she didn't know him at all, had got mixed up with him by mistake.

"I'm sure there's an explanation. He got stuck somewhere and couldn't phone."

"Why do you suppose he went out in the first place?"

"Oh, to post a letter or something."

"A letter? Really, Vera. . . ."

It was so long since Mrs. Flax had had to explain anything. And Mrs. Forsythe was an old hand at demanding explanations. The result was hopelessly lopsided. Mrs. Flax was beginning to stammer and overheat. "How do I know what he did? He's a grown boy."

"Please, Vera—there's no need to get excited. We're just trying to ascertain the facts."

It was awful. The only way to stop it was to say something oneself. It was as if Mrs. Forsythe had been trying to smoke her out all along—not intentionally, but with the instinctive guile of the old committee warrior. Betty pushed away her desolate plate and said, "Oh all right, if we have to talk about it." At least they weren't still chafing about her conversion; they had sighted a bigger worm and were making for that. Perhaps, come to think of it, they had been all along—perhaps they had noticed that something was wrong with Bert, and didn't give a hoot about her conversion.

Mrs. Forsythe was looking like Fu Manchu; Mrs. Flax had gone all pointless again. They both had their tricks for bluffing children. Betty had no idea what they were thinking, or what they wanted to hear. So she just told them everything.

3

It came out more in jargon than she would have expected, forgotten bits of Psychology 1 and Anthropology 2 strewn about like raisins: not because she thought in those words, but struggling for fluency, she found that stale words came easier than fresh ones—maybe there were no fresh ones, but only unfinished sentences in her head.

She hadn't meant to confide in them at all. But now she'd started, the hidden thinking of the night came out in a jumble. She felt a bit like the Great Detective summing up in Lord Ponsonby's library. "My own religious ambivalence had a lot to do with it. I blame myself. . . ."

Mrs. Flax gave a shivering snort, which took Betty off guard. "He wanted so much to convert me, it was a reflex from the early days. He couldn't even remember why he wanted to anymore."

Mrs. Flax added a furry, who-wants-to-convert-you look. Mrs. Forsythe on the other side of the table looked in turns knowing and quite blank as the story swam in and out of her range.

"As I see it, he wanted to reexamine the whole thing, but he couldn't afford to because his livelihood depended on his maintaining a certain point of view. Besides, if he'd reexamined too much, he might have lost his faith altogether and he'd never have sold another story anywhere."

"Bert would never have given up his religion," said Mrs. Flax.

"That's what I mean, he wasn't even allowed to have doubts. Bert Flax's faith was a byword, a company image. . . ."

"I don't know what any of that means, but I know that that boy would never have given up his religion."

"Well you may be right. If he hadn't felt he had to be a perfect, model, hundred percent serene-at-all-times Catholic, that he couldn't admit to any doubts at all, none of it might have happened."

"What happened?" said Mrs. Forsythe, who was having one of her aggressively blank spells. Her mother didn't like this kind of talk and made no effort to understand it. "Just tell us in simple words what actually happened."

Betty kept trying for a common language, and the two mothers took turns looking blank. "He wasn't like a priest, with a real role to play and somebody looking after him. If a priest ever got into that kind of hole, his bishop would say, 'That's enough, my boy, take a rest for a while, take a small parish. Don't worry, we'll look after you.' But Bert was just a self-employed child-raising professional religion-man, and he got stuck with it."

"Nonsense," said Mrs. Forsythe shortly. "Nobody has to do anything he doesn't want to."

"Nonsense," echoed Mrs. Flax, not even bothering to enlarge.

"Oh, look, it's not so unusual, Mother. Lots of people go to church to keep up appearances. Only Bert had to do it on paper, as well. And, I hate to keep harping on it, but there was the thing about me. Bert always wanted me to become a Catholic. And he used to think his own serene, untroubled faith would eventually do the trick. I could tell he thought that and, up to a point, I'm afraid he was right. So when he thought there was a chance, he made one last crazy attempt to turn on the serenity again, full blast. Me and Christmas were too much for him. . . ."

"I've never heard such high flown, pseudomystical rubbish," said Mrs. Forsythe.

"I quite agree," said Mrs. Flax.

Betty could see what they meant, in a way. It sounded much less convincing as she groped it out in words than it had in the secrecy of her skull.

"Look, he wanted me to have faith, but it came up at an awkward time, when he was having doubts himself. Suppose I were to wind up having it and he didn't. That may be why he took it out on his friend like that."

"What friend?"

"*You* know, his friend." Betty was coming completely unstuck. "His friend who came here the other night and said he was back in the Church. Bert was just furious. Everybody seemed to be getting the faith but him. And him, the famous faith-man—you don't know how these people feel about faith. It's a gift, you see, you can never count on it."

Mrs. Flax looked almost cynical on hearing this, and it occurred to Betty for the first time that she, too, must have her area of expertness. She might be inarticulate, but you didn't go laying down the law to her about religion, all the same.

"I'm not blaming the Catholic Church, mind you. I have great respect for it, in many ways," she sounded a tattered retreat. "But it meant something different to Bert, something crazy. It obsessed him. And now perhaps it's killed him as well."

She didn't believe this for a moment (and of course neither did they), but she felt obscurely that it needed saying. It would make them see the seriousness of what was happening, and make them give up this "dose-of-castor-oil is what they both need" attitude.

"I don't see how the Catholic Church could do a thing like that," said Mrs. Flax, with honest perplexity. And then with a sudden burst of vindictiveness, "I think *you* are more to blame than anyone. I think you're the one that changed my boy." She made a monumental effort to focus her usual, comfortable confusion and to convert it to rage. "Anyone who can make up a story like that is capable of anything—I mean about wanting a nervous breakdown, whoever heard of such things? And," her voice got firmer, "how do you know all this, anyway, what are you, a mind reader?"

It was an unsophisticated version of the "secrets of the human heart" theory, and Betty was chilled through for a moment.

Surprisingly, Mrs. Forsythe seemed to agree. "Betty always was very fanciful." She hadn't liked Betty's story either. There was a bond between her and Mrs. Flax that Betty would never have expected, motherhood or old-fashionedness or simplicity of heart.

She hardly heard Mrs. Flax making the most of it, "Smart-alecky college, crazy ideas, nothing to do for four years but make up theories." There was a definite chill. The search for a scapegoat led straight to her. "He was a good boy," emphasized Mrs. Flax, "a good, simple boy, before he was married. I don't know what crazy ideas Betty gave him to get him so confused, or what crazy standards Betty set that he thought he had to live up to. He stopped seeing his old friends, you know," she said to Mrs. Forsythe, who nodded with genuine sympathy. "And all the time, she was making up wild stories about him."

"She was always one for making up stories." They talked about her like any two mothers. Mrs. Forsythe mentioned her high school dramatics and her professor's remark about the spatulate fingers, and forgotten lies from nursery days. It became distressingly clear that her mother had, with cumbersome stealth, even read her diary. "Of course, imagination can be a useful quality" . . . "I quite agree," said Mrs. Flax "—if you don't take it too far" . . . "Exactly."

Betty tried to remember the old diary. Were there any references to Mrs. Forsythe in it? Probably. And later she wrote some stories about mothers for the high school magazine, in which she hardly bothered to disguise her model. It was cruel, that was a cruel time, but she had optimistically assumed that Mrs. Forsythe would never see the stories. She had seen them all right. "She wrote about crazy people, quite unlike anyone you ever met. There was a horrible mother, I recall. . . ." Betty winced. Mrs. Flax said, "Fancy."

"And now," Mrs. Forsythe wound up with a last withering blast, "she has started going to the Catholic Church herself."

"Yes, well," Mrs. Flax blinked uncertainly. That was something else.

"Oh, nothing wrong with that, I suppose. But for a girl with her creative tendencies. . . ."

"Yes, well."

The concordat was at an end. It was getting dark, anyway, and again there were the children. Mrs. Forsythe looked a little ashamed of herself and offered to help get them up. Nothing like this had happened to Betty since schooldays, when you had to sit still for anybody's smug bullying. Bert would never have allowed it to happen, this spontaneous ganging up. "What was that?" she said. "No, I don't think so." They wouldn't have dared to gang up with Bert around.

"Now when Bertram gets back, I want you to promise not to worry him," concluded Mrs. Flax. But no one was listening.

Big woman bent cautiously over a schoolgirl's diary, looking for clues. If Bert was sick, one might have to go back to that, to the "Betty is rather fanciful" days. As a prodigal daughter, she would be at Mrs. Forsythe's mercy. Her failure would be kept bright.

Mrs. Forsythe could probably see some of this, and her seamed face said, No it isn't like that, I wouldn't read your diary now, and she probably meant it with all her heart. But she wouldn't be able to help it. It would be too much temptation.

"It was very sweet of you both to come and help," said Betty. "Yes, I can manage all right." She kissed her mother as sweetly as she could. "I'm sure it's nothing, Mrs. Flax. I'll ring you." The two women looked so lonely again, but she couldn't help them. They wanted to stay but knew they couldn't after the way they'd talked. Mrs. Forsythe had been exhilarated by Bert's having shown his true colors; now she might be getting a little frightened: with evening coming on, and the silent drive home. Mrs. Flax looked as if she couldn't remember what she'd said, but that was no excuse either.

Betty Forsythe, the child-storyteller. She wanted to think about Bert, but her attention had been wrenched inward for a moment. While the two mothers washed their lunch off, Betty reflectively went over the same ground, remembering how it went; it wasn't just the diary. She used to make up those stories too—about things like her parents' money, and where maids came from, and whatever became of Mr. Forsythe, and write them down sometimes (she was a born writer, like Bert, and about ten million other people) and leave them lying about. For her mother's pain. She remembered leaving some of them in the attic, because the stairs were so difficult, her mother would never make it up there. They were probably still there.

There was one outrageous story, where she had Mrs. Forsythe riven with guilt about giving arsenic to her husband; she wanted to atone by handing over all her money to the poor; but she couldn't give it away fast enough, and they still had this great listless garden, a prison by now, and a house that didn't fit them and nobody much to talk to, and on top of that Mr. Forsythe buried round the back. It was all in fun; she was only eleven when she wrote it.

She never knew what became of that story.

The Forsythe girls were like two birds of prey. While her mother was downstairs talking about Betty's phases, Betty was busy investigating the Hollywood-Freudian possibilities on her new typewriter. Dominating women, and frigidity, and a lot of things like that were just beginning to break into movies. And Betty was the luckiest kid in her class: she had mother number 1A, who was usually showing in at least three houses in New York. Mrs. Forsythe had some revenge coming, all right. If she ever read the high school magazine, she must have seen the one about the husband dressing down his obviously frigid wife and walking out—poisonous little know-it-all high school story.

Why did Mrs. Forsythe pick today to open *that* set of wounds? Betty wanted to get things straight about Bert, and her mother said, "remember, remember *us*. . . ." Betty was only one of a hundred high school writers, using the thin material that lay to hand; but her mother had taken it right in the veins. Struggling up the attic stairs, sitting there with a great sad face, on the packing cases.

By the time she got to college, Betty had picked her mother clean and was ready for new flesh. She could run up humiliating dossiers on anyone in a twinkling (not that she was nasty, just average). Within five minutes, she could say, "What are you running away from?" ("Myself, I guess.") It was too much, and her reaction when it came was pretty violent.

That was where Bert Flax came in. She met him at a village party and she said, just conversationally, "insecure," and he said you never can read another heart and her heart suddenly thudded agreement, she didn't really know anything about anybody. When all the things you knew about people were horrible or dreary, ignorance seemed a wonderful possibility. She sealed up her mother gratefully like a tomb—she knew nothing about her mother. Bert had to be a mystery as well because, after all, it was his game. And she was allowed to be a mystery herself. It was, said Bert, a sort of reverence for people not to understand them too well.

"Analyze not lest ye be analyzed," he said. She had never met anyone so untouched by the fashionable culture; and she had no way of knowing at the time whether he was even good of his kind. She thought his cynicism about modern ideas must have something to do with the Scholastic tradition. She thought his writing was marvelously fresh and simple. She stopped chewing on her mother and stopped excreting cruel little stories; and even if she couldn't get beyond a sort of static healthy-mindedness, this new point of view was so much better than the sick spitefulness and impertinent guessing, that had passed for intelligence in her crowd. . . .

Bert had given her an alternative, and something that looked like health. He was charitable by rule, and it seemed like a great rule, after being raised in the best, private jungles. He was the kindest man she ever met, at first anyway; and sometimes it might have been just a rule—but at least he tried to keep it. His jokes about Father Chubb and O'Malley and the neighbors were never malicious; and he always turned them off with a "means well" or a "really a great guy" or a "been through a lot, spent the war on his back, mother died when he was thirty-six," any darn thing to keep from judging. Even his jokes about "Mother" were so superficial as to be almost impersonal . . . at first.

She got stuck at that point and couldn't remember what happened next, or why she was following this line of thought.

The toilets upstairs and down pranged simultaneously, and the mothers reassembled. She could feel alienation in the way they took their coats and the way they put on their hats. Dangerous nonsense, said the commissar hats. They would never like her version of what had happened to Bert. Look at what she used to say about me, said her mother's grim, lonely face.

The door slammed on her terror, and she heard the two mothers conferring again hotly down the drive and into Mrs. Forsythe's car. The house seemed awfully dingy now. The lights weren't bright enough. The living room was a deserted fairground, with toys strewn like wreckage. Where *was* he?

She rang Father Chubb, but Father was having his lunch in Larchmont. (With some patron of the arts, no doubt.) She rang the police, and all she could get was a lot of noise in the background and someone saying, "What was that? No, nothing's come in on that." Whoeveritwas took the name again, weary-voiced, and the brown hair and the thin nose.

She depended on him too much, especially now to explain what was happening. When had he stopped telling her things? He had always had his artificial moments, of course, when he suddenly remembered about being a good example to a non-Catholic wife. And when he had to create mood, for his creditors. But when did dishonesty become an infallible reflex?

The night when he swore at the Church, he might have been trying to tell her something he really felt. It was only part of what he felt. He was just trying to say, "Look, I'm having a little trouble. This role of mine isn't all roses." But he must have guessed that she didn't like it, that she wanted her serene man of faith, her plaster saint, back. (What she really wanted was the serenity without the plaster, but he'd forgotten how to separate them.) She and his half-witted fans said in effect, "Always stay the way you are," as if that was possible. But the Catholic image was one of solidity and calmness, and in certain circles, Bert was "Mr. Catholic. . . ." Then of course he got this idea that she might be converted, and he began to cover up in earnest. Nothing he did or said after that had any meaning.

The house was so incredibly lonely. (Bert said you don't need a crowd to be lonely; you can be lonely when there's no one in miles.) She didn't care if he marched in and said he'd changed his mind and become a Communist; she just wanted him back. To help put the children to bed. To make jokes about Mrs. Forsythe. To keep her company.

Teach you, Betty Flax, to parasite off someone else like that. Bert has faith, Bert has values. We'll let Bert do it. She remembered a letter he got once, "Dear Father Flax, I'm sure you're really a priest, because you're so wise"—it was good for another wince: Betty had made the same mistake. And Bert had fallen apart trying to keep her from finding it out.

4

The older children didn't really take naps. They went upstairs and tried to keep quiet. And they knew from the ebbs and swells of noise that something had been going on, and they wanted information. It seemed simplest to say, "We're looking for your father," although it sounded a bit like a Thurber cartoon. She couldn't bear pretending to them and hugging the secret to herself.

They seemed, in fact, elated by the news, and wanted to get right into their snowsuits and look for him. She compromised, and let them search in the garden. And she had the house to herself again, feeling very much Bert's crazy absence, tidying up mechanically, giving the house a brief neatness which no one would ever see. Then she went upstairs and put some makeup on, slowly and carefully.

At five o'clock the phone rang, and it was the two funny men in the booth again, the stuffed owls. Dave Gilhouley had had Christmas lunch over at the Flynns, and he and Matty, suddenly very close friends again, had gone back to Dave's place for a last, flatulent beer and had found Bert there, sitting quietly on the doorstep. They took him inside and sat him down on the sofa, and he was up there right now looking at magazines.

"He seems to be all right. But we don't know how long he was on the doorstep," said Dave. "*Reader's Digest*s, he's reading."

"On Christmas Day you'd expect a man to be with his family," said Matty, who must have been standing right next to the phone, but more to himself than to anyone.

"There's nothing doing here. He's just looking at these old magazines," said Dave. "Not talking or anything."

Betty shut her eyes and touched the lids. "Yes, he's not well."

"No, we figured that," said Dave. "Overwork, worry. . . ."

"It happens a lot," said Matty, "to a guy I worked with, for instance," as if to say, There's a lot of insanity going around at the moment, you've got to be careful. "They laid this guy off and in a few months he was as good as new."

She asked about a doctor, and it seemed Gilhouley had a doctor friend who was already on his way over. And Matty had a sister-in-law, who was a nurse and a great fan of Bert's. Betty didn't know whether they pounced or used guile on someone like Bert, no of course they wouldn't have to pounce, they would go quietly and like old friends down to the doctor's car, in their big overcoats, and they would drive over to the hospital, chatting quietly. Matty would ask the doctor questions about how things were going, was it true they had this new drug he read about in *Time*, is that so, is *that* so?

"I'm sure you've been a big help to him, Mrs. Flax," said Matty. "It could have been much worse."

"Me? A help?"

"Yes, I could see that, the night we were over at your place. We could see Bert was in good, kind hands."

She hadn't been any help at all. But it was hardly worth arguing about. Matty was another charitable man by rule, and would give her credit whatever happened. She took down the name of the doctor and the address of the hospital.

"And Mrs. Flax, one other thing. I want you to know that the Catholic Church begins where Bert Flax leaves off."

"Yes, yes, I'm sure it does," she said vaguely. "It was very sweet of you."

A big help—for godsake, how? "How was I a help?" she asked the phone, but Matty considered himself dismissed and had rung off.

She would feel the sting later—eating supper by herself, in bed, doing a thousand dreary dishes—you could never again tell when it would land. But right now, it all seemed just queer: another of Bert's inexplicable tricks during the spiritual season. It would turn out that he was doing research into mystical states or something. Her reaction wasn't the least what she would have expected, or thought proper.

She found herself daydreaming about what had really happened last night, when his head was buried in his hands and he wouldn't let her see it. Maybe he couldn't get it to look right for church any more. For so long, he had been forcing his nerves to weep, to curse, to pray, as if there was nothing you couldn't ask nerves to do; and suddenly the crazy, mutilated nerves had said, That's enough of that, but look at this, our own special dance; and God he was scared, he was sick, half mad with fear. (Stop that, Betty—just let me finish this bit.)

He suddenly knew what was wrong, she decided in her dream, he knew it right there in church. He was sick, he wanted to call it off, he wanted Betty to call it off. (It was like someone trying devil-worship for a gag and finding it actually worked.) Playing with sacred things, was what Chubb called it and—leaving aside Chubb's list—you might say your emotions were sacred things, your tears and rages were sacred, he suddenly realized that you didn't turn them on for kicks, or for money; your talent was a sacred thing; and your faith in God was sacred, you didn't pretend it was a whit stronger than it was, even for the sake of example; and, oh, there were miles and miles of sacred things, and Bert knew he had certainly blasphemed every last one of them, and there in church he might have heard a funny noise, and the tile floor opening (this was really getting wild), the crazy blind vengeance of the sacred things on their way, and he was scareder than any man who ever lived. And meanwhile, he couldn't stop grinning—a typical Betty Forsythe touch that. . . . She was surprised to find she could almost believe it had happened a bit like that, though: Bert could always make her see spirits.

Anyway, indications were that he was back at peace: no more responsibility, no more appearances to keep up. Not being able to "feel" appropriately wouldn't be held against him now. At St. Paloma's Hospital, and whatever nice quiet place they sent him to from there, he could act the sage if he still felt like it; or, if it took him the other way sometimes, he wouldn't have to answer for blasphemy, or anything else. The apostle of the wagging tongue had caught up with the blessings of silence. Anyway, Betty hadn't lost her knack for making up stories.

It probably wasn't like that at all, but just, "I give up." She couldn't blame him. What *would* Mrs. Forsythe say if he had lost his faith? What would she say if he had kept his faith, and lost his livelihood? If he had just been given a few months to turn round in, he might have worked something out, have decided what he believed in and how. But with five children and the American Christmas. . . .

The funny thing was, she supposed that none of this

would have been necessary if he had just been a plain uncomplicated windbag like the other inspirationists: he could have gone to his grave with his round tones, his relaxed manner and the untroubled face of a child.

But Bert wasn't an uncomplicated windbag. He wasn't even a natural hack. He was conned into it by public request. He wanted to do first-rate work, but he had trouble with it, and he did so much good the other way. (That was the going dogma, and even Betty had subscribed to it until sometime yesterday.) The worst of it was you couldn't even blame the Church. The Church hadn't asked him to write anything, wouldn't care if he stopped. Every institution kept up a froth of chatter these days; it didn't much matter who did the actual frothing. A million tons of stupid words had to be manufactured every year by somebody; but getting mad at those was like getting mad at New Jersey, as Bert used to say.

One false move and it was hysteria—giggles and tears with the kids trooping in silently to watch. Instead she turned her mind to practical matters: putting a husband together again, for instance, and raising five irreducible children on nothing a year. Today *would* have to be the very day when taking help from Mrs. Forsythe was shown once and for all to be unthinkable. (Or was it quite unthinkable? Did she really have the book on Mrs. Forsythe? It probably didn't matter; they would always turn on each other in a crisis.) Just getting through the next week would hurt nerves she wasn't used to using, and that was just one week, and there was no break between one week and the next. But of course Bert would be back this evening—reading the *Digest* was no evidence of insanity. Leaving his family on Christmas, not talking, oh God! She lifted her head and shook it. She had thought of a new needle to try on her mother, anyway: "Any Church that can get you into a mess on this scale must have something to it, don't you think, Mother?" she could just hear the snort, and the "It better have."

Outside on the damp, dead earth, more immediate problems were arising. Kevin had broken down under a variety of pressures: the pile of children sitting on him for one (they had finally given up searching for Bert), and the exotic Christmas melee in his stomach for another.

She brought him in all shiny and sniffling and took off his snowsuit and unfastened his diaper. Kevin's diaper, and its contents, were about all that was left of that particular Christmas.

But even Father Danny Mulloy couldn't win them all (see, *The Day Father Danny Lost—and Won*). And if there wasn't a Santa Claus, at least there was a Father Chubb, who still thought that five dollars got you somewhere; and, no getting away from it, a Mrs. Forsythe too, who had perhaps earned the right to be patron. Betty turned Kevin over and endeavored to keep her thoughts tolerably light.

5

In Bert's world, the statue of St. Jude would have come down and patted her on the back (and she would have run out in the street screaming). But the flesh tints were deader than dead; the whole church was hung over from the festivities, dank and gray in the evening light. Mr. O'Malley hadn't checked in; Father Terwilliger and Monsignor Flanagan were doubtless going "ho ho ho" over their Christmas lunch; the candles in front of the statue were a sorry mass of dripping. She knelt down and tried to think things over. Bert had reached some kind of turning point and she rather wanted to reach one too; to achieve a policy instead of just bumbling along.

There could be no more leaning on Bert anyway, the minor prophet of Bloodbury. He had done a whimsical series once about a talking statue; maybe she could find one this afternoon to help her out. Bert's church had been, in that sense anyway, a little too easy—full of chattering statues and winking cherubs and, oh, jolly bishops and priests with footballs and nuns with trombones, a marvelous place for a boy. But now the party was over and the church was empty and quiet. He'd got her this far, by rousing her curiosity. The next move was entirely up to her.

But she felt too weak to move at present. She wasn't used to commitment, if that was what was called for, didn't know quite how it worked. You couldn't take a step like this just to spite your mother or please your husband: yet she couldn't imagine a stronger or more lucid motive. The important issues kept dissolving in dreams. She thought about the first times she had been in this church, for wedding rehearsals and vague talks with Monsignor Flanagan about "the faith." Even the efficiency expert her mother had hired hadn't been able to counteract the first voodoo spell of crosses and vestments, the alien smell of Monsignor Flanagan's hands . . . she looked to Bert to explain but found that he seemed to be under a spell, too, strangely nervous and artificial, as if all he really wanted was for her to like the Church and the Church to like her, and the whole thing to pass off without embarrassment. As if the Church were a third mother-in-law.

She put it down to wedding nerves; with her mother bustling distastefully up the aisles and the efficiency expert barking crisp signals from the back, the Pope himself would have been nervous. Even Bert's clothes didn't seem to fit him in church; his face, never mind about his face.

But later, when her mother and the rest had subsided, he still seemed ill at ease as between Betty and the Church; he still wanted desperately for them to like each other—as hopeless a policy with institutions as with people. He answered her questions about religion with yards and yards of miscellaneous information, making the Church seem almost oppressively likable, but he never really got close to explaining why she felt the way she did about this building. Perhaps he didn't know.

She thought he was being devout, while all the time he was just hoping to make a sale. . . . Keeping calm required nice judgment. She sensed another picture, like a morose tapestry, spinning into shape—Bert finally at sea in his own church, grotesquely refusing the sacrament because he couldn't remember what it was for—and pushed it away and tried to think, without pictures, of what she *did* feel about this building. The walls were ringed with drawings of pain, Christ crucified over and over; that was supposed to help.

To begin with, it was just a feeling about this church, and not about the one in the next town, or St. Patrick's—let alone The Church, whatever that meant. Bert handled the abstractions, the Church, America, the Family—uncalled-for picture here of Bert keeping his pale vigil last night, a fanatic squire . . . oh God where was I? St. Jude's.

St. Jude's happened to be the only place of its kind she had found in Bloodbury, the only place where what was "out there" made itself felt even a little bit. She wished she could be more decisive about it. She had made rather a virtue of not thinking precisely; it was a recoil from a masculine mother, and now she was paying for it. All the symbols in St. Jude's were about trouble and the relief of trouble; scourging, falling, rising—curiously comforting. But whether any of it had actually happened, she was much too confused to say.

She talked to the statue (which was really the more reasonable way around, anyway) and said, "I hope Bert gets a good rest and comes back his old self." She looked at the statue and it didn't smile. She couldn't even smell roses. "And I hope. . . ." She supposed she still hadn't "got faith," whatever that meant—maybe she wasn't the type. Anything Betty Forsythe believed was suspect right there. But she enjoyed talking to the statues.

They're going to take you away if you go on like that . . . no, not funny, no more jokes about taking people away. On the way out, she passed the magazines and pamphlets. She saw one of Bert's standards: *Faith and the Layman* and was about to take it down; it really didn't belong in there. There was an ardent, clean-cut face on a green cover, looking up at a beaming cross, really! And a halo of question marks.

She changed her mind and just straightened it. Personally she thought the argument was for the birds, but a million voices, like angel voices, said it at once: "It might help somebody."

Who for instance? Nice old ladies who didn't need help anyway. People like herself who enjoyed basking in Bert's artificial sun lamp of confidence and goodwill. Vague, lazy people who wanted to be told that everything was going to be all right. (Wouldn't they have been surprised to see the greater consoler crouched over his bills last night . . . no please, Betty, not now.)

Out of respect for Bert and so as not to make a gap on the rack, she left the pamphlet where it was and went out to the car—which, luckily, she'd learned to drive last summer—and drove it home through the sludgy peace of Christmas evening.

She had at least one blessing to count on her way: that their credit with Mrs. Pelotti, the ancient baby-sitter, was good forever. Mrs. Pelotti had heard from her daughter that Mr. Flax was doing wonderful work for the Church, and she thought any man who did that deserved every break he could get. (No, she didn't read him herself—too intellectual.)

She also had one point of remorse to chew on: she had always known in her bones, hadn't she? that Bert was nobody's writer. Unfortunately she had lied to herself on this point. Or, at least, she had swallowed the crazy poison about his doing good, as if that somehow beatified bad work. If she hadn't been so dishonest, she might have had it out with him years ago, and he would have had at least one honest opinion to chart by. . . . You never know, it might have helped. Anyway, remorse later. Right now, she had to make some phone calls.

. . . As for religion—she found herself nodding vaguely at the dashboard—commitment in that area would probably have to wait until Bert got back.

And felt a stab of self-disgust over both the phrase and the thought that might almost have been the turning point she was looking for.

6

Dave Gilhouley had never seen a worse job of acting in his life. Worse even than last time. Come on Bert, we know you, he wanted to shout. He knew his old friend too well to be fooled by this stunt. Old Bert looked perfectly normal. He just wasn't talking. Dave had brought him in a whole batch of *Digests* from the hall cupboard, and his interest in them seemed mild but inexhaustible. Breakdowns couldn't be as tidy as this. Bert just didn't have the guts to throw himself on the floor, or whatever they did.

"They'll be here in a few minutes," said Matty, who had been phoning. "They were held up." Dave nodded. You could never tell what Matty was thinking under that blanket of charity. He wasn't going to call his old friend, anyway. If Bert wanted to have a breakdown, well, he probably had his reasons.

Really crazy. Trust a chucklehead like Flax to try a stunt like this. Oh, sure, a nice fellow—but there was always something a bit, well, soft about Flax. Tell you the truth, wasn't it people like Flax who used to make religion seem so jerky in the old days? The candle wax ardor in church, the synthetic wholesomeness outside. . . . Dave didn't know what kind of trouble Bert had been in, but he would have bet you ten years ago that Flax would buckle, whatever life brought him. When you were as soft and as dishonest as that. . . .

Gilhouley knew he was having a delayed reaction from Bert's bawling him out the other night. At first, he had been shaken, because Flax wouldn't accept him back in the Church (silly, but having a believer call you "evil" at that stage was no joke). Later on he managed to switch to shaky annoyance: at being made the butt of such a phony performance. So, he was biased, he admitted it. You couldn't take anything Flax did seriously.

Annoyance colored the past too. As he remembered it, he always had his doubts about Flax. See, what Flax used to do was this: he used to hang around all the time, but he wouldn't *do* anything. He'd say, "No thanks," when they showed the stag movies, and, "Not for me," the time they hired the call girl; but he wouldn't just go away, the way Flynn did. He'd wait downstairs until they were finished. . . . Talk about being evil . . . still in some peculiar way he made religion seem real, didn't he? even then. Unattractive, but real.

"He was a neat guy," said Flynn mostly to fill in the time.

Bert's eyes didn't even flicker, Christ (stop saying that) what a crazy afternoon. Nothing like a visit from Flax for laughs—what *happened* to him anyway? He must have been signaling for the man in the white coat the last time he came over, in November—nobody helps you these days until you put up the sign that says "I'm sick"—but what special thing had driven Bert up the pole? Did anybody know?

In the sluggish stillness of his apartment, Dave's mind wandered all over—funny what had happened about nervous breakdowns, for instance. . . . All kinds of unexpected people said, "Oh yes, that was the summer I had my breakdown." They just lost the use of their legs for a while, or got a fixed stare. It wasn't tragic, or even very important. The most trivial people could swing it. Bert was probably reading about it right now—"How I had my breakdown—and lived. . . ." Flynn's face was a permanent twist of reproach. Gilhouley was still pretty fouled up himself, wasn't he? thinking one thing, saying another, miming continuous concern, just like Flax, just like everyone. That was a nice wife Bert had, a bit skinny, it was hard to feel and think the right things—fancy having to make a living out of it.

Bert turned the pages of the *Digest* with lifeless fingers. Slightly staring eyes, the way they used to take off crazy people back in school. Come on, now, Flax, it isn't like that at all. You're getting it wrong, you do it like this.

Dave just couldn't tell if Bert was lining up a vacation or whether something serious had happened. Everything about him seemed as unreal as glass. There was an old copy of the *Passenger* lying on the coffee table—thirteen guardian angels in the house, for Christ (excuse me) sake—no wonder Flax wound up denying he was Bert Flax.

Only two nights ago, just before the blowup, Dave had tackled Bert about his writing; asked him he really believed in that stuff. In the first hot flush of reconversion, Dave was sure that religion was serious or nothing—you didn't fool around with it like that. . . . Bert had seemed hardly to hear him, to gird himself in smugness—and then had turned on him like a scorpion in front of the others, the public. Dave didn't want to be vindictive, but he couldn't help feeling that Flax had it coming to him—whatever it was that had come. Flynn would have to handle the compassion a while longer; Dave hadn't been back long enough for that.

Flynn was still handling the compassion twenty minutes later when the doctor arrived to take Bert away and find out what, if anything, was wrong with him.

On the phone, Mrs. Flax flatly refused to believe in Bert's nervous breakdown—as such. "The boy needs a rest," she said. "That's all."

Surprisingly, Mrs. Forsythe agreed; she made light of the whole thing. "A little strain, nature's way of getting us to take it easy," she explained.

Father Chubb was solicitous but said not to worry, a rest, a little rest.

Mrs. Flax pointed out that the same thing had happened to her husband, Bert's father, at exactly the same age.

Mrs. Forsythe confirmed that it was not unlike an attack she had suffered herself some years ago when she quite lost the use of her fingers.

Father Chubb remembered a case too.

Betty couldn't make out whether it was Bert or the breakdown that they weren't taking seriously. Certainly Bert had worn his credit down and down (even with this gang), with his phony writing and his phony manners; on paper you might call him sad but not tragic; in the flesh, he didn't quite make it either.

What went on inside his head was out of bounds, as far as these three jolly extroverts were concerned.

"Do you think he'll ever write again?" "Of course he will"—the hearty emptiness of Father Chubb's answer was the last word on that, too.

The other interesting thing about the phone calls was that all three (even Mrs. Flax) offered to pay his medical expenses.

Bert would have been amused by that; once upon a time.